The NightCrew II
Bloodlust

Brad Ricks

Published by Crystal Lake Publishing
Where Stories Come Alive!

Crystal Lake Publishing
www.CrystalLakePub.com

Copyright © 2025 Brad Ricks

Join the Crystal Lake community today
on our newsletter and Patreon!
https://linktr.ee/CrystalLakePublishing

Download our latest catalog here.
https://geni.us/CLPCatalog

All rights reserved
ISBN: 978-1-968532-09-3

Cover art:
Maarten Van Vuuren

Layout:
Edmund Stone: https://Linktr.ee/edmundstoneauthor

Edited and proofed by:
Jaime Powell, Jodi Shatz, and Monica Camarena

WELCOME
TO ANOTHER

CRYSTAL LAKE PUBLISHING
CREATION

To my sister Melinda,
Who somehow survived childhood
despite my constant attempts to try and kill her

1

Rory Brown stumbled down Burgundy Street. New Orleans was his favorite city, second only to Vegas. He loved the sights, the sounds, the partying, the alcohol, and the women. During Rory's undergraduate years, he had been too poor to appreciate the finer things in life. But now at twenty-five, finishing up his MBA at LSU, and working in corporate sales out of his home office in Baton Rouge, he had money to burn, weekends free, and no desire to slow down.

"You need to find a nice girl and settle down," his mother constantly harped.

"Why find a nice girl when there are so many not nice girls I haven't met yet?" he wanted to tell her. He knew better than to say that, though.

Instead, he just did what he enjoyed doing.

Rory staggered into a parked car on his right. He brushed his shoulder length blond hair away from his face and lurched toward the curb. His foot hovering a few inches over it, he closed one eye and squinted, focusing before hesitantly stepping down. At least he had enough wits about him to walk on the sidewalk instead of in the middle of the street.

Although some of the night's events lay behind the fog of alcohol and who knows what drugs, other memories he held onto with an iron grip. Like the image of Lily. It was her place he was stumbling away from. He'd seen enough women do the walk of shame from his own place to know exactly what he looked like. And he didn't give a shit.

Outside of the ache in his pants, Rory had no regrets about how he spent the past few hours. He couldn't remember the last time he'd been with a woman as hot as Lily. Now that he thought about it, he probably hadn't been. There were a few nights he couldn't remember; but he claimed that as deliberate and a win.

He came to a cross street, but he couldn't make out the name of it through his blurry vision. He nearly fell off the curb before regaining his stability and continuing down Burgundy. He was staying at a hotel just off the French Quarter. If he hadn't lost his phone, he'd have called an Uber.

"Fuck an Uber!" At four in the morning, there was no one around to hear or care if he talked to himself.

His thoughts went back to Lily. The vision of her gyrating on top of him. Her black hair was long enough that it brushed his legs as she had leaned her head back during one of her multiple orgasms. His hands tingled, remembering the feel of her silk skin and cradling her perfect C cup breasts. Her nipples perked so firmly they could cut glass.

Something awakened inside his pants. Despite the soreness from staying rock hard for almost three hours, he craved to be inside of her again.

As his loins started to wake back up, Rory felt a sharp pain in his chest. *Fucking heartburn.* He pounded his fist against his chest, hoping to help along whatever was stuck.

"Me, Tarzan," he joked into the early morning air.

But then a spell of dizziness hit him, and it stopped him in his tracks. That felt different. He couldn't count the number of times he'd been drunk, but he'd never felt that before. He reached for the side of a building and braced himself against it as the world spun. Maybe he overexerted himself or needed to rehydrate after his two colossal orgasms.

He tried to take a deep breath, but his lungs refused to expand. A ripping pain tore through his stomach. He doubled over and vomited hard enough to see an explosion of stars. With his sleeve, he wiped the puke from his mouth. Bright red blood streaked his shirt and more lay at his feet.

Rory tried to scream, but not enough air filled his lungs to make a sound. The words stuck in his throat. A vise grip constricted his chest.

Propped against a window, he jerked his head up, gasping for air, and saw his reflection. The image made him stumble backward. His face sunk in, and blood leaked from his eyes like tears. He shook his head, not believing his own recessed eyes. His arms tried to wipe the bloody tears away but only smeared them.

With another wave of nausea hitting hard, Rory staggered off of the curb and into the middle of the street. He doubled over again, throwing up blood and bile. Gasping for whatever air he could in between the bouts of vomiting, his vision darkened. He fell to his knees, collapsing in the middle of Burgundy Street.

2

"Do you thirst?" Thomas asked.

Michael White sat with his eyes closed on the hard concrete floor in the middle of the pitch-black room. He used it as a bedroom despite rarely sleeping. Sleeping was too difficult. Well, not so much the sleeping as the nightmares. Anytime he tried to relax, to meditate, to grow comfortable in this reborn form, images of Brittany, of Scott, of the skeleton children posed in school desks flashed before his eyes. If he was still human, he'd take something to help him sleep. Unfortunately, he couldn't lace blood.

Blood.

When he first met the Night Crew, he couldn't stand the sight of Thomas drinking blood. The thought of it, the taste of it, the feel of it disgusted him. Mike had his fair share of busted noses and split lips to know what blood felt like going down his throat. Sickening. Yet, now that sickness was all he craved. When he wasn't fighting off nightmares, he was thirsting for blood.

He listened for Thomas's footsteps, followed them in his head. The older vampire circled the young protege. Each step barely made a sound, but Michael heard each one. His ears were now those of an apex predator. *The* apex predator.

"Of course, I thirst. Hunger is all I think about," he replied.

Thomas stopped pacing in front of him.

"Focus your mind on something else. The hunger will always be there. It's the hardest thing for us to control. A fledgling with a good teacher can show restraint for a few days. I expect better of you than that.

"What are you focusing on?"

Mike opened his eyes. Even in the darkened room, his vampire eyes detected enough light to see Thomas standing tall a few feet in front of him. He still wore his signature leather trench coat. Just beyond him, Michael saw the outline of the door. He knew the refrigerator—*his* refrigerator—was only a few steps from it. His fridge, which contained pints and pints of blood, chilled to sweet perfection, just waiting for him to bleed the bags dry.

"What are you focusing on, Michael?" Thomas repeated.

"I'm focusing on running you over and grabbing one of my bags out of the fridge."

He could taste the thick liquid in his mouth, on his tongue, coating his throat. That metallic taste that was also so very sweet. He craved it, and it called to him.

Thomas knelt in front of Michael, maintaining his position between the fledgling and the door.

"Is that the most productive thing to be focusing on?"

"Right now, it's the only thing I can focus on."

Michael shifted his legs and sat up on his knees. The hunger ached inside of him.

"How beneficial are you to the team if you can't control your hunger? How will you be able to help Nate, Niki, and Josh? They expect you to lead them, yet you can't go more than a day without slipping into bloodlust. What's going to happen on your first assignment if one of them gets cut? Are you going to bleed them dry?"

Thomas spoke with a condescending tone that enraged Michael. Heat rose throughout his body. His eyes burned red as he glared at the person standing between him and relief. At that moment, Thomas wasn't his teacher, but his enemy. An object that stood in the way of what he needed. Of what he had to have. The desire burned deep, and the anger Thomas pulled out of him made that fire blaze hotter and hotter.

"Am I making you angry, Michael?" Thomas continued to chide. "The great Vampire Michael. Slayer of Silas. You know, he thought you had so much power. He believed that so much, he took you out of your happy little home and into this world. Do you really have that power, or did you just get lucky?"

Michael exploded off his knees and onto his feet. He bolted at Thomas with his unnatural speed. His eyes absorbed what little light the room held and focused entirely on his prey. He dropped his shoulders and collided directly with Thomas's stomach, thrusting his arms forward in a perfectly formed tackle.

But when Michael struck Thomas, his forward momentum stopped. Thomas held his ground against Michael's attack. Thomas's own power far surpassed the speed, strength, and agility of Michael's. Thomas grabbed him around his chest, spun him around, and tossed him back to where he originally sat.

"One day, you might be an alpha, but that day is not today."

Michael charged again. Fury kept his fiery eyes focused on his target. He lunged, hoping to drive the elder vampire to the ground, sprint through the door, and quench his unending thirst.

Thomas caught Michael by the throat, wrapping one hand around his neck. With the other, he grabbed Michael under the arm. He lifted the fledgling off the ground and slammed him onto the concrete floor. The floor cracked, and bits of cement crumbled to powder under Michael's back. Thomas held him in place, grinding him into the floor, chunks of rubble digging into his shirt and skin.

"Stay here. You obviously need more meditation."

Thomas eased his grip and spun around. His coat flared behind him, and in the next instant, he stood at the door.

"Once you complete another round of quiet solitude, you may leave. Focus on something other than feeding. The sooner you do, the easier this becomes."

He opened the door, delivering blinding white light from the hallway. It bathed the bedroom. Thomas stopped and turned back to his student, still laying on the ground on the broken concrete.

"You will be an alpha. You have the potential to be stronger than any of us."

Thomas closed the door, leaving Michael alone in the darkness.

Alone. As much as he knew he wasn't alone, as much as Jax, Niki, Nate, Josh, and occasionally Thomas reminded him that he wasn't alone, it didn't stop him from feeling that way. His entire world had been Brittany. Even after her death, his every motivation had been for her, to the point where she spoke to him throughout his quest for vengeance.

Without her, he was empty inside. A shell of the person he once was. A shell that had been transformed into this monster.

Michael stood and brushed the dust and rubble off his back. Despite the darkness, he was able to see his bed. He sat on it and pulled his legs in, crossing them. He lowered his arms and placed the back of each hand on a leg. He raised his head, arching his shoulders back, and closed his eyes, taking a few deep breaths.

He focused on the darkness around him. Over the past few months, he found himself more and more in tune with it. Once upon a time, that wasn't the case, but since his conversion, that was where he was at home. The darkness was his solace.

Mike thought back to the time before. Although a simple task to do, it was still extremely painful. His gift, what the doctors told his mother was called highly superior autobiographical memory, he referred to as his curse. A curse that was somehow worse than even becoming a vampire. Every painful detail of his life, every person he'd ever loved, every terrible thing that had ever happened to him, he relived in vivid detail. He tried to focus on the happier moments, but those revolved mainly around Brittany.

Each time her name popped into his head, he relived the torturous memory of holding her while she died in his arms. The gurgling sound as she choked on her own blood haunted him. While she lay dying in his lap, he vowed to avenge her. Who cared what happened to him. If he died while doing it, at least he'd be with her again.

But Silas had other plans for him. Silas. The devil who took Brittany away from him so that Mike could awaken to the real world. If it wasn't for Silas, Brittany would still be alive, and he never would've met the Night Crew. He could've continued living his life, never knowing monsters existed. Never knowing anything about the Council or the Accords.

The White family could still be living their best life in suburban America with a three-bedroom house, a two-car garage, two and a half kids, a dog, and shitty jobs.

But, instead of what could've been, there was what actually was.

Instead of that light, there was this darkness.

Brittany had died in his arms. Mike had tracked down her killer but had to be saved by Nate and Niki. He met Jax, Josh, and Scott. And later Thomas, Silas's brother. After a few close calls, he led the Night Crew to Silas's den. But before he could kill the monster that took his wife from him, the beast turned him into the blood-hungry abomination he was. And this abomination would've killed his new friends if not for the memory of Brittany, reminding him who he was, who the real enemy was.

The feel of Silas's cold, dead heart in his hand still resonated. He could still hear the sound of Thomas's machete slicing through Silas's neck, and the final look on Silas's face as his head fell to the ground.

Over and over, Mike replayed the events that led him to where he was. That led him to the darkness.

Thomas had repeatedly told him meditation would cure him of his bloodlust. Through meditation, he would find the way to control his hunger. Find the power inside of himself, blahdi blah blah.

If only Thomas lived with Michael's curse.

Michael sat alone in the dark, yet he wasn't truly alone. In the darkness, the ghosts came out. Each one held a story. Each one played a part. And each one had died because of him.

Not even sunlight banished the demons he lived with. Despite the vampire lore, sunlight didn't kill him. Instead, it just weakened him. It drove him back into the shadows, back into the darkness, but it couldn't absolve him of his sins.

Once upon a time, he had been Sergeant Michael White. He had been happy and optimistic. Now, he was a monster.

Michael took in a deep breath of air. His dead body didn't need oxygen. He did it out of habit. Breathe in, breathe out. He focused on that rhythm.

Thomas told him not to focus on feeding. He had at least accomplished that. Now, if only he could stop focusing on his past failures. His gift was a curse.

As the door opened and light flooded the room, Michael felt the hunger rage again.

4

At the corner of Burgundy and Toulouse stood The Maison Dupuy Hotel. It was shaped like a square, the pool inside the center courtyard. Balconies hung from the second floor, just above the Bistreaux restaurant, overlooking the sidewalk.

From the flat-topped roof of the five-story hotel, the four sisters watched Rory stumble down the street. They stood with their bare feet dangling just over the edge. Their talon-like toes gripped the ledge as their bat-like wings appeared nearly translucent against the night sky. They peered down at Lily's victim as he fell into a car and screamed obscenities at the ghosts inside his head.

Angie glanced at Lily and smiled. She'd seen how he looked leaving Lily's room. Lily had drained him to nothing. Any life he had left spilled out of him with each step he took. The alcohol and drugs had masked his awareness. Poor Rory was dead before he left. His body just hadn't realized that yet. But it was catching on quickly.

He moved under the sidewalk and out of their view. Moments later, the retched sound of vomiting broke the night's silence. His gasps for air reached all the way to their perch. As he ran into the middle of the street, Angie saw the terror that gripped him. Sheer panic lived in his eyes, and her smile grew larger. It had been some time since she had watched a victim slowly expire like this. Finally, he doubled over and collapsed in the middle of the street. Their show was over. Lily had provided nice entertainment. Angie would have to thank her older sister later.

As the sun broke the horizon, the four walked across the top of the Maison Dupuy Hotel and leapt off the roof. As they fell, they transformed into their desired appearances. Wolves in sheep's clothing. They landed one after the other next to the courtyard pool and then headed into the hotel and through the Bistreaux. As the first police cruiser pulled up to Rory's body, they strolled across Burgundy Street and lingered away from the hotel, watching.

"We're getting careless," Naomi said. With her dark complexion and hair that was short, spiky, and purple, she stood out from her sisters. "What if we draw the attention of the Council?"

"What Council?" Lily asked. She pulled her long black hair in front of her and ran her fingers through it. "We are finally free to do as we please."

The four huddled together on the sidewalk as the ambulance pulled up next to Rory.

"Shouldn't we go back if we are going to argue about this?" Angie snapped at Lily and Naomi. Her fiery red hair matched her personality. Even at this early hour, her red curls bounced off her shoulders and face.

Angie glanced over her shoulder as the emergency medical team examined the corpse on the road. Blood and bile pooled around the body. Any muscle mass he once held had withered to nothing. The rapid decomposition had already begun. In a matter of days, the body would be unrecognizable. Within a week, nothing but a pile of brittle bones and mushy mounds of flesh would be left.

She saw one of the officers, handsome, in his late twenties, staring in their direction. She gave him a wave and a smile, and the officer responded in kind.

"Angie," Lily said. "As much as I disagree with Naomi, now is certainly not the time to draw unnecessary attention." She pointed to onlookers on both sides of the street and on the balconies of the Maison Dupuy. "Be more subtle in your flirtations."

"You're no fun," Angie said.

"I'm the last person you could say that about. I was the first Samael created. If not for me, you three wouldn't even exist. It's me they call the Queen of Demons." She saw a few people, all men, looking their direction. "We should continue this conversation elsewhere, though."

With Lily leading the way, the sisters maneuvered through the crowd of gawkers, hoping to catch a glimpse of the dead body in the middle of Burgundy Street. With expert skill, they danced their way through, careful not to lay a hand on anyone.

After only a block, the street emptied. Early on a Saturday, New Orleans wasn't quite awake yet.

"Naomi," Lily continued. "Although that vampire's uprising failed, it was enough to open up the eyes of others. Why else do you think the Council disappeared so quickly? They know a single spark can create a blaze. The Council and those stupid Accords rested on such an unstable foundation. It took nothing to send them running."

"Ah, the Accords," Eileen said. "What a joke. All because some human army threatened us twelve hundred years ago. We existed for two thousand years before. Some even longer."

Angie didn't want to get into a history lesson. She was around for it. She didn't need to hear it.

"No one is paying attention to the body count anymore," Lily said to her sisters. "No one is sending hunters after us. We can continue to enjoy ourselves. Eat freely."

"And Samael?" Eileen asked.

"Yes, sister. With the Council indisposed, we can finally find the right sire to help us resurrect Samael."

Eileen and Angie, in unison, gave a cheerful, "Yeah."

Naomi remained silent, not contributing to their jubilee.

"Sisters, tonight, we hunt again."

"Sisters, tonight, we hunt again."

5

Nate Edwards burst through the door of their new headquarters with a bag in his hand. Dallas. Finally a city where he knew he could settle down. It had the nightlife, the restaurants, and the sports. Traffic sucked, but that seemed to be an issue wherever they went.

He walked into the large warehouse, passed the two decked-out SUV's that Intel had acquired for them, passed the row of shelving full of silver grenades, vests, guns, ammo, canned goods, and water bottles. Everything a team needed to survive.

Niki Davis strolled in close behind him. Nate paused and let her catch up. Life had changed so dramatically for them over the years. So many states, so many countries. He had wanted to be a world traveler but never would've guessed like this. At least with Niki, he had his person to enjoy the world with.

Niki strode up next to Nate, and he tossed his arm around her.

"Josh," she yelled in her Australian accent. "Where are you hiding, love?"

From the back of the warehouse, behind a set of cubicle walls designed as a make-shift room, Josh wheeled into view.

"Niki, you're loud," he said.

"You should hear me in bed," she quipped.

Nate saw Josh's eyes roll despite the dozen yards between them.

"Trust me, we can," he said in return. "How was your outing?"

"Definitely needed. Being cooped up in here is making us stir crazy. I'm hoping we get an assignment soon. I'm looking forward to trying out all the new gear over there." Nate tilted his head toward the shelves. "Oh, we got something for you." He tossed the bag at Josh, and it hit him in the chest.

Josh opened the bag. He pulled out a blue sweater with a white star on the front of it.

"Dallas Cowboys?" Josh asked.

"Of course. When in Rome."

"I guess it'll make good kindling. You know I'm an Eagles fan, right?"

"Give it to Mike, then," Niki said. "Where is our Supreme Vamp Leader at anyway?"

"Back in his room, meditating. Thomas said he's making progress..." He let the word hang in the air, implied doubt filling the room.

Josh grabbed his wheels and after a few quick thrusts sent him back to his office, he gripped them tightly and skidded to a stop. He held the sweater up over his head.

"Why would a vampire who doesn't get cold want a sweater?"

"How the hell would I know?" Nate responded. "Why does Thomas always wear that damn leather coat? Mike's from Texas. Doesn't everybody in this state like the Cowboys?"

"Not everyone," Mike said.

He stepped out of his room and into the warehouse. His skin was pale, and his eyes were sunken into their sockets. Thomas was supposed to be teaching him to control his hunger. He looked on the verge of starvation. And in his experience, a starving vampire could be more dangerous than an out-of-control one. He trusted Thomas knew what he was doing to Mike. At least, that's what he told himself.

"What's your favorite team?" Josh asked.

"The Cowboys," he said, derisively. "I was born and raised in Texas. If you don't want that sweatshirt, I'll take it. I may not get cold, but I'm not letting the star go up in flames to an Eagles fan."

"I thought you were in your room, meditating," Josh said, smiling.

"Super hearing," Mike said and pointed both index fingers at his ears. He looked over at Nate and Niki.

"You two look like you had a great time."

Nate smiled. He squeezed Niki close to him. "Of course. This is a town I could settle down in. Now, if only I could convince her."

"Oh, love," she said. "You know I can't yet."

"I know, but a man has dreams."

He bent his head down to kiss her. Nate knew how she felt. She still carried so much guilt for what happened. For what caused them to join the hunt in the first place. She had nothing to feel guilty about, but he couldn't convince her of that. Until she knew in her heart she was absolved, she wasn't going to quit.

"We will one day, love. Promise. Just still more to do."

6

Jason stood on St. Peters, staring at what looked like nothing more than another New Orleans warehouse. The exterior consisted of a handful of green double doors that opened outward from the middle and red brick that separated them. A large overhang stuck out just between the first and second floor and covered a large portion of the sidewalk.

He would've thought he was in the wrong spot if not for the wooden sign dangling from a flagpole mounted to the building. It read "REPUB-LIC" in big letters with "NOLA" in smaller print underneath.

The line of people waiting to make their way inside was also a dead giveaway. Republic New Orleans.

"You ready for this?" Jackson Smith asked, placing both hands on Jason's shoulders and giving him a shake.

The two men had been inseparable since the first grade. They grew up two streets from each other and shared every class they took. During high school, they both played football and baseball. With Jason McHenry standing at six foot even, and Jackson being one inch taller, they weren't bad at basketball, either. They had the height and build, but they preferred the break over the holidays and into the spring.

When it was time to apply for colleges, of course they chose the same one.

Jason stood close enough to the door to hear music playing from inside the club. He felt the bass from the sidewalk.

"Fuck, yeah," Jason answered.

He bobbed his head in sync with the music and swayed his body. He wore a pair of faded jeans that he'd been told showed off his well-sculpted ass and a tight-fitting T-shirt with the Punisher logo on it.

Jason had learned about this place from another friend of theirs. The friend had been in NOLA for work just after Christmas and couldn't stop talking about Republic New Orleans.

"Dude. It's the fucking hottest club anywhere," Chris had said one evening, stoned on Jason's couch. He pointed at Jason and Jackson. "You two fuckers need to take a weekend, rent a fucking hotel room close to the Warehouse District, and go. Make sure your hotel is close because the women are soooo fucking fine. And willing. I got so fucked up while I was there. I fucking woke up next to two chicks I couldn't even remember being with."

Chris had them at "hottest club". The rest were just details. That night, they'd picked the weekend and rented two rooms at the Embassy Suites, not even two blocks from Republic New Orleans. When they arrived, they immediately stocked each room with plenty of liquor and condoms.

With each passing minute, standing in line on the sidewalk, Jason found himself dancing to the music more and more. His excitement grew as they moved closer to the door. After thirty minutes, Jason made it to the solid wooden doors with golden handles. The doors waited open and beckoned them inside.

Once in, the sound level increased exponentially. At least three hundred people crammed onto the first floor. Jason couldn't tell how many might have been on the mezzanine.

"Want to go up or down?" he asked Jackson.

"Down for now," Jackson said.

He raised his arms above his head, bounced his head up and down, and moved his way to the center of the dance floor, joining the gyrating crowd.

Jason made his way to the bar at the side of the room and ordered a beer. He surveyed the area. Straight ahead, the DJ stood on a stage overlooking the legion of fans before him. He expertly twisted dials and spun records on the mixing board. With each new beat, the crowd responded in kind.

An LCD screen flashed images behind him, and spotlights swung overhead, shooting their beams of light randomly across the floor.

The whole environment was intoxicating. Chris hadn't lied. This place fucking rocked.

With one final swig, Jason turned to a trashcan and threw away his beer. As he did, a brunette leaning against the bar caught his eye. She stared at the dance floor, giving Jason ample time to gawk at her. She wore a black leather miniskirt that stopped only a few inches down her thighs. A purple blouse draped down the front of her. Even though it appeared to fit loosely, Jason easily determined she was a C, if not a D, cup. Her long brown hair split around her head, framing her face. The spotlights hesitated over her, making her glow.

Perfection.

"Hi," Jason said as he approached her.

"Hi," she responded, not taking her eyes from the dance floor.

"Truth or dare?" he said.

She shifted her eyes away from the DJ and the swarm of people and looked at Jason for the first time. Her gaze drifted from his sandy blond hair to his well-defined chest, the tight shirt and then dropping further. When her eyes reached back up to his, she gave a devilishly playful smile. Her body shifted slightly toward him.

"I'll bite," she said. "Dare."

"I dare you to tell me your name."

"Boring," she said and turned her attention back to the DJ.

"Boring? Is that a family name?"

She rolled her eyes but looked at him again.

"I'll give you one more shot because you're pretty. Dare!"

"I dare you to dance with me."

One side of her mouth rose up in a half smile. "That's better, pretty."

She grabbed the collar of Jason's shirt and dragged him onto the dance floor.

7

Jason let his hottie lead him through the throngs of people and onto the dance floor. He glanced around and saw Jackson behind a petite blonde. The blonde pressed her ass against Jackson's pelvis as they gyrated to the rhythm the DJ provided. Jackson's arm swept around her stomach, holding her close to him.

The tug on Jason's collar eased up, and he shifted his gaze back to this beauty. Placing a gentle hand on his chest, she stopped him from moving any further. They stood in the center of the dance floor.

She hiked the black skirt up even higher, giving Jason and everyone else an eye full of her toned thighs. She brought a hand behind his head, gently brushing the hairs on the back of his neck. Her fingers caressed down to his shoulder and then gripped. Hard. She bent her knees and dropped low to the ground in front of Jason, using his shoulder as leverage to rise back up in front of him. Her chest rubbed against him from his waist to his stomach and finally to his own chest.

His head swooned.

She grabbed the side of his leg and moved it forward. She inched closer to him, sliding his leg between her own. Both hands moved to the back of his head as she bent his lower, their foreheads touching.

Jason wrapped his arms around her back. He held her tight against him, as if he feared she'd fly away if he didn't.

As close as they were, his olfactory senses exploded with the smell of vanilla. The smell intoxicated him. It was sweet, but underneath held a strong, intense, and almost animalistic quality about it. He wanted to drown in her scent.

Her face leaned to the side of his head. With her lips so close to his ear that he felt the moisture, she whispered, "Eileen."

Eileen.

With the feel of her body against his, the aroma of vanilla, and now the timbre of her voice, everything else in the room faded away into nothing. The sound of music blasting through Republic New Orleans drifted off. The people who had stood so close to him moments ago, vanished. No large LCD screen. No beams of light. Only Eileen.

He moved and swayed but not to the music. He matched whatever movement her body made.

Her lips came close to his ear again. "You should buy me a drink, Jason."

A quiet voice deep in his head, some sense of rational thought, tried to speak up.

When did you tell her your name?

He dismissed the thought. Of course, he had told her his name. He must've. But that wasn't important. She wanted a drink. She needed a drink. Eileen needed him to get her a drink.

She gently eased away from him.

Jason felt a need to pull her back into him and not let her slip away, but his desire eased when she placed her hand on the back of his arm and led him to the bar. His feet tingled, as if they had fallen asleep, and he had no idea how he didn't stumble over them. All he could focus on was how she glided over the floor, smooth, as if her feet never touched the ground.

My Angel. Eileen.

He didn't know how long they'd been on the dance floor, but his throat screamed for hydration. He leaned onto the bar and waited for the large, bearded bartender to make his way over.

"What can I get for you?"

"Just a water for me, and she'll have..." his voice trailed off. He had no idea what she wanted.

Eileen placed an arm around his waist and leaned close to him. She gripped his hand with her other hand.

Jason cleared his throat. "She'll have a rum and coke," he finished. He didn't know how he knew what she wanted, but it seemed like he'd always known.

The bartender grabbed two glasses. He scooped ice into both, spun around, grabbed a bottle of rum from the shelf, and spun back. He gripped the handle of the bar gun and poured rum into a glass while pressing the button for Coke. With Eileen's drink done, he pressed the button for water over the second glass and slid it to Jason.

"Have a tab open?"

"Yes, it's under..." Jason hesitated. Oddly, he'd known what type of drink Eileen wanted but not his own last name.

"It's under McHenry," Eileen said with a smile.

"It's under McHenry," Jason echoed.

"Thanks." The bartender turned to the computer and tapped on the screen.

Eileen turned her back to the bar and watched over the dance floor again.

Jason mirrored her.

"How did you know my name?" he asked.

She brushed her hand over his arm again. "I heard when you ordered your drink earlier. I saw you before you saw me."

Eileen gave a playful smile, and even in the colored lighting of the club, Jason saw her cheeks blush. She took a drink.

He took a drink from his water and returned her smile. She had seen him first? If that wasn't an ego boost, he didn't know what was.

"This might be crazy," he said, leaning close to her, "but would you like to get out of here?"

She moved her hand across his face and behind his head. She pressed his head toward her and onto her lips.

Jason's entire body exploded in heat. His heart rate accelerated, and he felt a growing pressure inside his already tight pants. Her soft lips melded with his own, and her tongue explored the inside of his mouth, his dancing with hers.

After an eternity that didn't last long enough, she slowly pulled her head away from his, giving his bottom lip a slight nibble as their lips parted.

"I thought you'd never ask," she said.

8

When they were back on the street, Eileen's hand never left Jason's. She kept a tight grip on it.

Jason tried to pull her the direction of his hotel, but she tugged his arm the opposite way.

"Where are you going? My hotel is this way," he said.

"We're going to my place. It's just a few blocks this way."

"Your place, huh?" Jason said. His eyebrows bounced as he gave a cheesy grin.

She giggled.

"If you start to get cheesy on me, I'll leave your ass back in the club. Dozen other guys who would love to be in your position right now."

Jason felt a sting in his heart. The thought of not walking down the street holding her hand, of not being inches away from her, physically hurt. He needed her close to him as if she was a drug. It'd be easier for him to hold his breath until he passed out than it would be to leave her side.

"Sorry."

He straightened his back and put away his smile.

Eileen raised his arm and placed it over her shoulder, pulling in close to his side. Her hand traced up and down his arm. She cupped his hand and draped it lower so he could feel the smooth skin at the top of her breast.

The bulge in Jason's pants grew.

"When we get to my place, we have to be quiet."

"Quiet? I'll try my best, but I make no promises."

"Well, we can't be too loud. I live with my three sisters. We don't want to disturb them."

Jason stopped, brought his head down close to her, and kissed her. When he finally pulled back, he said, "So you live with your three sisters. Any chance of an orgy?"

She placed her hand on his chest and let out a loud, raucous laugh that caught Jason by surprise. Suddenly, she stopped laughing, and her face showed complete seriousness. "Not on the first date, dear."

He couldn't tell if she was joking. His eyes widened, and his mouth dropped open. "Wait...what?"

A coy smile crossed her face. "Come on. It's not much farther."

She ducked beneath his arm again, placing his hand back where it was, just below her collarbone.

Another block farther, she moved out from underneath Jason, turned in front of a two-story condo, sauntered up to the front door, and opened it without needing to use a key. Using her index finger, she motioned for him to come inside.

Almost tripping over his own feet, he rushed for the front door and wrapped his arms around her. He scooped her off the ground, his face buried into hers, as they stepped into the darkened condo. His hands roamed up and down her back, cupping her butt cheeks, and curling her legs around him.

She briefly pulled her face away from his and pointed up the stairs.

"That way," she said breathlessly, "second door on the right. Remember. Be quiet."

Her face went back to his as he strode up the stairs with her legs still wrapped around his waist. His hands ran up the back of her shirt and explored her back. He slipped a finger under her bra, pulling it back just far enough to slide his hand underneath it and cup her breast. Her erect nipple stood like a small stone pebble beneath his hand.

As they reached the door, Eileen eased her hand back and twisted the doorknob. The door flung open, and the two entered the room, intertwined. She nudged the door closed with her foot.

Jason took her to the bed and fell backward onto it, bringing Eileen on top of him. In an instant, her shirt and bra disappeared. A moment later, his shirt had done the same.

Eileen crawled off the top of Jason and stood at the foot of the bed, slipping her black leather miniskirt down her legs.

Jason responded by removing his pants. He shimmied up to the head of the bed as she walked around to meet him. He held his arms out as she crawled onto the bed. Their bodies collided.

The temperature of the room rose as they explored each other. Hands, mouths, and tongues trailed up and down. Jason was swept up in ecstasy, in her aroma, her taste, her feel. When his hard cock couldn't take anymore and needed to be inside of her, she crawled on top of him.

"Oh shit, hold on a second," he said.

Jason stretched his arms down to his pants.

"What's the matter?" she asked, hovering just above him.

"I just need to grab a condom."

Eileen brushed her fingertips across Jason's face.

"You don't need to grab one of those," she said.

Jason's eyes rolled back in his head. The sound of her voice flowed into his ears. The strong scent of vanilla filled his senses again. His hands found the sides of her hips as she reached between her legs and grabbed his throbbing cock, guiding it into her.

What the hell am I doing?

"Wait, no, you have me so worked up, I have no pull-out game right now. I need to wrap up."

He gripped her sides and held her steady. The tip of his penis brushed the folds of her lips. It took every ounce of self-control he had not to let her slide down the full extent of his shaft, but he knew he needed to put on protection first.

"It's fine. You can finish inside of me. I want you to impregnate me."

"What the fuck!" Jason exclaimed. "Fuck that. I don't need any kids running around."

He tried to shift his body out from underneath her and stretch to his jeans on the floor. A sudden feeling of hot lead erupted in his stomach. Eileen clamped her hand down on his cock and testicles, squeezing hard.

"Holy fuck, girl," Jason groaned. "Ease up before you crush something."

She released her grip and brought her face inches from his. Something about her eyes seemed off. He saw only black as if they didn't contain irises.

"I'm going to slide you inside of me, and you are going to impregnate me." The soft tones of her voice turned gritty, guttural.

Eileen sat back up, grabbed the shaft of his cock, and slammed herself down on top of it.

A mixture of pain and pleasure shot through Jason's body. Being inside of her felt like pure ecstasy, but the force that she drove into him sent pain rocketing up his hips and down his legs. Her muscles tensed around him, squeezing his cock to the point of pain.

He tried to force her off him, but he couldn't budge her. His hands moved under her legs to lift her off, but she overpowered him.

One of her hands went to his chest then crawled up to his neck, closing around his throat. She pinned him down.

Panic filled Jason as she slammed her pelvis into his. He was twice her size and should've been able to easily overpower her, but he couldn't move. Her fingernails dug into the sides of his neck. Sharp, painful razors bit into his skin, creating another fresh wave of pain. The grip tightened, cutting off his airwaves.

His eyes started to roll into the back of his head, and his neck extended further back, exposing more and more skin as the crushing grip grew. Trying to hold on, Jason thrust his head forward. What he saw sent him into utter terror.

Eileen, the beautiful, long haired, brunette angel with the perfect body, no longer thrust on top of him. Instead, a hideous creature rode him. Its skin, a sickly, gray color, clung to its body. What should have been breasts were lumps of wrinkled skin. Its hairless head with pointed ears displayed sharp teeth. The hand that held Jason's neck seemed more like a talon. A serpent-like tail waved above her head. The closest similarity that came to Jason's mind was a gargoyle.

In his hyper-adrenalized state, he found the strength to free himself from under the creature, sliding off the side of the bed, and collapsing onto the floor. Jason didn't even care about his clothes. On unsteady legs, he stood. Pain exploded in his abdomen. He peered down and saw blood covering his limp cock. Cuts ran down the sides of it with pieces of torn flesh flayed to the side.

Absolute fear gripped him, and he let out a blood curdling scream.

In a sound closer to a growl than a voice, the creature said, "I told you to be quiet."

The thing jumped off the bed, rushing at Jason.

Naked, he bolted for the door. Blood trailed from his groin and down his leg. As he stepped into the hallway, he turned to see the creature staring at him, still standing by the bed. He spun around and missed his footing on the top step, tumbling down to the bottom.

When he finally came to a stop, he was face down, staring at the carpet. He tried to move his arm, but his shoulder wouldn't work. He'd had enough sports injuries to realize it was dislocated. Before he could flip himself over, hands gripped his side and hoisted him on his back.

Two more of the same gray gargoyles with sharp teeth and talons for hands stood over him.

From the top of the stairs, the guttural growl said, "Sorry for waking you. I couldn't keep this one quiet. Eat up."

Jason's eyes went wide as the duo pounced on top of him, claws diving into his abdomen, ripping out his stomach and intestines, and feasting on his body.

9

Josh's head slumped forward and immediately shot back up as he tried to focus on the computer screen. The rest of the team had migrated to their own areas. Mike had escaped back to his room for quiet meditation while Nate and Niki snoozed the afternoon away in theirs. With the disappearance of the Council and Thomas training Mike, they'd been sidelined.

Josh kept waiting for the phone to ring.

When they were hunting Silas, the Night Crew had moved pretty routinely. Everywhere he stirred up trouble, they went. Things happened. They made a difference.

This boredom wore on Josh. When the Council first went missing, he had assisted Jax with a few leads, but those eventually dried up. Intel handled most of what Jax and his new team needed. Jax had Thomas by his side when Thomas wasn't teaching Mike. He knew without the Council, it wouldn't be long before the Accords dissolved. Once the word spread, there'd be chaos.

In the meantime, he fought to stay awake.

As his eyes closed and his breathing slowed to a relaxed rhythm, from somewhere far away, a voice spoke to him.

"Josh."

He gave no response to the voice.

"Josh."

He filled his lungs with a deep, full breath.

"Campbell!" the voice yelled.

Startled, Josh raised his head, his eyes shooting open.

A face filled the center of the twenty-seven-inch monitor in front of him. Josh recognized the buzz cut brown hair, squared jawline, and goatee immediately and sat upright in his wheelchair.

"Intel. Long time no see."

"Catching up on the beauty sleep?"

"Staying rested in the event we get tapped for a late-night mission, Intel," Josh replied.

"I appreciate the bullshit, Josh."

"What can we do you for?"

For the few years Josh had been part of the Night Crew, he only knew Intel's name as Intel. Intel gave him the assignments, logistical information, supplies, and made the arrangements. Intel was the all-knowing and all-seeing specter behind the curtain. Not until Mike joined the team did any of them know Intel had any other name. Despite the fact that now Josh knew Intel's real name was Austin Jeffries, former army grunt who had served with Mike, he couldn't break the habit.

Josh heard papers shuffling.

"What are your thoughts on New Orleans?" Intel asked.

"Great city. Love the food. Laissez les bons temps rouler." Josh smiled and took a breath, staring at the head on the monitor. He changed to a more serious tone. "What's going on in New Orleans?"

"I got ahead of myself." Intel removed his glasses, placing them in front of him. He then cupped his forehead, and massaged his temples.

"Need some Motrin?" Josh asked.

"My ulcer says no." He put his glasses back on his face, resting them gently on the edge of his nose. "Be straight with me, Josh. How's he doing?"

"Mike? He's getting better. Good days and bad days."

"Don't sugar coat it. You know better than that." Intel stared straight ahead.

Josh could feel Intel's eyes penetrating his soul. He didn't know how Austin had been when he'd worked with Mike, but to hear Mike talk about it, he loved to joke and get into trouble. This version, though, the Austin who was Intel, had all the makings of an interrogator. He pulled information out of Josh just by thinking about it.

"I want the team to get out there. We're all going stir crazy cooped up in here, but I'm worried about putting him in the field too soon. Mike's still having control issues. The last time Thomas was here..."

"I heard," Intel interrupted. "Thomas got to slam him into the floor."

"What if something happens on a mission? Things get violent, things get out of hand. If Nate or Niki gets cut, or an innocent bystander, anything where there's blood, I don't know if he can keep himself from losing control and vamping out."

Josh paused for a moment. If Intel was asking him his opinion and not just defaulting to another team, there had to be a damn good reason.

"What's going on? How bad is it?"

"Bad enough that we may need to worry about crossing that Michael-Vamping-Out Bridge sooner rather than later."

"Fuck," Josh said. He dropped his head backward and stared up at the ceiling.

Maybe boredom was better.

10

After Intel disconnected the call, Josh moved to his workstation and pressed the alert button on his desk. A sharp alarm bell rang throughout the warehouse. It reminded him of a fire station alarm, rousing the fire fighters from their bunks and making them race to the truck.

A notification showed up on his monitor, and he opened it. Everything Intel had told him about—pictures, autopsy reports, and articles—popped up on the screen. He left it open for the team.

Nate and Niki left out of their room. They looked as if they had just woken. Niki still wore boy shorts and a tank top. Nate wore baggy shorts and pulled on a tank as he strode to the table.

Mike stepped out of his room in jeans and no shirt. With his skin pale, Josh would've thought he was sick, if he didn't know he was actually dead. Mike went to the fridge, grabbed an insulated water bottle, and began sipping it. The straw turned a dark red. The more he drank, the more his skin livened up.

Once the team sat at the table, Josh spun around.

"I got a call from Intel."

"What did Austin have to say?" Mike chimed in. His demeanor seemed more upbeat than he'd been recently. "Did you tell him I said hey?"

"Didn't exactly get a chance for any of that," Josh said. "We have an assignment."

"Killing some vampires?" Mike asked.

"You know we do more than just kill vampires, right, love?" Niki asked.

"Outside of the rumble with Silas, we haven't done anything but sit in this warehouse. I get the recuperation and all, but I think we're ready for field work." Mike turned back to Josh, sitting at the head of the table. "What's the assignment?"

"New Orleans," Josh said. He held a controller in his hand and pointed to the monitors on the wall around them. With a click of his finger, the picture of a man in his twenties flashed on the screen. His eyes were closed, and his head rested on a metal table. Morgue picture. Josh clicked again and the image changed to another man dead in a street.

"There's been over a dozen people killed so far. All men, young and healthy. Most appear to have died of natural causes, but a healthy twenty-three-year-old doesn't just die of a heart attack or lung failure like he's in his eighties."

Another click showed a face with slash marks across it.

"Two of the bodies have been ripped to shreds."

"Does Intel think the crimes are related?" Nate asked.

"He does, but the New Orleans and Louisiana authorities do not. There's no reason they would. The going theory is there's a wild animal on the loose."

"And the organ failure?" Nate asked, leaning his elbows onto the table.

"A street drug of unknown origin."

"So obviously the authorities are wrong," Niki said. She pushed her chair away from the table, leaned back, and tossed her feet onto the table, crossed at the ankles. "What does Intel think?"

Josh clicked another button, changing the screen from the image of a man whose body was riddled with claw marks to a marble statue. The sculpture captured the form of a beautiful woman, with sensual curves, a voluptuous chest, and long, flowing hair. Attached to her back, two bat-like wings extended. The sculptor shaved the wings thin, nearly translucent, with a ribbed bone along the top and splitting each wing into three segments. Where her hands should be, bird of prey- like talons hung instead.

"A succubus?" Niki asked.

Nate leaned back in his chair, and Michael stared at the screen, his brow raised with a puzzled look on his face.

"I thought they didn't exist anymore," Nate said. "Extinct sometime during the Middle Ages."

"I had the same thought," Josh said. "As did Intel. He triple checked every record they had regarding succubi. It's the only thing that matches the MO."

"Hold on a second," Mike interrupted. "I know I'm the new guy and haven't watched many horror movies, but let's back up a minute. What's a succubus?"

Josh shifted his eyes up to the monitor and clicked through a few more images. Pictures of beautiful women with bird-like claws and serpent tails flashed by. "I'll start with the lore. A succubus is a female creature, demon actually, who seduces men. She drains her victims of their life force, sort of like a vampire drains blood. A succubus needs to create a bond first, though."

"A bond?" Mike asked.

"She needs to jump your bones," Niki said. "Fuck your brains out."

"Thanks, Niki, for putting that so delicately," Josh said with a smile.

"Anytime."

"Yes, the bond is usually created during sex. According to legend, Adam's first wife, Lilith, became a succubus. She wanted to be Adam's equal and was banished from the Garden of Eden for not obeying Adam."

"Harsh," Nate said.

"Adam's first wife? You're telling me there are creatures that go back to creation?" Mike asked. "When I first met you, I thought you were joking about werewolves and vampires. Now we're adding the Garden of Eden and sex demons?"

Josh laughed. "I think some of that is embellishment. Plus, the odds that Lilith survived that long are slim."

"So, this succubus just goes around having sex and killing men afterward? Like some kind of black widow or praying mantis?" Mike asked.

"Well, this is where the lore gets a little dicey. Unlike vampires, a succubus can't create other succubi. They were created by a demon named Samael. Now, he's an interesting character. In some writings, he was the angel who tempted Adam and Eve. Think of him as a precursor to Satan. Some say he was an archangel."

"Archangel," Nate said. "Like Michael and Gabriel?"

"Correct, although just like Lilith and the Garden of Eden, there's probably quite a bit of embellishment that's gone on over the years. That being said, Samael was destroyed a long time ago, which is why the Council believed succubi went extinct. No more Samael; no new succubi. But, if there is a succubus, then she could be looking for the perfect mate to sire a child. Said child could be the reincarnation of Samael."

"Why hasn't she tried to raise him before?" Nate asked.

"We don't know that she hasn't. Hell, we still don't have confirmation that one even exists. Maybe it is a new street drug. Either which way, that's why you're heading to New Orleans."

Michael slowly nodded. "Well, that makes perfect sense. Your creator was killed, but if you get knocked up by the right person, he could come back as your baby. This job doesn't get dull, does it?"

"Just think about it," Niki said, her feet still propped up on the table. "You'll have forever to learn about all of this stuff. Plus, you never forget anything. One day, you'll be the most knowledgeable man in the world. Also known as the average female."

She started laughing, and Nate pushed her feet off the table, which only brought on more laughter from her.

Josh rolled his eyes.

After Niki's laugh slowed, she said, "Oh, I needed that. What else do we need to know about a succubus?"

"Well, this isn't so much for you, Niki. At least, I don't think so, but her touch is addictive. That's one thing that's pretty consistent amongst the legends. You can become completely infatuated with her with just a touch of her finger."

Michael nodded. "Got it. So, on top of all my other training and meditation, I need to add in how to kill a sex demon without her touching me. Speaking of, how do we kill a succubus?"

"Ah, well, that's something you guys are already experts at doing. You kill her the same way we kill pretty much everything else. Cut her head off. Then, I'd probably burn her body for good measure."

11

Alone in his room, Michael White felt a heavy weight on his shoulders. They'd just received their first mission, their first assignment with him as the supposed team leader. He was the newest person. How did he get voted to lead?

Of course, he knew how. After he had rescued the team not once but twice, the writing was on the wall. He and Thomas had worked together to save Jax, Nate, and Niki from Silas when he held them in Club Starlight. Then, when the Night Crew went after Silas in the abandoned school, he saved them again. It had cost him his own life, but he had saved them. Now he was cursed to exist as this immortal being.

And their team leader.

During their huddle, he had intentionally appeared gung-ho about the idea. The others were going stir crazy and needed a mission; needed to work. He wasn't going to say he wasn't ready and hold them back. That's not what a leader did. He was going to nut up and accept the mission.

Mike stared at the closed door. Even in the darkness of the room, his supernatural vision picked up the subtle light around the edges of the door frame. Just beyond the door, calling to him, reaching out to him, lay the refrigerator.

In the days following his transformation, the fridge had stayed in his room. He had stayed close by it, barricading himself inside with it. He didn't trust himself. Couldn't trust himself.

How could he? Silas had tried to use him as a weapon against his team. If not for Thomas stepping in, and Brittany—or her vision (ghost)—he would've bled them dry to quench his thirst.

No, he didn't trust himself then. And Michael doubted if he could trust himself now.

But what choice was there?

12

It was a ten-hour drive to New Orleans. The four of them loaded into a large Escalade with heavily tinted windows, primarily for Michael's sake. That much extended sun exposure concerned him.

Intel informed the team their temporary base of operations would already be stocked with supplies, so they didn't have to worry about cramming everything they might possibly need into one vehicle.

Niki drove first, but as the sun dipped below the horizon, Michael felt his strength grow. With his night vision far surpassing hers, he swapped to the driver's seat. The dark Escalade flew down the interstate. Since Michael didn't need the headlights on, the SUV soared like a stealth missile down the highway.

It was the first time he'd been behind the wheel since his transformation. Aside from the relocation to Dallas, he'd rarely stepped beyond their warehouse walls. For the first time in a while, he felt in control of something. Not necessarily of himself, yet, but it was a start.

They reached Baton Rouge as the sun began to reemerge. That also seemed like a great time to stop for breakfast. As Nate, Niki, and Josh went inside a diner off Interstate 10, Mike sipped from his insulated bottle in the back of the SUV. He sat curled up, focusing on the vibrations of the highway.

The other stimuli, though. Those worried him.

He stared at the carpeted floorboard. When he glanced up, he saw people walking into the diner. He heard their heartbeats. His eyes detected the rhythmic pulsation of their jugular veins just under the skin of their necks. Most people couldn't feel it with their hand against their neck, but Michael could see it. The heat from the blood pumping through their bodies emanated all the way to him. The sweet smell cut through the doors and windows to entice him.

Pulling the hood of his jacket over his head, he curled further into a ball. The red tinted straw of the bottle still rested between his lips as he sucked the O-negative blood into his mouth.

What the fuck am I thinking?

"You don't know how strong you are."

He hadn't heard her voice since the day he'd changed. Since she stood before him and forced him to see who the real enemy was, she'd been silent. Looking back on that moment, he still questioned if her spirit really was there, or if his psyche fought so hard to retain his morality that he conjured her image.

Really, he couldn't fucking care less. He just wanted to hear her voice, feel her touch again. Finally.

Mike inhaled deeply, hoping to catch a hint of her aroma.

This is harder than I realized.

"Did you think it'd be easy?"

Well, Thomas makes it look easy.

The voice in his head changed to Thomas's. "It's a daily struggle, but one you can handle."

Mike smiled, thinking of Thomas's words once more. Of course, he'd be buried somewhere up there. Mike hadn't done much else but listen to Thomas drill him for the past few months.

Three car doors opened around him. The smell of gasoline, exhaust fumes, hot rubber, and maple syrup filled the interior. Michael squeezed his eyelids closed at the harsh morning sun barging in.

"How was your breakfast?" Nate asked from the front passenger seat.

"Rare," Mike said, cowering further into the seat behind Nate, trying to escape the encroaching sun.

Josh lifted himself into the SUV and closed the back door.

The rear door opened, and Niki loaded Josh's wheelchair in. She closed it, strolled to the front, and hopped into the driver's seat.

"Whatever happened to chivalry? I had to put Josh's wheelchair away, and I'm driving. Glad to be along with you three strapping lads."

"Well, I'd help but..." Josh said and pointed at his legs.

"Mikey drove us here through the night and wouldn't enjoy the sunbath. Nate, my love, what's your pitiful excuse?"

She started the Escalade and backed out of the parking lot.

"I know how much you like being in control."

Niki patted the side of his face. "Only in the bedroom, my dear."

Everyone settled into their seats as she drove the remaining hour and a half to New Orleans. Michael stared out the window, watching the Louisiana landscape flow past them. As he saw the wide stretch of Lake Pontchartrain and the surrounding wetlands, he knew the city lay straight ahead.

Niki took them into the heart of New Orleans and through the French Quarter. She continued until she hit Washington Square. From there, she turned down a side street, into an alley, and stopped the car.

"This is it," she said.

In front of them was an old French-style house. The bottom floor had a series of green doors against sandstone colored brick. The second-floor rooms had balconies that overlooked Washington Square Park. It was the size of an entire city block. Trees absent of leaves lined the park, skeletal in their appeal.

"Doesn't look like much," Mike commented as he brought Josh his chair. He kept his head covered by the hood of his jacket and slipped his pale hands back in his pockets the moment he put the chair down.

"Thanks," Josh said. "And it's not supposed to look like much. Rather it have flashy neon lights with 'Night Crew' plastered on the front?" He spread his hands in the air in front of him as if the building had a marquee sign.

"Well, no," Mike said with a smirk.

He helped Nate grab the few duffel bags of clothes and hoisted them inside.

The interior lived up to the impression the exterior gave. With the exception of the latest in technology already wired and a room stocked full of blades, guns, and ammunition, the interior decor showed an abundance of wear and tear. The floors were cracked, their glued-on tiles peeling. Cracks also ran up the walls. Plaster patches covered holes and dotted the sandstone-colored walls in stark white spots.

Each room contained a bed with no box spring. Just a mattress laid across a twin bed frame, one step above a cot. Michael had never thought he would, but suddenly he had a longing for a nice army cot.

Do not tell Austin.

Niki stepped out of a side room and into the living area where a large table sat. Laptops lined the table. Josh, Nate, and Mike joined her.

"You know, Mike," she said, "when Jax was team lead, we had better accommodations than this."

Josh chuckled. "Ah, give him a break. It's his first mission. He didn't know to book us in the Marriott. He'll do better next time."

"When I first met you, I woke up on a cot in a warehouse," Mike said. "Don't give me any of that bullshit."

"By the way, you don't have to stay covered up or hide here," Niki said to Mike. "I doubt you're the only vampire in town. This is NOLA. It's like Vampire Mecca. Let your freak flag fly. And as long as whatever other vampires are in town behave, we won't have to hunt them while we're here."

"Find the succubus and kill her," Mike said. "That's the mission."

"Exactly," she confirmed. "But we do need to get you registered."

13

Josh stayed at their new headquarters, getting equipment set up exactly where and how he wanted it. The rest of the crew started strolling down Royal Street.

"Registered?" Mike asked.

He wore his jacket, but left the hood off, and shoved his hands into his pants pockets. Although the sun was out, the cloud cover made the outdoors less unbearable. He maintained his focus on Niki and Nate, ignoring the sounds and smells coming from other people on the street. Footsteps, heartbeats, and the sweet scent of blood.

"New Orleans has always been a haven for vampires," Niki said. "Long before Anne Rice and *The Vampire Chronicles*, the city just had an appeal, a draw. The voodoo history, the atmosphere, the night festivities. No one knows exactly why, but it just was.

"During the early 1800s, a socialite named Delphine LaLaurie had a certain affinity for torturing and murdering her slaves. Rumor was, she had taken a few lovers who were vampires, so she used her slaves to keep them fed and happy.

"When the Council found out, there was an uproar. Sure, the vampires themselves didn't break the Accords, but had a human kill for them."

"So, the registry was established to know who was here?" Mike asked, assuming the end of the story.

"Pretty much. They hoped having a list of who was in town would dissuade those with ill intentions. With as many vampires and witches, not to mention other creatures here at any given time, can you imagine the bloodshed if it was open season?"

Mike shook his head as they crossed Ursuline Avenue.

He loved the architecture here. The styling was unique only to New Orleans. They walked under awnings that served as balconies for the second floors. The occasional banner of purple, yellow, and green provided vivid colors to the already vibrant atmosphere.

"What happens if a creature doesn't register?" Mike asked.

"When that happens," Nate said, "the assumption is they are new, didn't know, or forgot. They are highly encouraged to register. Refusal means you must leave town immediately. You only get one warning. After that, you are barred. If you're found in town after being barred, you are reported to the Council and that's when a team like us gets involved."

"So we're the police," Mike commented.

"More like enforcers," Nate corrected.

They crossed Dumaine Street. To Mike's right, was the sign for the New Orleans Historic Voodoo Museum. A strange smell caught his attention. Notes of grass and wood with certain floral elements. He couldn't tell if he liked the smell or not. It made him pause for a moment.

"Sage, love," Niki said.

Mike held a confused look on his face. The aroma in the air still lingered heavily on his senses.

"You had a look on your face," she continued. "I'm guessing you are smelling burnt sage from the voodoo museum. It's used for cleansing and healing. Very common. We don't typically pick up on it unless closer, but I can imagine you're getting a nose full."

"You can say that," Mike said, continuing his walk down Royal Street. "It was odd. I felt equally drawn to it but also repulsed."

"We're here," Niki interrupted.

Mike had lowered his head, engulfed in the fading aromatics from the burnt sage, instead of observing his surroundings. When he lifted his head, he saw they'd stopped at the corner of Royal and St. Ann. He stood next to a building with a soft, red-colored exterior. It was almost pink, but not quite. A white sign hung from a metal pole at the corner of the building in order to be seen from any direction. In small black lettering across the top of the sign were the words "THE NEW ORLEANS". In large lettering at the bottom, Mike read the words "Vampire Cafe". The "I" in vampire was used as the stem of a decorative wine glass drawn in the middle of the sign.

"You've got to be kidding me," Michael said. "The registration is inside a place called 'The Vampire Cafe'?"

"Hiding in plain sight," Nate said.

"Or New Orleans just doesn't care," Niki finished.

She stepped in and was followed by Nate.

Michael went in last. The smell of burnt sage vanished. An intense aroma of blood hit him. Colors along the street sharpened. The hues became brighter, crisper. He knew his eyes had flared red. He also realized his breathing had accelerated. The smell hit him so hard, he backed out of the cafe.

"You ok?" Nate asked him.

Niki strolled up to the bar and spoke with the bartender.

Mike shook his head. "I can't go in there. Too much blood."

"That's fine. Niki is handling it. We can wait out here."

Nate led Mike around the corner of the building. He peered into the window of "The Vampire Cafe". Bags of what looked like blood sat on the tables next to bottles of red wine called "Vampire". Small, decorative coffins, fangs, roses, and bats filled the interior of the cafe. The silverware was placed together in the shape of a cross on the tables.

Mike chuckled. If he had better control of himself, the place would've been comical. "So, what's in the blood bags?" he asked Nate.

"Sangria. Pretty cliche, isn't it?"

"It's a place Brittany and I would've loved." Mike paused.

He thought of Brittany and a vacation they had taken two years prior. A lifetime and a half ago. The Ultranet in his head threw up images of them driving through New Orleans. They had stopped for food at a small Cajun place on their way to Orlando.

Before the memory could go too far, he forced himself out. He tried to avoid memories of Brit when he could. The pain was still fresh. Raw.

"Hey, boys," Niki said, leaving the cafe and stepping over to them. "Miss anything good?"

"Just admiring the scenery," Mike said. "Get everything taken care of? Do I have permission to move about the city?"

"Actually, the registrar isn't here anymore. Too many tourists. Go figure. He lives in the Garden District now."

"Garden District?" Nate asked. "Monster registration must pay well." He turned to Mike. "No offense."

"None taken," Mike said.

"Oh, this is for you," Niki said. She tossed him one of the blood bags he'd seen on the tables.

"I don't drink Sangria."

"That's not Sangria. Bartender said it's on the house. A thank you for killing Silas. Silas was always an ass to him."

Mike inserted the end of the bag into his mouth and took a long, slow drink. The soothing effect of feeding washed over him. He felt more at ease sucking on the bag.

Niki took out her phone and opened her Uber app. She peeked up and saw Mike watching her. "I'm not walking there. These boots are made for ass-kicking, not walking, specifically not walking across town."

He nearly choked on the blood in his mouth. He coughed up a fine mist of red while laughing at Niki.

"Our Uber is around the corner. Finish up your lunch."

Michael drained the last of the bag and tossed it into a nearby trashcan. Once their Uber arrived, Nate and Niki slid in the back. Michael opened the front door and paused, standing just outside of the car.

He turned his head from one side to the other. Another strange scent caught his attention, but unlike the earthy smell of burnt sage or the sweet smell of blood, this one wreaked of something else. Hints of spice that sent him back to his time in Afghanistan, along with the pungent smell of rot and decay.

Standing there, he closed his eyes and tried to follow the smell. He searched for the source, seeking the direction the wind had carried it. As quickly as the smell washed over him, it vanished. Nothing in the air but the normal city scents.

"Come on, Mike," Niki said. "The driver's waiting."

He sat in the car and closed the door.

14

She slipped inside a parking garage a block away from the Cafe, hoping she wasn't noticed. When dealing with vampires, Naamah knew better than to linger. Their predatory senses could detect the slightest whiff of sweat or the faintest beat of a heart. She saw him hesitate before getting in the car but reassured herself anything could've caused that moment of pause. It didn't have to be her.

Better to be safe than sorry, though. Especially with a vampire who hung around two hunters.

Walking the streets of New Orleans, her short, spiked purple hair and darkened complexion made her less noticeable than her sisters. They preferred the attention, whereas she knew survival depended on being inconspicuous. She blended in with everyone else around her, disappearing amongst the locals.

She felt the most comfortable in this form. It was the closest she could bring herself to the form of her youth. The version of her before she was transformed into a monster. If her father would've seen her now, he might have recognized her. Well, if she went back to her long, brown hair. She preferred the purple and spikey, though. It fit her personality better.

Naamah still held on to vivid memories of the time before. She remembered when the Romans took control of her Syrian homeland. Her family fleeing... or trying to. She remembered the cries of her mother and father as she was hauled away. Her "sisters" would say they gave her a gift by turning her. They gave her the strength to enact her revenge on the soldiers who ripped her away from her family, but at what cost? She'd lost count of the generations of her family she'd seen grow up, have children, and die. The cycle repeated over and over, and Naamah could only watch from afar.

She had long hoped to return to her ancestral homeland. To step her feet back into the sands once again. To feel again.

Her sisters chided her for such desires. They didn't understand why she wouldn't want to live in such a lustful society. One where women could be the aggressor and men loved it. The man's lust had made their existence so easy. It made feeding and hunting barely a sport. With the simple touch of a finger, they could take a man wherever they wanted, and no one batted an eye. They preferred their new looks and more modern names.

"Better to catch prey," they'd said.

Things wouldn't be the same if they returned to their homeland. Women had to cover themselves. They didn't have rights or privileges. They'd have to keep a man around to do the simplest of tasks.

On and on, her sisters lambasted her with reasons why North America was the best place for them. Whether it was the decade they spent in Los Angeles in the twenties, or Las Vegas in the seventies, or New Orleans now, the hunting grounds were fertile. They'd talked about maybe Nashville next. It was a bachelorette party haven, and where there were bachelorettes, there were eligible bachelors.

Naamah navigated the streets, keeping her head down, blending in, and staying invisible. Although she despised her sisters, she needed to tell them what she saw. If her sisters were careless, the attention could be deadly for her as well. She hoped this would give them some caution.

The trip home took longer than usual. Walking always did. When she arrived, she found the other three relaxing in the living room.

"Why the rush, Naomi?" Lily asked. She held an empty martini glass in her hand and used an olive skewer to pick between her teeth.

"A new vampire is in town," Naamah answered.

Angie moved her feet off the ottoman and sat up. "What's so special about that? Vampires come into town all the time."

Naamah strode over to an empty chair and sat. "He is still a fledgling, but there is something different about him. He has a very strong aura. Nothing I've seen before."

"Was he cute?" Angie asked. A smile spread across her perfectly symmetrical lips.

"He's accompanied by two hunters. A large Black man and a thin white woman."

"A vampire hanging out with two hunters," Lily said. "How could you tell he was a fledgling if he had such a strong aura?"

"He couldn't stand to go into The Vampire Cafe."

The three sisters erupted in laughter. Eileen slowed her laughing first. "The irony," she said. Her voice took on the pattern of a Southern belle. Her latest incarnation she was still perfecting. "A vampire couldn't go into a bar named for their kind. Unable to control his bloodlust, I take it?"

"So it seemed," Naamah said.

"Well, his aura may be strong, but fledglings are weak," Lily said. "There's nothing to worry about."

Naamah sighed. She loathed their arrogance. Although Naamah was the youngest of them and Lily the oldest, she feared that one day that same arrogance would get them all killed. Lilith, Eisheth, and Agrat had pushed their luck for a millennium before Samael turned Naamah.

How many more times can you continue to tempt the Fates?

"I want the new vampire," Angie said. "I would love to slowly drain all of that strong aura out of him. Whichever way I can."

Her sultry smile brought laughter from the other two.

"I'm sure you'd like to," Lily said. "Enjoy your toy, then."

"Lilith..." Naamah started.

"Lily," she snapped.

"Sorry. Lily, do you think we should show some caution? If the vampire is with the hunters, it's possible he's also a hunter. They could be here on assignment, searching for us. Are you going to let Agrat, I mean Angie, throw herself onto him?"

"Who's left to send hunters, Naomi?" Lily asked.

The condescension in her voice hit Naamah harder than a slap.

"I can handle myself, little sister." Angie stood and made her way to the staircase. "Vampires are fun. Good pets if you treat them right."

15

From the moment they entered the Garden District, Mike felt as if they entered a living, breathing museum of both architecture and history.

More than a few of the opulent homes were famous. He recognized Buckner Mansion as they went down Jackson Avenue. Season three of *"American Horror Story"* had featured it as the primary setting. The regal stone and cast-iron front gate with large lanterns, the wide wrap-around balcony with Corinthian columns, and the veranda with Ionic columns were unmistakable.

The farther into the nineteen-block stretch of the Garden District they went, the more the large live oak trees shaded the walkways. Even though it had just passed midday, Mike felt the sun's rays ease. The difference was staggering, and he understood why they preferred to hunt at night even though creatures like vampires were stronger then. When he was weak, he felt trapped. He felt like a cornered animal. Held down by the oppressive sunlight, desperate to escape any danger, however he could. But at night, when the weight of the sun wasn't holding him down, he wanted to stay and fight. Use his predator reflexes to their maximum potential. Destroy any and all aggressor and feast on their blood.

The driver took them past house after house. Each one unique in its architecture and easily considered a mansion. Some with ornate marble columns and wide balconies, one odd colored pink with cast-iron adorning the front of it, and another pink house with large palm trees hiding its features. No two houses looked the same, yet each seemed to perfectly fit its surroundings.

Another turn had the three of them across from Lafayette Cemetery. The driver came to a stop.

"Here you go," he said.

"We appreciate it," Niki said.

Niki and Nate opened their doors and stepped out.

Michael, staring at the cemetery, hesitated. Something felt off about the area.

A loud rapping on the window startled him. He turned his head. Nate stood next to the door, bringing him back to the moment.

"Thanks," Mike said to the Uber driver. He opened his door, stepped out, and closed it.

The driver quickly sped away. Off to pick up another fare.

"You ok?" Nate asked.

Michael glanced down the darkened aisles of the cemetery. Brown leaves littered the stone sidewalks. Mausoleums lined the pathway. Family crypts were filled with centuries of bones and long-dead memories. The coverage of live oak trees seemed exceptionally dense, as if the sunlight itself died amongst the graves. Something from the cemetery called to him. He felt an urge to go inside. An unnatural longing.

"I...I don't know," he said.

"Death attracts death," Niki said.

The pull was strong. Staring into the gates, he saw movement. Figures in the shadows, hiding. He couldn't tell how much was his mind playing tricks on him, how much was the wind shifting around the leaves, and how much were creatures like him who felt the same calling. Creatures that wanted to stay longer with the dead. Maybe it was his own dead body ready for rest. A cemetery, the place where the dead should be, the place where his head should be laid for the long sleep.

"Mike," Niki said, refocusing him again. "This way."

She grabbed his arm, pulling him away. If he had wanted to stand his ground, she wouldn't have been able to budge him. He didn't want her to pull him, but he also needed her to. He didn't go willingly, but he didn't fight. Apathy won the battle, and she turned his body and headed to the house in front of them.

"The Registrar lives here?" Mike asked.

The sound of his own voice felt distant. He shook off the feeling from the Lafayette and refocused on the task at hand. Get him registered and find out any information they could.

"That's what the bartender at the Vampire Cafe told me. Like Nate said, monster registration must pay well."

Like most houses in the Garden District, an iron gate sat at the entrance to the property. The lawn was perfectly manicured. Each blade of grass exactly the same height. The edging, a perfectly straight line.

This time, the two-story grand mansion appeared to be a mashup of styles. Greek revival columns ran across both the front porch and the large balcony. On the other hand, the estate also had Italianate flourishes and hexagonal windows. The mix came together in an elegance that matched the other Garden District estates.

A shrill shriek cried out as Niki pulled back the gate, opening it.

Who needed a doorbell with a noise like that?

Not at all to his surprise, before they mounted the steps to the porch, the front door swung open. An unassuming older man, short in stature, his head nearly bald, stood in the doorway. He wore a white shirt and brown pants held up by the suspenders running over his shoulders. Despite having small but thick round glasses on his face, he squinted at the three of them standing on his front porch.

He glanced at Niki, gave an audible puff from his nose, then turned to Nate. He made the same noise before peering at Mike. That's where his gaze stopped. He tilted his glasses down onto the tip of his nose, gawking over the top of them, and then pushed them back up to his eyes.

"Vampire, I see." His voice had an equally unassuming quality. He spoke very matter-of-factly, like having a vampire step up to his door was a usual occurrence. "Come on in. Let's get you registered."

16

When they walked in the door, Michael knew a home with such an elegant exterior would have an equally stunning interior. The mansion didn't disappoint. A large crystal chandelier hung over the entryway. The floors were hardwood, and a small wooden staircase with a solid oak handrail rose to the second floor. Instead of pictures on the walls, they were covered with an Italian style wallpaper, adding to the elegance.

The Registrar directed them around the staircase and into a living room. Large windows with red velvet drapes lined the back wall. Light flooded in through the windows, filling the room with natural light. Three more crystal chandeliers hung from the high ceiling of the living room. Paintings by Monet and Renoir hung on the walls. Michael guessed each painting's worth at over six figures. From the living room, he could see a dining room with a mural painted on each wall.

The decadence of the mansion was overwhelming.

The Registrar directed Nate and Niki toward a couch in the center of the living room. He then pointed to a single wooden chair with a red cushion for Michael. The chair sat across from a tiny wooden desk. It was the only thing that felt out of place in the extravagance of the house.

Michael sat, and the diminutive old man strode to the other side of the desk and pulled up a large leather office chair. The word Serta was stenciled across the top of it. When the man sat, the chair dwarfed his small demeanor. He looked like a child sitting in his father's chair.

He rolled the chair to the desk, then pulled a ledger book out of the drawer. Without saying a word, he turned a few pages before stopping. He grabbed a clear Bic pen.

"This is quite the home you have," Niki said.

"It was a gift," he replied.

"A gift?" Nate asked. "That must be some friend. I wish I had friends like that."

"This house belonged to Anne Rice. The author of the Vampire Chronicles."

"We know who she is," Niki said. "That's amazing. Someone gifted it to you?"

"She did," he said.

He spoke as if talking about the late author and a gift of this manner was nothing out of the usual. But of course, he knew Anne. And why wouldn't she give him her old house?

"I'm sure there's quite the story there," Nate said.

"Mmmmhmmm," the Registrar said.

Michael sat in the chair, silent. When they were outside, the towering live oak trees had blocked out the sun, draping shadows across the sidewalk. In here, the windows at the back basked the room in natural sunlight. He shrank in the chair, trying to cower away from the draining sun.

The Registrar jotted a few notes in his ledger then peered over the top of his glasses at Michael.

"It's on purpose," he said.

"What's that?" Michael asked.

"The sun coming through the windows. I move my desk throughout the day to follow the sun. I get more vampires than anything else. Some just want to see Anne's former home. She wrote most of the Witching Chronicles here, you know," he said. "Their make-believe home is designed after this very house.

"Anyway, New Orleans gets a lot of vampires in general. Most aren't escorted by hunters, though."

"How did you know we're hunters?" Niki asked.

He turned his gaze to Niki, tilted his head down to the knife strapped to her hip, and peeked over the top of his small glasses again. He raised his brows and picked his head back up.

"When you've been around as long as I have, there's not much you can't tell just by looking. Pretty hard to surprise me. I doubted you two were just best friends with a vampire, so you must be hunter escorts."

He looked back at Michael, then at Nate and Niki. Both of them had originally rested back against the couch but now leaned closer with their elbows on their knees. The Registrar had gotten their attention.

The old man pointed his finger at Michael while still looking at Nate and Niki. "This one is a fledgling. Hmmm. A fledgling escorted by two hunters. Either he got himself into trouble..." He shifted his gaze back to Michael, glaring at him from over his glasses again. "No. He's also a hunter, working with you. Just still a baby."

"That's impressive," Nate said.

"How did you know I'm a fledgling?" Michael asked.

"You're paler than you should be. Guessing because Lafayette called to you when you were outside. Also, the way you shrank away from the sun. Dead giveaway. Betas... and especially Alphas... they don't care. Some get angry, but most just ignore it. But you've been trying to hide from it. Averting your eyes."

He made a few more notes in the ledger.

"Alright. Name?"

"Michael White."

The pen flew across the ledger.

"Duration of your stay?"

Michael glanced over at Nate and Niki and shrugged his shoulders.

Niki spoke up. "That's something we don't know. We are on assignment."

"On assignment? Usually, the Council notifies me in advance when someone is working in the area. But, with all the mess going on with them, I guess it's understandable. So, what's the nature of the assignment? Who are you hunting?"

"That's something else we wanted to talk with you about, actually," Niki said. "You document all the comings and goings of every creature in New Orleans, correct?"

"Of course." He sat his pen down and stared up at her. "New Orleans is a must-see destination for monsters. Anne didn't help with her books.

"'Anne', I told her. 'This city has enough creatures of the night already. Set your books in Florida.' But no, she insisted on them being here because of how popular New Orleans already was. The number of vampires and witches who come through my door each week is amazing.

"I tell you what, it scares me to think what'll happen if those rules go away. If a few start to think it's open game, there'll be a slaughter. There're not enough hunters to keep everyone in check.

"Who, or what, are you hunting?" he finally asked.

"A succubus," she answered.

"They're extinct." He said it like one would say the world is round and the sky is blue.

"Intel thinks one may be dropping bodies here."

Michael and Nate sat back and glanced at each other. They made an unspoken agreement to let Niki handle the talking.

"I heard rumors about a few out of towners dying on us. Been wondering myself if it's someone on my registry. I was thinking maybe a witch the way they've been expiring. What makes Intel think a succubus?"

"Because of the murders that look like animal attacks. I agree a witch could explain some of them, but once you add in the ones ripped up, though..."

"I can see that. I can see that." He took the glasses off his head and sat them on the desk. He rubbed his eyes, as if nursing the start of a headache.

"I'll tell you what," he started, placing his glasses back onto the bridge of his nose. "I don't have a succubus in my registry. As far as I know, they are extinct. Samael was the only one who could make them. He was killed by Charlemagne himself in 799. That next year, Pope Leo III crowned Charlie the Emperor of the Romans."

"Because he killed Samael?" Michael asked.

"Naturally. You kill Satan himself. You get a reward from the Pope."

"Satan himself?" Confusion shot across Michael's face.

The Registrar looked at both Nate and Niki with disappointment. "The training program must have gone downhill for new recruits. Who's the team lead?"

A smile cracked across both of their faces. In unison, they pointed at Michael.

The Registrar took his glasses off again and tossed them on his desk. "Sweet tea and jambalaya," he hollered as if he just cussed them out. "I know the Council's on their hiatus, but someone's got to be making the decisions. Who used to be the team lead before this kid?"

"Jax, ah John Sanchez," Michael said.

"Oh, that explains it." He picked up his glasses and stared at Michael through them. "You working with Thomas? His brooding is wearing off on you." He paused a moment. "Wait a minute. You're the one who killed Silas, aren't you?"

Michael nodded.

"Well, that makes a little more sense." He went back to his ledger and made some notes.

"Oh, you asked about killing Satan. Sorry. I got distracted. Happens in my old age." He sat his pen down.

"So this goes back to the Garden of Eden. How well did you listen in Sunday School?"

"Pretty well," Michael said, adding in a shoulder shrug.

"Good, I'll give you the rest of the story as Paul Harvey used to say. So, Adam had a first wife named Lilith. She was made at the same time from the same clay that Adam was. Seeing as how she wasn't made any differently, she didn't want to be subservient to him. Most scholars like to use more fanciful language, but the gist of it is, she wanted to be on top. They had a huge fight, and Lilith left the Garden. Definitely different nowadays where the husband sleeps on the couch, but we've been enlightened, I guess.

"Anyway, Lilith left, and Adam complained to God. So God put Adam to sleep and made Eve from Adam's rib. When Lilith left, she met Samael.

"In Talmudic lore he was an archangel. He's also referenced as the Adversary, which is what Satan actually means.

"In Midrashic texts, he's the Angel of Death and the Head of Satans. Yes, there are multiple of them. Isn't that a wonderful title, though? He engineered the fall of Adam and Eve by using a snake. The text says he rode the snake like a camel. That part's weird.

"Where was I? Oh, Lilith. So, she meets Samael, they have sex, and in doing so, she becomes the first demon. And it's only by having sex with Samael that a succubus could be created."

Michael nodded. He finally made the connection. "And since he hasn't been around for sixteen hundred years..."

"Then no more succubi could be created," the Registrar finished. "As they were killed over the centuries, and evidence of them disappeared, it was assumed the last of them had been destroyed."

"If we assume there's one in New Orleans," Niki said, "where should we start looking?"

The Registrar thought for a moment. He took his glasses off and put the end of an arm into his mouth, nibbling on it. "All the victims I've seen were from out of town. Check missing persons. Find out who reported them missing. Was it someone traveling with them? Find out where they had been.

"With this many bodies, wherever she's hunting is fertile ground."

17

"Josh," Niki said into her phone as they stood out in front of the Registrar's mansion. "We need some information."

"What can I get for you?"

"Either missing persons' or coroner's reports. Need to know who reported them missing and/or who identified the body. Preferably the most recent victim."

She glanced up at Michael. He stood on the front porch, speaking with the Registrar. Nate wandered to the road and jogged across the street to Lafayette Cemetery. He paced in front of the large fence, trying to read the names on the mausoleums.

Clicking noises came through the phone.

"Is this morning recent enough?" Josh asked.

"God, I hope so," she said.

"Body was discovered of a Jason McHenry. Well, most of a body."

"Chalking it up to an animal attack?"

"So far? Undetermined. Coroner's report showed signs of claw marks, but they can't match them to any animals. He has notes that suggest a serial killer masking his work to look like an animal attack. Someone's getting smart," Josh said.

She heard how impressed he was through the phone. And for good measure. It was rare that someone started to peel back the layer of the world around them. Most people wanted to stay oblivious. Life was easier that way. She would've loved to have stayed oblivious to this world. To still have their son. She'd trade every good thing, every life she had saved, for the one she wasn't able to.

She swallowed hard, forcing the thoughts away and hardening her heart and soul again.

"Who identified Mr. McHenry?"

"Looks like..." More clicking from the keyboard. "Jackson Smith. Childhood friend. They were here together on vacation."

"Where's Jackson now?"

"Staying at the Embassy Suites. I'll text you the address. You're pretty close. He's been ordered not to leave until they completely rule him out as a person of interest."

"Thanks, Josh," she said and hung up.

Mike shook the Registrar's hand at the same time and strolled down the sidewalk. His eyes gazed down, avoiding the cemetery.

"You all good?" she asked.

She'd never been a part of training a fledgling. She'd taken the head off her fair share but had never seen one grow from fledgling to Beta to maybe an eventual Alpha. It reminded her of training a baby or a toddler. But she knew Mike had what it took to be the person they needed.

"I'm good," he said. "Ignoring the pit in my stomach."

After a pause, he continued. "It's strange."

"What is?"

"The pull. I stood in the cemetery where I was buried. Watched my funeral from afar with Jax standing next to me. I didn't feel it then. This place is different. According to our friend back there, he said the history and the ghosts make it that way. Some powerful voodoo priestesses have been entombed here. They have a draw similar to what has drawn creatures to New Orleans for centuries now. It's in the earth."

"This place *is* different," she echoed.

Nate walked back to them.

"Looking for someone you know?" Niki asked.

"Trying to see if I could find Marie Laveau's tomb."

Niki popped him on the back of the head.

"What was that for?" he said. A look of surprise splashed across his face.

"She's in St. Louis Cemetery, not Lafayette Cemetery." She shook her head and rolled her eyes at him.

"We have a lead. The person who identified the latest body. His name is Jackson Smith. Josh just sent me the address. I'll get us an Uber."

18

After the short Uber ride, the three of them arrived at the Embassy Suites. As they entered the hotel, Michael kept shifting his head. His eyes danced from one side of the lobby to the other. Only a dozen people or so scattered around the elegant room, but Michael felt as if every eye was on him. He knew he didn't have reason to feel that way, but yet, there it was.

He pulled the hood of his jacket up around his head, trying to shrink inside of it. He shoved his hands in his pockets. Any amount of exposed pale skin was too much.

They marched through the lobby. Niki pointed out the elevator, and they veered over to it. Standing, waiting for the doors to open, Michael kept his eyes trained to the floor.

His ears picked up so much more than he wanted to. He heard conversations happening in the lobby. A couple at the counter received their room keys. A man in his forties scheduled dinner with a business associate. Two women talked about their creole lunch.

He could close his eyes and not see. He could breathe through his mouth and not smell. But listening? He wished he knew a way to not hear.

A bell dinged, and the elevator doors opened. Michael let out a sigh of relief. The elevator car was empty. The three of them stepped on, and Niki pressed the button for the fifth floor. The doors closed before anyone else joined them, and Michael let out another sigh.

Nate glanced down at Niki. "How do you want to do this?"

"Well," Niki said. "He's probably been questioned by every cop this side of the Mississippi. Feds?"

Nate held his arms out to his side and dropped his hands up and down. "Do we look like Feds?"

To Mike, the answer seemed obvious. Niki was right. Every flavor of law enforcement had probably interrogated Jackson Smith in some way, shape, form, or fashion over the past twenty-four hours. They had probably accused him of killing his best friend.

It hadn't been long ago that Mike had lost his wife, his best friend. He related to the loss Jackson felt. He at least had the ability to confront Silas and attempt to stop him almost immediately after he'd killed her. Jackson had to identify the desecrated body of his friend with no answers as to why. Mike knew what would help.

"Why not just tell him the truth?" Mike asked.

Nate and Niki turned to each other and shrugged.

"Worth a shot," Niki said. "You want to run with this one, Team Leader?"

Before Mike could answer, the elevator dinged again, and the doors opened. Mike stepped out of the elevator car. "What's the room number?"

She told him as he headed down the hallway, leading the way.

"I guess he's running with it," Niki said from behind him.

Mike made it to the door and rapped three times on it with his knuckles. When the door opened, he first noticed Jackson's sunken eyes. Sleep must've been a rare visitor.

Mike recalled his own appearance following Brit's murder and was reassured that his assumptions were correct. He reached into his UltraNet and did what he had hoped he wouldn't have to do. He revisited the night she was killed. When he held her in his arms as she took her last breath. He tapped that emotion and drew empathy for it.

"Jackson Smith?" Mike asked. He lowered his head inside of his hoodie, hiding his eyes from Jackson.

"If this is about Jason, my attorney said you have to call him," he croaked. His voice contained gravel. A throat obviously sore from alternating between swallowing emotion to tell the same story over and over and releasing that same pent-up sorrow when alone in the dark.

His eyes drifted beyond Mike to Nate and Niki. Nate and Jackson stood at the same height, both towering over Niki.

Mike took the moment to really look at Jackson. Aside from the sunken eyes, his short brown hair stuck up in places and desperately needed to be washed. He wore gray sweatpants and a white tank top. Based on the aromas coming from Jackson, he could use a shower in general. In Mike's short time as a vampire, he hadn't had the displeasure of garlic yet. Josh had been gracious enough to keep it stashed away. Mike imagined garlic had the same pungent effect as Jackson and his hotel room.

Jackson moved his arm to shut the door.

With his reflexes, Mike shot his foot out and stopped the door from closing. He leaned in, drawing himself closer to Jackson, pushing past the smell. He placed his hand on the door but kept his head down.

"We're here to help you," Mike said.

Jackson held strong on the door, but it wasn't a challenge for Mike to hold it open.

"Help me how?"

"Closure. We can tell you the truth about what happened to Jason."

"The truth?" Jackson's voice started to waiver. "How would you know..." he started to ask but his voice trailed off. His eyes grew large. Michael sensed Jackson's heart rate double in speed.

"We didn't do that to him, but we know who did and are trying to stop it from happening again. We can offer you closure but need to know a few things first."

"How do I know you didn't kill him?"

Michael took a deep breath. He raised his head, his eyes glowing red at Jackson. At the same time, he pushed the door open, easily overpowering the athletic young man.

"Because if we wanted in, we wouldn't have asked nicely."

Jackson stumbled a few steps backward and fell on the floor. He raised his arms in front of him as if they could provide protection. "Please. Please don't hurt me."

"We aren't here to hurt you, love." Niki stepped in front of Michael. She placed a hand on Mike's chest and offered her other hand to Jackson. "My friend was telling you the truth. We are here to help and to explain what we believe happened to Jason. We just want to chat."

She turned to Michael. "Very subtle."

Jackson grabbed her hand and rose to his feet. "What is he?" He pointed to Mike.

"Someone who's gone through worse than you have," Niki answered. "Shall we?" She motioned for the group to move farther into the hotel room.

"I...I'm sorry for the mess. I'm usually more put together than this."

"Completely understandable," Mike said. His eyes went back to their normal dark blue shade. "I lost my wife a few months back. I don't think I ate for a week."

"Was it the same way that Jason died?"

Mike smiled at the question. At least he was getting conversation with Jackson. He focused on using the empathy he pulled out of those retched memories.

"Different but the same at the same time. I sought revenge, and although I got it, I lost myself along the way."

The hotel room had one king-size bed, a dresser with a large flat screen TV on it, and a desk. Instead of a window, the back wall had a door that led to the balcony. A bottle of Johnny Walker sat on the nightstand, nearly empty, and another bottle peeked out of the trashcan. It reminded Mike of his own hideaway before joining the Night Crew. Well, minus the balcony.

Jackson pushed some clothes off the bed and grabbed a chair from the desk.

"It's ok," Niki said. "We won't be here long."

He sat the chair down and stepped to the balcony door. His gaze drifted outside with his back turned on his three visitors.

"What killed my best friend?" Jackson asked.

Michael knew the strength it took to vocalize that question.

"A creature that we're here to kill," Mike said.

"Is it one like you?"

"No, different than me. But extremely deadly. We think she's responsible for a dozen deaths in the past few months."

"She?" Jackson's voice rose in pitch.

"Yes, love," Niki said. "She. Does that mean anything?"

"Maybe. We were at a club. Republic New Orleans. It's over in the Warehouse District. I hit the dance floor almost immediately. Saw a few hotties who I wanted to..." he trailed off and glanced at Niki.

"You're not going to offend me. I kill monsters for a living."

"I was on the dance floor. I saw him talking to a smoking hot brunette by the bar. Next thing I knew, they were dancing. He had a look in his eyes like he'd seen heaven.

"I didn't blame him. She was gorgeous. Like cover of *Sports Illustrated* beautiful. Legs, ass, tits...sorry. Anyway, I kept dancing with the group I was with, and he left. I figured he was getting some of the best ass I've ever seen him with. After two days without hearing from him, I started to get worried. His phone was dead, he wasn't in his room, but all his stuff was there. Like he just vanished. So I called the cops. I gave them his picture, and the next day, I got the call and had to..." Jackson choked up. He swallowed hard. Mike knew he was using the physical action to push down his emotions.

"It's ok," Mike said. "Take your time."

Jackson wiped both of his eyes. "I had to identify him. But it was hard. I recognized a tattoo on his chest. His face... I had to call his mom. They're on their way. I don't know what I'm going to tell them."

Niki spoke up. "Tell them it was an animal attack. And know that we'll handle the rest."

"Does any of what I said help?" He wiped more tears from his eyes.

"Gives us a place to start," she said. "You focus on grieving and accepting."

"Like she said," Mike added. "Know this is taken care of."

"Who are you guys?" Jackson asked.

Mike looked at Nate and Niki. So many sayings from TV shows came to mind. He thought about saying, "If you have a problem, if nobody can help, and if you can find them, maybe you can hire, the A-Team." Or "Sometimes bad guys make the best good guys. We provide...leverage."

"We're friends," Nate jumped in.

19

"Josh," Niki said. She placed her earpiece in her ear as they left the Embassy Suites. "We have a starting point."

"The Republic?" Josh asked.

"How the hell did you know that?" Niki's astonished tone made both Nate and Mike turn to her.

"I looked at where the majority of the bodies were found and last known locations. Republic sits dead center. I think that's her hunting ground."

"That's the last place Jackson saw Jason alive. And we have a description."

"That'll help, but I'm not sure how useful it'll be," Josh said. "According to lore, a succubus could change her appearance."

"It's at least something for us to start with."

"True. You all head back here. I have the schematics for the club. I'll also plug in her description and see what I can find off of any cameras in the surrounding area."

"Sounds great." She hung up the phone and looked at Nate and Mike.

"We good?" Nate asked.

"Tonight, we're back on the hunt!" she shouted. She held her hand up, and Nate gave her a high five.

A few people walked by with questionable looks on their faces.

"Is this a thing?" Mike asked.

"We did the same thing before saving your ass that first time," Niki teased.

"You saved my ass once. I saved your ass...twice?" Mike responded with a smile.

"Mike, in this lighting, you can't even tell how pale you are," Niki said as they stood in line to enter Republic New Orleans.

The mention of his skin tone made Mike shove his hands into the pockets of his brown leather jacket. Standing there reminded him of the last time he'd been to a club, waiting in line at Club Starlight with Thomas. He hoped he wouldn't have to burn this one to the ground.

Niki hadn't minded the black miniskirt, silver belt, boots, and shiny black top when she put them on.

"It shows off my legs, don't you think?" she had asked Nate.

"You know I'm always a fan of your legs, beautiful," he'd responded.

But, as the three of them waited in line, she huddled next to Nate. Once the sun set and a cool breeze started to blow off the Mississippi River, the temperature plummeted.

"This line better hurry the fuck up." She slid her arms under Nate's shirt and pressed them against his stomach.

"Damn, babe! You're a Popsicle."

"It's moving pretty quickly," Mike said. "Do you want my jacket? It's not like I need it."

"You keep it," she said. "Makes you more attractive."

"Thanks," Mike said with an eye roll. "That makes me feel more confident."

"What's the matter, love? Nervous?" Niki gave a coy smile. She pulled her arms out of Nate's shirt and turned to Mike.

"A little," he admitted. "Nate and I are supposed to snag the attention of a sex demon who is hunting young, attractive men. Neither of us really fall into the mid-twenties category. We're both fit, but I'm pale as a ghost."

"You'll be fine." She tapped Nate on the chest. "But Nate and I are in support roles. You have the lead."

The line moved closer to the door. Mike heard the music and smelled the alcohol.

"Wait, so I'm trying to attract the sex demon on my own?"

"That's right," she answered.

"We discussed both of us."

Niki glanced at Nate. She wrapped her thin arm around his large bicep. "I don't want a sex demon hitting on my man. Plus, we thought it a good chance to let our little bird shine."

"Last time I checked, I'm supposed to be the team leader."

"You are, love. Don't worry. I guess Jax didn't let you read the fine print."

"What fine print?" Mike asked. Maybe he should've had more questions when Jax so willingly told him he was the new team lead.

"The fine print where, occasionally, we make sure you can attract a succubus," Nate said. His smile extended from one ear to the other.

"We didn't have this problem in the military." Mike shook his head.

"We're almost there," Niki said. "Comms check. Josh, you hearing us?"

"Loud and clear. Don't worry, Mike. Just turn on that charm of yours."

Charm?

He recalled how nervous he had been asking Brittany out on their first date. And that was after months of getting to know her. Not some random person at a club.

The line moved closer, and the trio headed inside.

21

Michael ventured to the bar and ordered a beer, handing the bartender his credit card. He stared at himself in the mirrored wall behind the bartender. Peering through the assortment of alcohol bottles, he didn't recognize the person staring back. So much had happened in such a short amount of time. At least the others kept their humanity. He was a wild animal, leashed only by the slimmest grip on his sanity.

The barback sat the bottle in front of him and popped the top off.

"Thanks," Mike said.

"You really going to drink that?" Josh's voice spoke clearly into his ear.

He turned away from the bar, holding the beer in front of him, and surveying the dance floor.

"I want to. I miss the taste of beer." He brought the bottle up to his nose and breathed in the hoppy aroma. "Smells really good. What happens if a vampire drinks something that's not blood?"

"After you violently spit it out?" Niki asked. "Nothing really."

"So I take a sip, spit it across the floor, drawing every eye in here to the weirdo at the bar. Glad you stopped me."

"Glad we could help," Josh said.

"Why don't you work the dance floor, Mike?"

"I'm getting there."

Mike stared at the swarm of people on the dance floor. At the far end, he saw Nate and Niki gyrating against each other in rhythm to the music.

The music, with its constant thumping bass, reminded him of the sound of a heartbeat. At first the lights didn't bother him, but the more he surveyed the room, especially on the dance floor with the giant LCD screen behind the DJ, the more the lights became a nuisance. The smell of multiple alcohols wafted his way. The bitter smell of whiskey combined with the fruity smells of mixed drinks and sweat and pheromones. His senses fired up. He panicked and clenched his empty fist. In response, he sat the beer bottle down before he broke it.

"Mike, did you hear what I said?"

He closed his eyes, dialing back the sensory input.

"Sorry, Niki, what was that?"

"Do you remember the description that Jackson gave us?"

"Yes, I remember." He hoped the frustration he felt didn't come across the comms. Mike didn't want Niki to think it was directed at her.

"Focus on that. Search the crowd for someone matching her description."

Michael opened his eyes and trained his predatorial sight on the dance floor. Brunette. Long hair. Absolutely gorgeous. At least that dropped out all the blondes he saw. And those who weren't *Sports Illustrated* beautiful.

He shifted all his focus on the crowd, pushing past the smells and sounds. Passed the radiating heat of the bodies on the dance floor. The beating hearts forcing blood through their veins.

"Hi," a woman about his age said. She had short black hair that reminded him of Joan Jett. "I saw you standing here alone. Would you like to dance?"

"No, thanks," he answered.

"Oh, come one. You sure?"

"Yes, sorry. I'm looking for someone."

"I'm right here," she said flirtatiously. "But, if you change your mind, I'll be over by the bar."

She walked away.

Michael kept his eyes honed on the dance floor.

"Mike, she was cute," Niki said. "You should've danced with her."

"Aren't we on a mission?"

"Yes, but if you are just stiffly standing there, you aren't really blending in. You look out of place. Let loose. Enjoy yourself."

"I'm not sure I can do that, yet. You know it's only been a few months since Brit died. You were there," Mike said.

"Not saying settle down and propose. But it's ok to let yourself go. I'm sure she would've wanted you to."

"Niki," Mike started. "Don't presume to've known her." He had to swallow down the hot anger rising in his throat. "I'm just...not ready. Let me focus on the mission at hand for now."

"Sorry, love," Niki said. Her tone eased and had sincerity in it.

"It's ok. Aside from not being ready to enjoy myself like that, I also don't have the control I need just yet. Standing here, I'm forcing myself to focus on certain things. I can hear everyone's heartbeat. Can see their veins just under their skin. As I'm looking for a beautiful brunette, I can't help but think about how much blood is pumping across the dance floor. It screams to me. If I don't concentrate, I could slip into bloodlust. I'd hate it if you had to remove my head in the middle of this club."

"We'd hate it, too," Nate said. "You do what you need to do. We've got your back."

"Josh, anything in the surveillance cameras?" Mike asked, shifting the focus back onto searching for the succubus.

"Plenty of beautiful people. A few gorgeous brunettes, but they're with groups of people. My guess is, she'll either be alone or already with an attractive young man if she's even there."

"It's been a few days since the last kill. If this is her hunting ground, she'll be here soon." Mike thought for a moment. "As fast as the bodies have been dropping, she'll be here tonight or tomorrow."

He scanned the dance floor again. Bodies pressed against bodies, writhing in rhythm to the music. Sweat glistened off their skin. Smoke obscured some people, leaving only vague shadows, but he saw enough.

Mike swallowed hard. He needed a drink.

He tilted his head to the second floor. People hopped around to the music and leaned against the railing. So many people crammed into this small place. He had to find a way to get out of his own head.

He swallowed again and smacked his lips. His tongue brushed past the sharp points of his teeth. His throat screamed for thick, warm blood.

Hair stood up on the back of his neck, as if a breeze had gently kissed there. He glanced around as a strange sensation swept over him.

Warmth spread from there and traveled across his body. He hadn't felt warmth or cold since his transformation. Just numbness. His thought sensors must be on overload creating phantom feelings.

He shook his arms by his side, then did the same with each leg. His whole body gave a shiver. His breathing relaxed, and tension in his muscles melted away. As the heat spread into his stomach, he calmed.

Michael shot his eyes up with a sudden realization.

For the first time in months, he didn't thirst or crave blood.

As the warmth spread across his body and the thirst vanished, for the first time in months—decades, it seemed—Mike felt in control of himself. He smiled at the sheer sense of peace and calm that washed over him.

Did I do it? Did I finally break free of the bloodlust? Did I achieve what Thomas has been harping on me about?

With the renewed sense of purpose, he trained his eyes around the club. He sensed them go red at his will, and the supernatural vision allowed him to focus on individuals, without the worry and concern he had only moments ago.

Scanning the dance floor, he saw Nate and Niki, still dancing, but their eyes patrolled everything around them.

In the air, he caught a scent. It had a familiar quality and a pleasing sweetness. He picked up hints of pepper and vanilla, but underneath those was something else, as if they were only there to mask the true scent.

He tried to tap into his UltraNet to identify it, but for the first time that he could remember, he couldn't access it. His memory bank, that steel vault that retained everything he'd ever seen and heard, every memory good or bad he'd experienced, shut itself off.

Mixed emotions welled up inside of him. He'd never been disconnected from it before. Those memories were always at his disposal when he wanted them, but also when he didn't. Their absence when he needed them felt like a dear friend who had left.

Simultaneously a feeling of relief forced its way in. Did this mean no more vivid memories of things he didn't want to remember? Of...?

Her name escaped him. His wife's name. The memories of holding her as she...

His head drifted from one side to the other. His mouth felt dry, almost like cotton mouth after a night of drinking. The focus he had in his eyes dissolved, and he blinked a few times to correct a swimming sensation coursing through his head. He had to catch himself from losing his balance and stumbling over.

Mike hadn't had a feeling like this in a long while. Drunk. Could a vampire get drunk? What if he drank blood from someone who had a high blood alcohol content? Even then, he'd only drank blood from the bags they got from the banks. That blood had been filtered, and all impurities had been removed.

What the hell is happening?

That smell drifted past him again. Pepper and vanilla with something hidden underneath. What was that smell?

He squeezed his eyes tightly shut, trying to force open his UltraNet. It was there. It had to be.

Bursts of electricity shot down his spine, starting at his neck and radiating up through his skull and down to his lower back. Hairs on the back of his neck stood at attention, and the frustration he felt at not being able to access his memory bank faded.

This time, he realized it wasn't a breeze and spun to his right.

Standing next to him stood a woman just shorter than him. She had curly red hair that bounced around her head and shoulders, as if it had a life of its own. Her cheeks glowed with a red tint that seemed to be accentuated by the color of her hair. Her button nose and meadow green eyes added a perfect symmetry to her face.

The scent grew stronger as he gazed into her eyes. Inside them, he saw the greenest valley nestled between the greenest mountains. Her eyes were beautiful, vibrant, and alive. Mike found himself floating in them, transported, drifting off to parts unknown, and parts he didn't need to know. Lost, without a care in the world.

She was thin but in a healthy way. Not as if she had starved herself but rather ate all natural foods with no added chemicals. Her red, shimmering top formed to her shape, and Mike could tell she wasn't wearing a bra.

As he stared at her, she brought her hand back to her side, dropping away from his shoulder.

23

"I'm Michael," he said. His voice sounded airy and ethereal. The words floated out of him.

"Angie," she said. "Nice to meet you, Michael."

She raised her right arm, and, with the tips of her fingers, she brushed his left cheek.

Her touch electrified his skin. When she took her hand away, Mike's cheek held on to the phantom feeling of her fingers.

"Would you like to dance?" he asked.

"I'd love to."

Angie held her hand out, and he reached up with his. His arm felt weightless as he grasped her hand, careful not to apply too much pressure. He held it as if cupping a delicate rose.

She moved in front of him, raised her arm over her shoulder, and led him to the dance floor.

"You go, Mike," Nate said.

He heard Nate through the comms. Although it was secured in his ear, delivered directly into his ear canal, the words came from miles away.

Mike found himself transported beyond his body. His mind wasn't in control. He was there, operating purely on muscle memory. He let himself go, his body independent of any actions, free from inhibitions.

"Josh, you should see this chick Mike is dancing with," Nate said. "Pretty hot."

"Oh really," Niki said.

"Of course not as hot as you, beautiful," Nate said. "But for Mike, I mean, he didn't do that bad."

"Mike, you there?" Josh asked. "Mike?"

He heard but didn't respond. He didn't care what was happening in his ear. That was nothing more than a distraction from Angie. He felt himself on a high as he danced next to her. His hands traveled up and down her arms and sides. Her ass pressed against his crotch. He felt alive again. It was the first time he'd really felt that way since...

Since...

Again, he tried to pull her name from his head, but it wasn't there.

Whose name are you trying to pull? he asked himself.

He didn't have an answer to the question.

Angie bent down in front of him, her hands touching the floor, then rose back up, sensually leaning back against him. She reached behind her, rubbing her hand from his hair down to his face. She tilted her head to his. Her red lips, full and wanting, hovered nanometers from his own.

Before he leaned in to kiss her, she spun around, facing him. She grasped the back of his head and turned it slightly so that her lips almost touched his ear.

"Vampires usually aren't in here unless they have permission to feed in the wild," she whispered. "Do you have special permission?"

He turned his face to her, staring into her eyes. The green meadows sucked him in again.

"You aren't an Alpha. Why aren't you at one of the approved vampire dens? You aren't even a Beta. Just a fledgling. Are you lost, little child?"

Her words came to him as velvet. Although she spoke down to him, he hung on her every word. He wanted to hear more of her voice. Needed her to speak to him more.

"Guys, we have a problem," Josh said.

"We hear," Niki responded. "Either she's the succubus or she's something we've never heard about."

"Mike," Josh said. "Mike, are you able to respond?"

The sound buzzed in his ear like a fly. He batted it away, paying no attention to it. He just wanted to hear her. Needed it like he used to need blood.

Angie wrapped her arms around him and pulled him closer. Her body locked onto his.

Every inch of Mike's skin reached for her, wanted to be closer to her, absorb her into him. He could drown in her and be satisfied. He clutched the back of her head and pulled her lips to his, passionately kissing her. Their tongues danced and intertwined.

"Nate. Niki. You need to move."

"On it," Niki said.

Angie eased away from Michael, gently pulling their lips apart. A touch of saliva connected them before breaking. Michael felt his heart crack as she pulled away. She nibbled on his lower lip before drifting up to his ear again.

"Michael, lose the earpiece and follow me. I know where we can be alone."

"Mike!" Josh screamed. "Don't do that. That's a bad idea."

The buzzing sound of the flies increased their volume.

"Mike!" Niki shouted. "Mike, don't..."

He reached in his ear, removed the ear bud, and dropped it on the ground.

From across the dance floor, two people he thought he might've recognized swam their way to him.

Angie grasped his hand in hers and led him away from the dance floor.

Niki watched Michael get led off the dance floor and toward the exit. Between them, the dancing swarm must've tripled. Every gap was filled. Through the strobing lights and fog, Niki tried to keep her eyes on Michael while swimming her way through the crowd. With each forward movement she made, they somehow grew further apart.

"Josh," she hollered. "Can you track him?"

"On it. Pulling up surveillance cameras now."

"He took his fucking earpiece out. Why would he do that?" She slipped her arms between two couples and elbowed her way through them.

"She touched him," Nate said.

She heard him in her earpiece. She didn't have the luxury of making sure he kept up with her. If they got separated, at least he knew her location.

"Niki, good news." Josh clicked on the keyboard as he spoke.

"Get out of my damn way."

Niki shoved the couple who stood directly in her path. They stumbled backward, and she stepped where they were. Michael and Angie stepped through the exit.

Shit!

"What's the big deal?" a guy in his mid-twenties yelled at Niki after making sure the girl he was dancing with wasn't hurt.

Niki ignored him and pushed on. She was almost off the dance floor.

"Did you hear me?" the man shouted.

"Is there a problem?" Nate asked.

Niki glanced back.

The man's head ended at Nate's shoulders. His head craned in an attempt to look Nate in the eyes. A smile briefly spread across Niki's face as the man shrunk in Nate's looming presence. Any bravado the man possessed had evaporated as he physically deflated.

"Not a problem," he said, timidly. "Just...she could've asked."

"We're in a hurry." Nate's deep voice caused the man to flinch.

He backed up and turned to his dancing partner. They moved to another side of the floor.

"Did you hear me? I've got good news."

"I lost Mike so whatever you have, great. Give it to me," Niki snapped.

"He dropped his earbud but still has his phone. I'm tracking him through that while watching the surveillance cameras."

"That's good. I'm almost to the door. She didn't look anything like how Jackson described her. She was thin. A red head."

Niki paused after clearing the dance floor and waited for Nate to catch up. She still needed to rush before anything bad happened to Michael, but at least Josh had him located. Hopefully, Mike could take care of himself. Thomas had talked about the strength inside of him. It's what had attracted Silas to Mike in the first place. Niki could only pray he found that power before he lost his head.

"We thought she might have the ability to change her appearance. I'd hoped she kept the same one, but I guess not," Josh answered before shouting out. "Holy shit!"

"What's wrong, Josh?" Nate asked.

"They're moving incredibly fast. Both of them. Even if you had made it outside when they did, there's no way you could catch up. I'll keep an eye in the sky. You two move faster."

"Fuck you, Josh."

They hurried to the exit and burst onto the street, pushing anyone who dared to block them out of their way.

"Where'd you stash it?" Niki asked.

"Around the corner," Nate answered. "Behind a dumpster."

The two ran to the edge of the street and turned. A dumpster sat against the exterior wall of the club. Niki reached the metal container first. Her nose filled with the rancid smells of alcohol, piss, and vomit. She brought her hand up to her nose and turned away.

Nate dropped back behind the dumpster and lifted the black duffel bag into the air. He tossed the strap over his shoulder, letting the bag drop to his side, and turned back to Niki.

"Ready?" he asked.

"You going to be able to sprint with that around your shoulders?"

"Just watch."

Michael no longer felt connected to himself. Whatever force had previously grounded his mind to his body no longer did its job. He was there. He watched through his eyes. But the numbness that spread disconnected him. He felt...nothing. And it was amazing.

Except for the hand she gripped. That hand was alive. His hand was the umbilical cord feeding him everything he needed or wanted. There was no craving for blood, no fear of the bloodlust. Only the intoxicating touch of Angie, the beautiful, fiery red head who led him to parts unknown. As long as she held his hand and the warmth from it radiated, he was in ecstasy.

His legs moved, one step at a time, but at a pace he'd never traveled before. The streets blurred past him. Mike knew he had the ability to move quickly, but he'd never traveled this fast.

As a predator, he could attack prey in an instant. He'd heard stories about how fast a vampire could be on a person's throat. Although he'd only drank blood prepackaged from the banks, he realized the power was there. Silas had moved with exceptional speed. Mike had moved quickly when trying to attack Thomas during his training session, and Thomas was even quicker in putting Michael on the ground.

They continued out of the warehouse district and into a residential neighborhood. Through the connection he shared with Angie, he received the message to slow his pace. Somehow, his disconnected legs received the request, and their pace dropped to a slow walk.

"I'm right up here, my pet," she said. Her words fell on him like silk.

Mike saw the two-story condo. It had gray siding and three small steps leading up to a white door. It looked like a typical suburban condominium. A large bay window was on the left side of the house. A few windows with shutters sat on the second floor. He had a hard time believing an angel like Angie lived in such a plain house. Actually, he wasn't sure what he'd truly expected. He hadn't thought much of anything outside of the touch of her skin against his.

"Follow me." She brushed the side of his face.

She led him up the three steps and opened the door.

"You may sit, pet," she said, releasing his hand. "I need to change into something more...fitting. Be good and don't disappoint me."

As she let go, Mike gazed at his hand. The electricity coursing up his arm ceased. The warmth faded, and numbness took its place. He needed her touch again, but he also needed to do what she said. Peering into the living room, he saw a couch and sat. The residual tingling in his hand remained.

The farther she sauntered up the staircase to the second floor, the more he wanted to go with her. Each step away from him left a sharp, dagger-like pain in his stomach. Through the numbness, he felt the pain rip through him. Never before had he craved something so bad that its absence sent such anguish through him. She had told him to sit, so he sat. The last thing he wanted to do was make her unhappy. He'd rather wallow in his agony waiting for her than disappoint her.

Is this what an addict feels like?

Was he addicted to her already?

Mike tried to remember how he got there. He tried to remember why he was in New Orleans to begin with. He placed his head in his hands. His brain was mush. His UltraNet wasn't working. Something deep within him screamed that he should be panicking right now, but Angie had told him to sit, so he sat, not wanting to displease her.

Turning his head from left to right, he glanced across the room for a clock. Something, anything, to tell him how long he'd been sitting there. Had it been a few minutes or a few hours? The moon still hung high in the night sky, so it couldn't have been that long. The smell of vanilla and black pepper perfume wafted in the air. Underneath, the unmistakable smell of death and decay lingered.

He quickly shook his head from side to side, reminding him of the times he had tried to sober up after a late night out with his unit. He slowed his head and took a deep breath.

Focus, Maggot.

Startled, he sat upright on the couch as if at attention. Muscle memory from the voice of his drill sergeant. He hadn't heard the man yell at him in over a decade, but his body still reacted. It knew. Even if his brain wasn't working like it should, his body did.

Sitting with his back straight and his shoulders back, he closed his eyes. The voice had to originate from somewhere, and there's only one place it could be stored. Had he finally unlocked it?

Michael concentrated. He thought about the white room, pictured it in his head.

Find it, dammit.

The room needed to be lined with shelves full of books. The ambiance of a library with a computer sitting in the middle of it. He forced the image in his head as footsteps coming down the stairs reached his ears.

Abandoning the search, he opened his eyes.

Angie dressed in a red teddy that matched her hair. The curls still perfectly shaped her face and bounced off her shoulders. A black lace shawl draped across her, the thin fabric almost translucent. Just a faint shimmer. The tightness of the teddy gripped her stomach and exaggerated her breasts.

She walked from the stairs to the living room in black high heels. "Stand, pet."

Before his brain gave the order to his legs, they operated independently and raised him up. He felt weightless within the drug of her presence. The few words she had spoken brought a relaxing calmness to him. Each word delivered a reinvigorating dose of drugs. Intoxicating.

The closer she stepped, the more drawn he felt.

She placed her hand on the side of his face, and he placed his own hand on top of hers, embracing the softness of her touch on his cheek. He closed his eyes. His senses filled with the scent of vanilla, black pepper, and rot.

Angie drew close to him and gently kissed his lips. A surge of electricity sparked across Mike's lips and through his face. Pleasure he hadn't felt since... since...

Brittany! his brain shouted back at him.

He stumbled back as if a wave had struck him. Pulling away from her hand, his eyes shot open.

"I...I can't," he stuttered, taking another step back.

Angie smiled. Her bright red lips spread across her face in a devilish grin. It screamed *yes, he could. Yes, he should.* It beckoned him to her. She tossed her head from one side to the other, her fiery red hair bouncing whimsically.

"Yes, you can, my pet." Her words were a drug.

He struggled against falling into her grasp once more. Struggled against the seductive sound of her voice, the IV drip of dopamine she delivered. Her red hair caused images of Brittany to flood back. Whatever locked away his UltraNet vanished. Memory after memory rushed back as the dam opened wide. Along with it came a deep feeling of regret, remorse, and guilt.

With his right hand, he reached up and touched his lips. A lingering tingle vibrated there. He hadn't kissed anyone since Brittany. Hadn't wanted to. Had no desire to. Even with Angie in all her beauty in front of him, he didn't want to. He was in New Orleans on an assignment. An assignment to seek out the succubus.

"No," he said. He tried to retreat but was trapped between her and the couch, just behind his calves.

"You are a strong fledgling, aren't you? You are fighting the call. Impressive. How long do you think you can hold out, though? I feel your desire for me. Give in to it. Be a good pet and heel."

With each word, Michael found it harder and harder to resist. He needed an escape, to distance himself from her. He picked a leg up and placed it on the couch. He raised himself into the air and nearly fell over backward. Everything reminded him of an awkward teenager. What happened to his predator abilities? Where did his agility, his strength disappear to?

On legs that felt like Jell-o, he walked across the couch cushions and hopped onto the floor. He stood behind a chair that had been next to the couch, keeping it between him and Angie.

"Pet, don't run. There's nothing to be scared of." The words flowed from her like velvet.

"I'm only here for your pleasure. Your strength will keep me satisfied. Neither of us will need to feed again. Tell me, how does it feel to not crave the taste of blood? I can make the craving stay away forever.

"How'd you like all of your pain to vanish? No more worries. No more memories of your wife."

At the mention of Brittany, Michael froze behind the chair. Whatever hold she had on him, whatever spell he was under, boiled away in the fiery anger that rose within him. His breath steadied, and his eyes sharpened. He didn't have to see to know his eyes were burning red.

"Did I hit a nerve, pet?"

"I am not your pet," he growled.

The world became clearer as the last of the fog lifted. As it did, a ripple ran across her body as if thousands of worms lived just under her skin. The red teddy which held firm to her torso slipped to the floor. The naked form in front of him contorted and shifted. Her perfect breasts sagged and melted, leaving gray sacks of flesh clinging to her chest. Fingers melded together into sharp talons. The red curls that had danced so lively on her head shriveled and withdrew into her skin. What was left was a gray, hairless creature with bird-like talons, eyes as black as her soul, thin, membranous wings, and a smile filled with ravenous fangs.

The beast that was formerly Angie, stretched itself upright. Its arms, nothing more than bones with skin wrapped tight around them, reached to the ceiling. Her wings extended out and left large gashes deep in the sheetrocked ceiling. Her black gaze found Michael, and he felt her stare burning into him.

His face turned away from her.

"What's the matter, pet? Don't you still find me beautiful?"

The voice that had held him captivated was now deep and guttural. Nothing was left of the red-headed beauty who had led him to her lair.

26

Josh's eyes darted from one screen to the next while his fingers flew across the keyboard in his lap. One monitor showed a beacon with Mike's position. It hadn't moved for almost half an hour. Josh prided himself an optimist, so he felt confident that Mike knew what he was doing and was in full control of himself. But there was also that voice in the back of his head which kept nagging at him. How many team members had they gone through over the years since he'd been part of the Crew?

It was because of the incident that left him in the wheelchair that Jax brought him on. He was the only remaining member of their original team, not counting Jax and Thomas since they were off handling bigger issues. Nate and Niki didn't join the Crew until after. Each person Josh had befriended was gone. He could see why it was so easy for Thomas to put distance between himself and new members, but Josh wasn't wired that way. His role was different. He was their support.

"What do you have, Josh?" Niki asked in between gasps of air. Her voice blared from the speakers of Josh's computer.

"He's still at the same address, hopefully. I can only track his phone. If he ditched it there..."

"We know," Nate replied, breathless.

Josh glanced to the monitor with the blinking dot that represented Mike. Nate's and Niki's dots still showed almost a mile away but closing in fast. They were sprinting down the street.

After placing the keyboard on the top of the table in front of him, Josh pushed himself back a foot and stretched his arms into the air. He shifted his neck from side to side, dropped his hands, and rubbed his eyes. His body needed sleep. He used to be in a good routine of sleeping during the day and running operations at night. The past few months had taken him out of that routine, and he felt the effects wearing him down.

He grabbed the Red Bull on his desk and took a long swallow, then pulled himself back up to the table and grabbed the keyboard.

"You're almost there. It's on your right."

A loud crash of glass blasted over the speakers, startling Josh.

"Nate? Niki? What was that?" he screamed into the empty room.

"Someone respond!"

27

Michael glanced behind the large gargoyle-like creature that was once a stunning red head. From where he was, he doubted he could make it to the door behind her. The window was next to him, but she was too close to make even that. Deep inside, the craving for blood returned. At that moment, he wished he'd indulged more before they had left on the hunt. He could've used the fuel to figure out how not to be killed.

In his head, he heard Josh's voice from their briefing in Dallas, comparing a succubus to a vampire.

"You're nothing like a vampire," he said.

"Me? Like a vampire?" the beast growled. It flashed a mouth full of glistening sharp fangs and bellowed what Michael assumed was a laugh. It sounded like a cross between a cackle and dry heaving. "I am nothing like a vampire! I existed for a millennia before the first vampire was ever created."

Mike kept his feet moving from one side to the other, searching for the best opportunity to sprint past the succubus and escape from his current trap.

"You still crave blood. When you evolve, you'll no longer crave such a meaningless fluid. I've evolved beyond blood. I drain the very life force from someone. Nothing as primitive as blood."

With one long talon-tipped arm, she swiped at Michael. He danced to the side, but the tip of her claw scraped his chest. His shirt opened, and a line of beaded blood spread from the gap.

"You're quick for a hungry vampire," she said.

He glanced down at the slice running from left to right just above his belly button and the growing trail of blood. "Not fast enough obviously."

"I wanted you to be my little pet to do with as I pleased. Instead, I'll just take your head."

Her hand whipped out from her side again as fast as a snake striking. The talon extended, sharp as a blade, ready to separate Michael's head from his neck.

He shifted out of the way, feeling the breeze from her hand as it passed no more than an inch from his neck. His hands shot to his throat just to make sure it was still intact. Before he had a chance to counter, the force of her wing crashing against his shoulder threw him into the wall, cracking it and sending a cloud of pulverized sheet rock into the air.

Michael's head spun, and for a brief moment, he was back in high school, in the midst of a fight as a sophomore. Jennifer, a cute brunette who sat a few seats in front of him in algebra, hadn't understood the homework. After school, they hung out, and he helped her with the assignment. They laughed and had a great time until her boyfriend thought they were having too much fun.

As if it was yesterday, Michael saw the senior tower over him, grab him by his shirt, and haul him to his feet. Before Mike knew what was going on, the angry boyfriend swung a right hook and connected just above Mike's ear. Stars erupted, and a piercing sound exploded within his head.

Mike's world swam in front of him. Jennifer stood up, her mouth moved, but he couldn't hear anything beyond the high-pitched ringing in his head. The senior reared back to punch him again and would've delivered another deafening blow if she hadn't grabbed her boyfriend's arm and forced him to release Mike.

He wavered on his feet and tried to raise his own arms but lost his balance altogether and fell back onto the bench. Mike continued to sit there, dazed and confused, for almost ten minutes.

He coughed a cloud of dust particles from the wall, bringing him back to the present. The dying remnants of stars faded from his vision. With his hands on the floor, Mike pushed himself off and jumped to his feet. His upper body radiated with pain, more sensation than he'd felt since becoming a vampire.

"That all you got, you ugly bitch?" he asked, brushing crumbled chunks of wall off his shoulder.

Angie let out a roar that shook the light fixture above them. She drew closer to him, with nothing but the couch separating her from Michael. Her hands swiped at him. Her wings with their bony structure swung again, trying to make contact.

After being stunned once, he now dodged both her razor-like talons and her wings.

Her legs brushed against the couch cushions, and Michael jumped on the opportunity. With all his might, he kicked the couch, ramming it into her thin, skeletal legs. The wood inside the couch crunched into her bones, and she let out another roar. This one was the unmistakable sound of a hurt animal.

The force had caused her to stumble back, and seeing her off balance, Michael jumped onto the back of the couch. He used the additional height to his advantage, leaping off and cocking his arm back as he did. His fist flew forward as he collided with her, connecting with the side of her face. For a moment, he felt solid bone underneath her skin just before it collapsed under the impact of the punch. He landed on the ground in front of her as she continued to stumble backward.

Her eyes burned with rage, and her mouth curled into a vicious snarl. Fangs were broken or missing from where his punch had connected. She spat on the ground and shattered teeth ricocheted off the floor.

Michael jumped back onto the couch behind him, turned with his arm reared back, and swung again while in the air. This time, his complete momentum shifted directions. Her wing swung into his side, catching him right under his raised arm, square in the ribcage. The force of her swing flung him across the living room. Before he realized what was happening, he crashed through the large bay window and landed on the sidewalk in front of the house.

Face down on the concrete, his side burned like a chunk of red-hot iron sat inside of him. He tried to take a deep breath and immediately decided against it. Shards of pain had exploded inside of him when he did. Broken ribs. Multiple broken ribs.

He pushed himself to his hands and knees and stayed in that position, assessing the damage. Blood dripped from his face and dotted the sidewalk. He lifted his head, fighting past pain from the needles stabbing into his neck. He reached to the back of his neck and yanked out a shard of glass embedded in his skin.

Through blurry eyes, he saw two figures rushing his way.

"Michael?"

He blinked a few times, clearing his vision, and recognized Nate and Niki sprinting toward him.

"Oh, thank God," he said, rolling onto his back. His arms dropped to the ground and stretched out across the pavement.

28

Niki skidded to a stop when she saw the body crash through the window of the house and roll to a stop on the sidewalk. Nate bumped into her as he slowed, nearly knocking her over.

"Nate? Niki? What was that?" Josh screamed into their ear. "Someone respond!"

"We hear you, love," Niki finally said.

The crumpled mess on the sidewalk raised onto its hands and knees, and she immediately recognized who it was.

"Michael," she hollered.

Niki and Nate raced to him. As Niki drew closer, she saw blood drip down his face onto the sidewalk. He must have taken a decent beating.

"We have him, Josh," Nate said and Josh's sigh of relief was audible.

He dropped the duffel bag on the sidewalk as they both grabbed Mike by the armpits and helped him to his feet.

"What the hell happened to you?" Nate asked.

Mike coughed and spat out a wad of blood. "I found the succubus."

"No shit," Niki said.

"She's big. Watch out for her wings." He bent over and placed his elbows on his knees, then raised up and popped his back.

Mike's shirt was in tatters. Shards of glass from the window pinned it to his chest. A large cut ran across the front of it and dried and fresh blood splattered the entire thing.

"Do you have any fight left?" Nate asked.

"If I need to."

"Good," Niki said. "Let's go kill this bitch so we can go back home."

She unclasped her belt and whipped it by her side a few times. The luster of the silver whip gave a dull shine in the moonlight. From her boot, she pulled out a knife.

"Hiding anything else?" Nate asked. A coy smile spread across his face.

"Wouldn't you like to know." She returned his smile.

Nate bent down to the black bag that he'd somehow managed to keep with him and unzipped the top of it. He grabbed three machetes and handed one to Mike. He tried to hand the other to Niki, but she waved him off, so he dropped it back into the bag. Reaching in one last time, he pulled out the shotgun.

"You two want anything else?" Nate asked.

Niki, with her whip coiled in one hand and her knife in the other, shook her head.

Mike tossed the machete from one hand to the other and then back again. "I'm good."

Nate stood and attached the machete's sheath to his side.

Leading the charge, Niki turned to the house and bound up the few steps to the door. With a quick kick, the door frame exploded inward. She saw the staircase directly in front of her. The living room was to her left. It looked like it had hosted a ferocious battle. The broken couch was shoved against the dormant fireplace, scratch marks streaked the ceiling, and a Michael-sized crack decorated the wall. The cool night air drifted in through the shattered window.

What she didn't see was the succubus.

"Come on, bitch. Where'd you go?"

Niki stepped into the entry way, easing her boots down on the floor to minimize noise. There were doorways past the staircase. As Nate and

Mike maneuvered in behind her, she motioned for the two of them to head upstairs.

"Come out, come out, wherever you are," she sang.

Her eyes danced around, and she kept her head on a swivel. The entire house was dark. The further in she moved, the less the full moon and streetlamp helped.

"Upstairs." Nate's voice whispered into her ear. "Multiple bedrooms. Checking room one."

"Entering kitchen," she responded.

The kitchen was relatively small. Only the essentials - sink, dishwasher, stove, refrigerator - lined the wall. A four-person dining room table was in the kitchen. There were no decorations or knick-knacks, no personal items. This place could've been a model home, left perfectly like this from the realtor. There was nothing to give the impression that anyone lived there.

With her back against the wall, Niki kept the entire room in view as she circled it, checking each dark corner.

"Room one clear. Checking room two."

She made her way back into the hallway, continuing to peer into the downstairs shadows. Michael hadn't said much about how the succubus had changed. Only that she was big and to watch out for her wings. Obviously, the myths about her being a shape shifter were true. The redhead at the club wasn't tall nor did she have wings. She also didn't look that strong. Niki doubted she could've thrown a vampire, even a fledgling, across a room and through a window. Not the beanpole she'd seen.

"Room two cleared. Checking room... holy shit."

She heard Nate yell, followed by the sharp roar of a shotgun blast. Above her, the floor rumbled as if a series of weights had been dropped all at once. Niki ran down the hallway and sprinted up the stairs.

"I think they found her," Josh said.

"You think?" Niki exclaimed.

When she reached the top, Nate was there picking himself up off the floor. The wall across from the open door sported an indention the size of his back. She ran to him.

"Fuck, that girl can hit," he said.

"Where's Mike?"

"In there." He pointed to the room. "She knocked me across the hall and then grabbed him."

From the bedroom, Niki heard, "Back to play, pet?", and turned away from Nate to the open door.

In the middle of the room, with her wings extended wide blocking the window, the succubus held Mike in the air, her talon-like fingers gripping him around the neck. His arms hammered against hers, trying to break free. When that didn't work, he tried to pry her claw away from his throat.

She flipped the knife around in her left hand and unwound the whip, letting the silver links fall to her side.

"You looked much better as a redhead," Niki said, entering the room. The end of the whip drug across the floor. "You must've been beaten with the ugly stick a lot as a child."

Angie turned her head away from the struggling Michael and locked eyes with Niki. Without turning her attention away from Niki, she tossed Michael across the room as if he was a weightless ragdoll. He collided with the wall, breaking through it and landing in the next room.

"I don't usually play with girls," Angie said. "But for you, I'll make an exception."

The succubus dropped both hands to her sides and extended her razor-sharp claws.

29

Niki's eyes danced around the room, taking inventory of what she had at her disposal. There was nothing between her and Angie. A full-size bed sat against the wall to her left. She barely made out a dresser behind Angie against the wall.

The claws on Angie's feet clicked against the hardwood floor as she shifted in place, waiting for Niki to make the first move.

As fast as she could, Niki ran straight at the gargoyle in front of her. Remembering Michael's warning about Angie's wings, she kept her eyes glued to them. When Angie swung one in her direction, Niki angled to the right and dropped to the floor, using her momentum to slide past the oncoming wing.

It passed inches from her face. The moment it cleared her, she planted her boots into the ground and sprung back to her feet. As soon as she landed, she whipped her arm out, sending the thong of her whip at Angie's neck.

Angie twisted her body just before the cracker reached her and batted it away with the skeletal wing. At the same time, she shot her arm out and backhanded Niki into the corner next to the dresser. She turned completely around and aimed the bony tip of the wing toward Niki. The wing flew forward and Niki ducked out of the way. The wing struck the wall, puncturing a hole in it.

Chunks of wall rained down.

The succubus pulled back and swung her fist. It collided with the dresser, shattering the side of it.

Niki dropped to the floor and tried to crawl away, but Angie hit her in the chest and pushed her back into the corner. She held her hand against Niki's chest, pressing her into the wall.

Struggling to catch a breath, Niki wrapped one hand around the bone thin arm and tried to pry it away from her. With her other hand, she used the knife to slice through the gray skin. The ends of the talons pierced into her despite her efforts to hold the arm in place.

Niki glanced up and saw a wing extending above her. The tip, a sharp point made of bone, aimed at her head. She wiggled and fought against the hand but couldn't move. With each twist Niki made, the sharp claws dug deeper into her chest, pinning her in place so the wing could make the fatal blow.

Just as the wing began its final approach into her skull, a loud blast echoed in the room, and Niki's ears rang. The deadly wing disappeared, and shards of bone and tissue fell and covered her. The pressure on her chest eased, and the piercing talon pulled out of her skin.

Angie screamed out in pain and spun around.

Nate stood in the doorway; the shotgun pressed against his shoulder. A thin line of smoke rose from the barrel. He pumped it, ejecting the spent shell and loading a fresh one in its place. He pulled the trigger and clipped the other wing.

The bone broke across the top, and the membranous wing dangled next to her side. Angie tried to move it, but it flopped harmlessly, unable to rise.

With Angie's attention focused on Nate, Niki scrambled to her feet, grabbing the whip as she did. Fully extending it, she spun around and wrapped the thong around Angie's neck, pulling as hard as she could. Angie fought against the whip, but her struggles only increased the tension around her neck. When she violently pulled her head up and back down, Niki shot forward. She used the momentum to slide behind Angie. With her knife outstretched, she cut across the back of Angie's legs just behind her knees. Niki felt the knife cut through muscle and grind against bone.

The succubus buckled to the ground.

With the whip still around her neck, her body shifted and transformed. In an instant, she was the red-headed beauty they'd seen at the club. Except the two destroyed wings didn't disappear and limped grotesquely against her naked back.

Niki, still standing behind Angie, pulled the whip taut, making sure she couldn't escape its grasp. Niki edged her way closer, looping the whip around again and again as she did. When she was close enough, Niki placed her knee into Angie's back and held on tight, strangling her.

Angie's hands reached for the silver around her throat, leaving gashes in her skin as she tried to claw her way out.

Nate stepped closer; the shotgun butted against his shoulder ready to fire again. Slowly, he lowered it and sat it down behind him. With his hand by his side, he gripped the machete and slid it out of its leather sheath.

Angie stopped fighting and stared at the silver blade.

"You have no idea who I am," she croaked out.

Still holding the whip tight, Niki said, "You're a succubus about to lose her head. What does it matter who you are?"

Beneath her knee, she felt Angie's back rise and fall as if she was laughing.

"What's so funny?" Niki asked.

"I am no ordinary succubus. I am Agrat Bat Mahlat. One of the last wives of the archangel Samael. I am the whore of Babylon, a queen of demons, tempter of David. I was already ancient before history began. You are nothing more than insects, existing for mere seconds of my life. Who are you to me but the fly that buzzes around a camel's shit?"

Niki pulled back on the whip. "Unfortunately for you, this fly is taking your head."

Nate raised his arm, bringing the blade to his shoulder.

"Samael will rise again. You will fail."

Niki felt the tension on the whip vanish as Nate swung with all his might. His machete cut through cleanly just above the whip and just below her jaw line. Angie's eyes darted from side to side as the head fell from its perch and rolled across the floor. The whip slid off her neck, and her body fell to the ground. Black blood pulsated from her neck and spread across the hardwood floor.

Mike struggled to open his eyes. The ringing in his ears sent sharp pains through his head.

Everything hurt.

Face first in a pile of rubble, he coughed out a plume of white dust and blood. He tried to push up onto his arms, but they collapsed underneath him, and he crashed back to the ground. So, he rolled onto his back.

Despite the pain, he eased his eyelids open. His vision blurred, and the tinny ring muffled any surrounding noise. Lying there, he felt the world spin around him. His UltraNet flashed the memory of a mission in Afghanistan when an insurgent had blown himself up in a house twenty feet from Mike's unit. The concussive blast had shot him backward. It took a week before he'd regained his hearing, and during that week, his equilibrium was screwed up and the world kept tipping back and forth.

He heard muffled sounds, as if he had cotton balls stuffed in his ears.

"Mike?" a voice asked. "Mike?"

In front of him, the little bit of light coming from the window disappeared behind a large black mass standing over him.

Somewhere inside his head, Mike heard a moan.

"You weren't lying, Mike," the voice said, still muffled by the cotton balls. "She was huge."

Mike forced his dry tongue across his even drier lips. The grit from his mouth ground against the soft tissue. His initial thought was water, but then his stomach turned over just thinking about it. He reminded himself that he didn't drink water anymore. He'd need blood to recover.

"Is she dead?" he choked out, his voice hoarse and his throat scratchy.

"Headless," Nate's deadened voice answered. "How are you feeling?"

Nate reached his hand down. Mike fought through the pain in his shoulder and lifted his own hand up to grasp Nate's. With one quick movement, Nate hoisted Mike to his feet.

Once vertical, Mike braced himself against the edge of a dresser, letting the world balance back out. His head radiated red-hot pain, but the ringing in his ears subsided. His vision cleared up, allowing him to see the damage to the room and then the wall. A jagged hole created a new walkway between the two rooms. But it wasn't just the sheet rock that was broken. Two shattered wooden studs also testified to the damage.

"Bitch threw me through two separate two-by-fours!," he said. "No wonder my whole fucking body hurts."

He bent his head down, placed his hand on the wall, and stepped through the makeshift doorway. Before him was the headless corpse. Broken wings stuck out from the back, and thick blood covered the floor.

Although he still felt hunger pains, nothing was right about that blood. It smelled rancid, putrid, and sour. If he'd had anything left in his system, he was certain he would've thrown it up.

As he picked his head up, he saw Niki standing over the head. She looked beat to hell. Her hair was frazzled, and her shirt was torn. Small puncture wounds across the top of her chest produced droplets of blood. Mike couldn't smell it from the overpowering stench of Angie's blood, but once he saw Niki bleeding, his mouth watered.

Immediately, he bolted out of the room, ran for the stairs, and headed down to the first floor as fast as he could. He continued to the street and began pacing. His senses sharpened to their predatorial form. There was movement in the trees and leaves rustling across the ground. All around, there was the percussive chorus of beating hearts—people sleeping in nearby houses. Their blood pulsed through their veins. Red. Sweet. Delicious.

Footsteps approached from behind him, and he spun around, ready to pounce on his prey.

Nate was hunched over the duffel bag they'd left on the sidewalk. He reached inside and grabbed a bag.

"Here," he said and tossed it to Mike.

With quick reflexes, he snagged the bag out of the air. He had seen what it was before it had left Nate's hand. As soon as his fingers clasped the cool, plasticized PVC, he shoved it to his mouth. His teeth pierced the bag, and his mouth filled with the sweet, coppery taste of blood. Within seconds, he drained the bag dry. As he did, he felt his eyes lose their heat. The surrounding sounds died down as his senses returned to a state where he could control them.

Once the bag was sucked dry, he withdrew his teeth and raised his head. His eyes met Nate's and a wave of shame washed over him. He had lost control. He should've been better prepared, but he wasn't.

"I'm sorry," Mike said.

"Don't be. We know you are still figuring things out. Give yourself some grace and credit. You could've attacked Niki when you saw the blood, but instead you ran outside. Even if you don't realize it yet, that took some serious control."

Michael smiled but deep down he expected more from himself. Nate was right, but Michael still strove to be better. He would be better.

"What are you looking for?" he asked Nate.

"Found it." Nate pulled a bottle of lighter fluid from the duffel and a lighter. "Time to torch her. Want to watch?"

"No, thanks. I think I'm going to sit out here and find out if there's a single spot on my body that doesn't currently hurt."

Nate stretched his arms out and moved his shoulders back and forth.

"I hear that. There's a hot bath in my future. The bitch threw me into a wall."

"She threw me through one."

They both laughed, and Nate made his way back into the house, ready to set fire to this problem and leave it behind them.

Michael strode to the curb and sat. The blood helped him regain his composure, but his head still felt off. And he'd need another few blood bags before his body healed.

He placed his hands behind him and leaned back, gazing up at the stars. "Thank God, we don't have more of those.".

The scent of burnt flesh wafted into the air.

Josh rubbed his fingers across his eyes, wiping away the sleep that had built up. Exhaustion had taken its hold, and he struggled to stay awake. The stress of the evening's adventure hadn't helped.

While the team was on a mission, he made it a point to always record the audio and video streams. He sent them to Intel, and Intel uploaded them to whatever archives the Council kept.

He played back the audio of when she had spoken. Josh listened to her final words, and then the sound of the machete swishing through the air.

After downing the last of his coffee, he replayed the audio and listened again. He ran his fingers through his hair. Every single word she said made him feel uneasy. A knot formed in his stomach. He couldn't help but think they'd missed something.

For a third time, he rewound the track.

"I am no ordinary succubus. I am Agrat Bat Mahlat."

He hit pause, pulled up a web browser, and searched the name "Agrat Bat Mahlat". He hovered his mouse over the first entry.

"Wikipedia, of course," he said to the empty room, his voice echoing off the bare walls.

Josh right-clicked on the first few links, opening each in a new tab. He quickly scanned each webpage before minimizing his browser. With a click of his mouse, Josh initiated a Skype call.

"Intel here."

"It's Josh. Did you review the audio I sent?"

"A few times now. It's concerning."

Josh clicked on the browser in his taskbar, maximizing it back to full screen.

"Especially if she was who she said she was," Josh said, clicking through the open tabs. Wikipedia, Encyclopedia, Occult-World crossed the top of the browser window. "From what I've read, she was pretty spot on with her titles. Either this succubus was well versed in lore..."

"Or she was the real deal," Intel finished. "That's the part that's most concerning to me. How did the Council lose track of a creature that ancient? Hell, if what she said was true, she should be on the Council."

"Most of what I'm reading comes from rabbinic literature or the Zoharistic Kabbalah," Josh said. His eyes darted across the computer screen. "She was known as the dancing roof-demon, a queen of the demons, and an angel of sacred prostitution. Those are some wonderful titles."

"Oh, keep reading, it gets better," Intel said.

Josh clicked from one tab to the next. His eyes scrolled the page as fast as his fingers did. "Agrat had been an alternate wife to Adam if he hadn't chosen Eve. Along with Lilith and a few others. When Adam chose Eve, the others left the Garden of Eden, and Samael took them as his wives."

Josh knew that wasn't the story they told in Sunday School. So, assuming she was the true Agrat bat Mahlat... "Are we confirming Adam and Eve and the Garden of Eden?"

"I wouldn't go that far. The written accounts are from oral traditions which came from local myths, storytellers. Based on what we do know of her, how hard would it have been to tweak the stories and make her larger than what she was?"

"Well, she seduced Michael without any problem so it's probably not that much of a reach."

"Remind me to give him hell about that when his head is clear. After as much shit as he gave me when we were deployed together... Oh, I'm going to enjoy this."

Josh heard the smile in Intel's voice.

"What about this last part?" Josh asked and hit play.

"Samael will rise again. You will fail." Angie's final words hung in the air.

Both men were silent, letting the words sink in.

"A veiled threat," Intel said, but his voice lacked conviction. The statement sounded more like he wished it was a veiled threat.

"Or a promise." Josh vocalized the concern he knew they both shared. "I thought only a succubus could bring Samael back from whatever hellscape he's in."

"That's the lore."

"If that's the lore, and those were her dying words, what's the likelihood there's another one?"

"Another succubus?" Intel asked. "Before now, I would've sworn they were extinct. Now, we're contemplating more of them. For fuck's sake, Campbell. How could they have hidden so well for so long? Without Samael to make more, they've had to exist for over a thousand years. Hell, in Agrat's case, probably triple that."

"Beautiful women who prey on unsuspecting men who want to get laid? Who can seduce them into doing whatever they want with just a touch? How hard would it be for them to hide in plain sight? As long as they don't leave a string of bodies, how would we ever know?"

"Which begs the question, why are they leaving a string of bodies now?"

Josh leaned back in his chair. He crossed his arms in front of him and dropped his head. He said the first thing that came to mind. "What if word of the Council's disappearance is causing a ripple? Believing no repercussions, creatures are comfortable enough to break the Accords.

Has anyone else seen an increase in activity? With any creatures? Vampire uprisings? Werewolves? Banshees?"

"Nothing out of the ordinary," Intel answered. "If it is the Council's disappearance, and this is the first instance, I tell you what, between you and me, this scares the shit out of me."

Naomi felt the pain surge through her body. Wave upon wave pierced her as if her very soul—if she'd still had one—was being ripped away. Her head exploded with a shrill cry. She'd experienced pain before, but something of this intensity hadn't happened since before the Accords were written, before the Council took over. Not since Samael was executed.

Her skin rippled, and she forced herself to stay in her human form. She could've allowed herself to change, but she hated the other form. This was her, and this was how she wanted to stay.

The excruciating pain dragged her to the ground in agony. She fell onto her hands and knees, pressing them into the cold stone beneath her. The thick air of their tunnel was dank and humid. It tasted foul and rotten. She tried to breathe through the pain, taking in large gasps of the putrid air. With each deep inhale, she stifled a scream. From somewhere else deep within their tunnel system, she heard the screech of one of her sisters, then the other. She wasn't the only one feeling what just happened.

Finally, after a few seconds of eternity, the pain vanished. Silence filled the gap. A nothingness existed where a shared connection used to be. Naomi felt a hole inside of her.

Down the corridor, the sound of shoes striking the floor echoed off the stone walls and ceiling. Multiple sets ran her direction—both Lily and Eileen—creating a chorus of footfalls reverberating throughout the underground lair.

"Angie!" Lily screamed as she and Eileen ran to Naomi. "Angie needs us."

Naomi raised her head; her hands and knees still pressed firmly into the ground. Sweat stuck to her face. Tears of blood streaked down her cheeks.

"Angie's gone," Naomi replied through clenched teeth.

She took a few deep breaths, trying to ease the phantom pain still resonating through the void left by the absence of Angie's connection.

"She was arrogant, and now she's dead, Lilith."

Both Lily and Eileen stopped running a few feet from Naomi. Eileen placed her hands behind her head and lifted her head to the stone ceiling. Loud sobs escaped her as she collapsed to the ground. Her bloody tears testified to her pain.

Lily strode the last few feet to Naomi and slapped her across the face. The strike was so quick that it took a moment for Naomi to register what had happened as her cheek flared in pain.

Naomi jumped to her feet, her hand rising to the place on her face where she was sure a red print matching Lily's hand started to form.

"How dare you?" Lily shouted. "She was my sister."

"She was my sister, too," Naomi shouted in return. Her voice echoed down the corridor. Red tears welled up in her eyes. "But she was arrogant. All three of you have been arrogant and careless. She wanted the vampire as a pet, but I told you he was with hunters, and he had a strong aura. Did that matter to you? No, it didn't. You were convinced the Council's disappearance meant you had free reign to do whatever the hell you wanted. Careless. And now look what happened!"

"We'll kill the hunters for this. And if the vampire is strong enough to be the one, I'll take him for myself," Lily shouted at the top of her lungs. Her black hair fell in front of her face in matted tangles. Even though she stayed in her human form, Naomi saw the beast lurking just beneath the surface, wanting to break out of its shell.

"Did you not hear what I said?" Naomi replied. "Even now, you are insisting on carelessness! Between the three of you, you've killed more in the past few months than in the previous century. You are the oldest of us, our leader since our creator was killed, but you are leading us to extinction. We are the last of our kind. There'll be no more of us, especially with your insistent foolishness. If you continue to lead like this, we'll all end up as piles of ash somewhere."

"We will not be the last of us," Eileen said. She finally stopped crying. Red streaks traced her face. "Lily will use the vampire to raise Samael, and then Samael will make more of us."

"Fuck Samael," Naomi snapped. "He was a cruel master who treated us as slaves, concubines. Why would we want him to return? Why not just go back to how we used to live? For a thousand years, it was the four of us living as queens, seducing whomever we wanted, getting whatever we wanted. We stayed off the Council's radar by not being careless. We didn't kill, and it worked. We survived!"

Naomi paced as Eileen and Lily stood there with their mouths agape.

"I doubt Agrat said anything about us. They didn't know we existed. They don't have to know we still do. Let's leave this town and go somewhere else."

Lily shook her head and clenched her fists. "Leave our home for the past hundred years because of hunters and a fledgling vampire? Who do they think they are? Who do you think we are? They'll pay for killing her. If you don't want to help, that's fine. Eileen and I will string the hunters up by their toes and flay every piece of skin from their bodies. We'll make the vampire watch before using him.

"You, Naomi, are a disgrace. Samael will return. I, being the oldest and your leader, will bring him back. I suggest, somewhere in the dark depths of your soul, you find the way to love him again when he does.

"But for now, we have hunters to kill."

In the room he had claimed, Michael's bed sat against the corner. It was the sole piece of furniture in the room. No dresser. No nightstand. Just the four metal legs of the bed frame touching the floor. The thin mattress, which might as well have been a bedroll, rested on top of the metal frame.

At first, Mike had thought it was one step above an army cot, but now he realized it was more akin to a prison bed, just without the top bunk. The more he contemplated it, the more real it became. He was trapped in a prison, just one of his own making. Prison was meant to separate those who were a danger to society away from everyone else. Wasn't he a danger to society? To those around him? For their protection, he needed to be isolated.

Two full bags of thick red blood rested next to him on the bed. An empty littered the ground. The vibrations of their temporary housing reverberated across his back as he sat pressed against the corner of the wall. He doubted anyone else could feel it, but he certainly could. A rhythmic pulsing flowed throughout the walls. He wasn't sure if it was the plumbing or the electrical wires. Or it could have been the energy of New Orleans, the spirits here. For that matter, just residual pain in his back from being thrown through a wall.

The moment they walked back in, he grabbed the sustenance his body craved. The sweet, metallic fluid his thirst called out for. He'd snatched a few out of the fridge as Josh relayed his conversation with Intel.

Mike wanted to ignore him. He couldn't go out into the field again. He needed to believe that Angie was the only one.

He felt the heat rising in his throat and across his face. Heat that only came from a deep, fiery anger. He tormented himself, reliving what happened. Reliving everything from the slight touch of her hand to jeopardizing the entire team. Even more, to how he had acted when he had seen the faintest amount of blood on Niki.

He replayed the events over and over, using the recorder in his brain as castigation.

Long before he heard the knock at the door, he sensed someone coming down the hallway. He heard their pulse. Smelled their sweat.

"Hey, Mike." Nate's voice accompanied the rapping on the door.

"Not in the mood, Nate."

Despite the objection, Nate opened the door. "I know you aren't, but I'm also not in the mood to let you beat yourself up."

"It's what I do." Mike shifted his legs, but kept his back against the wall, still feeling the vibrations, feeling them talk to him, call to him.

"No, it's not. I remember the guy who was determined to track down his wife's killer. Faced an alpha all on his own. I was there when you stood toe-to-toe with Silas in the club and rescued us. Don't tell me feeling sorry for yourself is your MO. Not when it's been taking action."

Nate walked to the wall on the other side of the room and slid down to the floor.

"I'm not going to say I understand," he continued, "but I'll say what I can see. Being a vampire, a good one, is a struggle. I see it with Thomas, and I see it with you. Whatever's in the blood that changes you, it wants to be bad. The vamps we go after, the ones who are bad, they don't seem to struggle like you guys do. They give into the evil, feed it, and let it consume them. You're fighting a demon inside of you that constantly wants to be unleashed."

Mike raised his head and let it rest on the wall behind him. He looked up at the dingy ceiling, aged by years of smoke stains.

Still staring up, he said, "When she touched me, all of that went away."

"All of what?"

"Everything you just said. The addiction. The hunger. There was none of it. Her touch replaced it all." He lowered his head and brought his eyes to Nate. "Ever since I became this, I haven't been able to quench the thirst. Feeding helps ease it, but it never goes away. I feel it just under the surface, ready to be called upon at any moment. Ready to be unleashed so I can bleed the world dry. It. Never. Ends.

"But when she simply brushed her hand across my face, it vanished. I don't exactly know how to explain it, but while she held my hand, it was like she was my dealer providing a slow drip of drugs into my veins. For the first time since Silas, I wasn't thirsty. I wasn't craving. Even now, even though I know what she was, part of me desperately needs that again. Part of me..." Mike searched for the right words to express what was inside.

"Part of me wishes she had a different hair color."

"Reminded you of her?"

"Of course. And get this, Angie knew her name when I couldn't remember it. All my memories were gone. It was like there was a lock on my brain. Not only did her touch entrance me, but it gave her a connection to me. She had access to everything and then shut me out.

"That's probably where she messed up, actually. Being disconnected felt so strange, that it took me out of her spell. But when she mentioned Brit, that was it.

"But, Nate, what if Angie had picked a different hair color? And had never said Brit's name? I don't know if I could've resisted. She had me."

"But you did resist. Don't beat yourself up over this. As of a week ago, we thought these things were extinct. We learned more in a few hours than the Council has known for centuries. And we won. We took a beating, but we won. So, stop beating yourself up. That winged bitch did enough of that for you. We just need to recharge and hope Josh and Intel are wrong about more."

Nate rose from the floor and brushed off his pants.

"What about Niki? I almost attacked her."

Nate turned to Mike and started to laugh.

"Yeah. Okay. I wouldn't worry about that. It's not the first time a vamp has wanted to get a taste of her. Plus, I think it's funny how you think you could've taken her. She'd have wrapped you in her chain like you were a steer and dragged you out of that house kicking and screaming. And then poured one of your bags down your throat. She's a tough one."

The image of being hogtied by Niki brought a smile to his face, and he started laughing.

"You're probably right. Even at full strength, I don't think I could take her."

"You and me both," Nate said, laughing as he left.

Mike leaned his head back against the wall again and let the vibrations sooth him.

Mike stayed in bed with his back pressed against the wall the entire day. The darkened window hid the sunlight. He didn't need to fall asleep like everyone else. So instead, he listened to the vibrations of their temporary headquarters. He felt them resonate throughout his body.

While meditating, he heard everyone else's heart rates slow as they drifted off to sleep. All four of them needed to rejuvenate; meanwhile, Mike found himself praying Austin and Josh were wrong.

His aching body was still sore from the fight. If he had to fight a second? If this one was pissed by her friend dying? They were truly fucked.

"Hey, Brit," Mike said to the empty room. "Haven't seen you in a while. God, I miss you and could sure use your company right now."

He grabbed the last bag from the bed and began to sip from it. The thick fluid filled his mouth and coated his throat. It wasn't warm blood straight from the tap, so to speak. Thomas had warned him about sinking his teeth into someone. He was to avoid it as long as he could.

"There's nothing more addictive than feeling the heart pump warm blood directly into your mouth," he'd said.

So far, Mike had managed to keep to the bags and planned on making sure he stayed that way. He couldn't risk anything else. Couldn't risk becoming one of the creatures his team hunted.

Another sip and half the bag remained. Mike dropped his hands to his legs, sinking into the vibrations. With his stomach full, he closed his eyes, willing his body to transform whatever nutrients it required to do its work and repair him.

"Although, I haven't seen you," he continued, his eyes still firmly shut. "I'm just going to pretend like you're in the room, that you're right here next to me."

Using his UltraNet, he summoned a memory of Brittany. She sat next to him on the bed. He sat wearing boxers, propped up, reading a book. She lay on her side facing away from him with her iPad in her hands. Her red hair spilled across the pillow, and the blanket was pulled up to her shoulders.

Mike thought of that night. It was pretty much like any other night. It wasn't special. It was normal. But he guessed, in its own way, that made it special.

He placed himself inside the memory.

"I forgot about you today," he said. "In all of my years, I've always remembered everything. But the thing we fought today had the ability to make me forget."

"How'd that make you feel?" she asked, still looking at her iPad.

"Empty. Hollow. And the worst part was, when I couldn't remember, I felt vulnerable. She controlled me. I wasn't in control of myself."

"But you found your way."

"Yeah, but this was my first mission as a vampire. I did better as a human. At least then, I did some major ass kicking. I took down a whole club full of vampires, killed a corrupt cop, saved the team a few times. But now, I can't control my cravings. I've been seduced by a beautiful creature. Gotten my ass kicked and thrown through a wall. I almost attacked Niki."

"Can we go back to the 'seduced by a beautiful creature' part?" Brittany asked.

Mike heard the smile in her voice.

"Michael White. It's ok," she finally said, still facing away from him. He knew he could make the image flip, but part of him didn't want to see her face right now, didn't feel like he deserved to.

"I'm dead. You're not. Hopefully, you'll get to live an untold number of lifetimes. Just because you're undead, doesn't mean you're dead. One of these days, you may find someone and love again. Don't feel guilty. I love you. I need you to be loved.

"And as for the vampire stuff, you'll get the hang of it. Were you the special forces guy when you were in basic? Hell no. You were a skinny, bumbling private just like everyone else. You thought you were special, but you quickly found out you weren't. And then you learned. And you excelled. You did it then, and you'll do it again. Be patient with yourself. Allow yourself some grace."

Brittany hadn't met him until he was out of the military. He knew the words coming out of her mouth were his own. He just needed to hear them coming from someone else. Coming from her.

He let the memory slide away and opened his eyes.

The room was empty.

A glance at his watch told him it was mid-afternoon. Everyone else was resting up for the second outing in a few hours. He eased himself against the wall and sunk into the relaxing hum that engulfed him.

"These lights are getting on my last nerves," Niki shouted to Nate and Mike.

The three of them stood at the bar inside the Republic. Nate had ordered drinks for them. Although Mike wasn't drinking, having one in front of him helped him to blend in. She saw their reflection in the mirrored wall behind the rows of alcohol.

They looked like an interesting trio. The faint memory of a bruise still showed on Michael's face. Niki had noticed he was also still favoring his arm. Other than that, he seemed to have almost completely healed.

If not for the overly-caked-on makeup she'd applied, she would've looked like an abuse victim. A small cut split her lower lip in half. When she smiled, she felt the sting of it pulling apart. If she wasn't careful, she'd taste blood as it ripped open.

Her body ached. She decided against the more alluring attire she wore the previous night and went with a comfortable pair of jeans and a relaxed, plain T-shirt.

It hadn't been apparent that Nate was beat to hell until she had rubbed her hand across his shoulders. He had winced every time she did. Now it was a game to get his attention.

"I'm not saying I'm getting old," Mike said, turning to face the other two, "but this music is loud."

"Oh, we're getting old," Nate said. "After last night, I could've used another few days to recover."

Niki checked her watch. It was almost one in the morning. They'd been there since before ten. Nate had been hit on twice, which made her both jealous and inflated her ego, but neither female gave signs of being a succubus. Michael had walked the club a handful of times and also had no luck.

"If there's another, I don't think she's out tonight," Niki said. "Maybe we scared her off."

"Or Angie was lying," Mike said.

"Love, I'll drink to that," she said and downed the last of her Tito's and Coke.

"I took you for a whiskey girl," Mike said. "Or Foster's."

"Don't believe the commercials. Foster's is not Australian for beer." She exaggerated her Australian accent, making all of them smile. She felt the sharp pain on her lip, followed by a faint taste of blood.

Mike turned his head away from her.

"Is your vampire sense picking up anything?" she asked.

"You say that like I'm Spiderman using my spidey tingle."

"Let's go with that, Vampireman."

He turned around and placed his back against the bar. Niki watched as he closed his eyes and took a deep breath. When he opened them, they blazed red.

"Angie had a distinct smell. She masked it with perfume but there was a rot underneath. There's a lot of smells in here right now, but nothing like that."

"Anything else?" Nate asked.

Niki stared into the mirror, watching the crowd dancing behind her. Thomas had talked a lot about how sensitive vampire senses were. They could pick up the smallest detail out of a crowd. He'd said it was how predators of any species found the weakest in the herd and pounced. It was how a lion could single out one gazelle, separate it from the rest, and feed their pride. Vampires were no different. They were predators seeking prey, seeking food, seeking blood to survive.

She wondered what a place like this felt like to a vampire. The constant bombardment of sounds, smells, contact. Hopefully, Mike had learned enough to separate the anomaly from the pack. And to minimize the impact of the sensory overload. A vampire with a migraine didn't sound like someone fun to be around.

He closed his eyes and when he opened them, they were back to their normal hue.

"Nothing. The vibrations from the music are so loud, it's hard to focus. As soon as I try, they drown out everything else."

"You must really be feeling the bass," Nate said.

"I'm going to call it for tonight," Mike said. "Our only source is a soul-sucking bitch's dying threat. I don't give that much credence."

"I agree with you there," Niki chimed in. "Let's get out of here. I'll call the Uber."

Mike shook his head. "I think I'm going to walk. Need the brisk, midnight air to clear my head."

"There may still be a succubus out there, Mike," Josh said. He'd been so quiet the whole night, Niki had forgotten he was listening.

"You're still awake over there," Nate responded.

"Just been enjoying the music," Josh quipped. "A dying threat or not, we have to stay vigilant, just in case. A lack of readiness will get you killed."

"You sound like Jax," Niki said. "Josh, you can track each of us, correct?"

"Of course."

"We can all use the fresh air," she said. "Nate, you're with me. We can walk Bourbon Street. Mike, clear your head."

36

Once outside the club, Michael lowered his head and started walking. He headed in the opposite direction away from Nate and Niki. As he walked onto the street, he pulled the collar of his jacket up to hide his face.

Maybe I can hide from the world, be anonymous.

Part of him wished he actually could. But he knew it wasn't, and doubted he'd allow himself to hide away even if he could. Another part of him, though, the part that tried to save Martin those many years ago, still lived somewhere inside him. It was just a matter of finding that version amid the mess he had become.

As he let his feet lead the way, he felt phantom vibrations traverse his body. They felt just like they had when he'd sat on his bed earlier. Small electrical impulses danced up and down his spine. Light sensations ran across his stomach and down his legs. With his hand, he reached for his back, scratching at the tingle as it made its way throughout his body.

"Josh," Mike began. "You still with me?"

He heard a slight click in his ear as Josh unmuted his own mic.

"I'm here. What's up?"

"Just wanting conversation. Need to get out of my own head."

"No worries, man. I get it. Yesterday was rough. Hell, the past few months have been rough." Josh paused for a moment. "So, how's the weather out there?"

"I'm guessing...cold?" Mike shook his head. "Anything new from Jax or Thomas?"

"I wish. Everything's still a mess."

"I'm going to pull the newbie card. So, dumb it down for me. If we stopped Silas, what the hell is happening? And why not just elect a new Council?"

Josh fell silent.

Mike scratched at his stomach. These sensations didn't sit right with him. Maybe it was a combination of his healing ability and the cold night air. Whatever it was, it unnerved him. It reminded him of a limb falling asleep and the tingling sensation as it woke back up. Was this part of the vampire maturing process? His body regaining feeling? If so, he wished Thomas would've mentioned it, so he could've prepared himself. Granted, maybe Thomas didn't remember. He would've gone through this process over two hundred years ago.

"I'll start with the Council. Did Jax, Thomas, or Intel ever talk to you about how it's made up?"

"Only that they're the leaders of the different species."

"They are the oldest and usually the strongest members of each. It's not so much an elected position as an inherited one through age and power. Not every species has a representative. If that was the case, there'd be too many members to get anything accomplished."

"How many seats are on the Council?"

"It's changed over the years, but before the disappearance, there were eleven.

"Vampires have a controlling majority with five seats. They are the oldest species and seen as the strongest. Werewolves are next with three. Demons have two seats and magic wielders have one."

"Demons and magic wielders? Explain that one to me." He glanced from one side of the road to the other. He heard the raucous sound of a party a few blocks over. His hand traced the electrical impulses up to back of his neck, before dropping back to his side.

"Think witches and warlocks. Harry Potter shit. There aren't many of them left. Unlike vampires and werewolves who turn people, magic wielders have to be born. From what I've heard, they used to do a lot of inbreeding to keep the magic bloodlines alive and pure, but that had its own set of consequences. Disorders and deformities.

"Demon is kind of a catch all group. If we had known about the succubus before, she'd have been part of that group. Banshees fall under demons. That group gets all the weird shit.

"Electing a new Council isn't an easy process. In the rare circumstances that a Council member dies, there's typically in-fighting and slaughtering before someone new takes the seat. Can you imagine the bloodshed trying to fill each of them all at once?"

"Where did they go?" Mike asked. "Why did they leave?"

"Silas played a political game. He wanted to create enough chaos to seize power. Instead of a Council, he would've made himself emperor. Everyone else would be relegated to weak advisers. Silas built a following. Unlike those in the past who've tried to do the same, he had a movement that waited for the right time and the right people, including some Council members."

"If he had some of the current members, then did they really leave, or go into hiding? Or are they prisoners somewhere?"

"Those...are really great questions we don't have answers for."

Michael thought about everything Josh said. As an amateur student of military history, things were beginning to make sense. "So, Silas tried to build a huge clan of vampires, all loyal to him, like what we saw in Texas with the hives. Betas run them like local command posts, filling the ranks while he creates more hives.

"Once his army grew large enough, once he had enough support from certain alliances, the Council would vanish, and the only one left to lead, without all of the bloodshed, would be Silas. The clans would vote in their own dictator. Especially if they believed this would at least allow them to still be heard."

"That's the going theory. The Night Crew did a great job of snuffing out as many hives as we could, but we couldn't get them all." After a heavy pause, he continued. "Silas still has a loyal following."

Michael looked up and scanned around him. The street was dark and quiet. The buildings looked like warehouse after warehouse. He had no idea where he was or how he'd gotten here.

37

As they left Republic, New Orleans, Niki reached out and grabbed Nate's hand.

"Bourbon is this way, love," she said as she led him down St. Peter's.

"You sure?" Nate asked.

Niki shook her head and rolled her eyes, dropping her head to the ground. As long as they'd been together, he knew better than to doubt her sense of direction. They'd lived in Los Angeles and Detroit before The Incident. In both places, he had no sense of direction. The man could get lost walking to the mailbox. In their apartment building. That was not her fault.

The Incident. That's how she had to refer to it. Capital T. Capital I. The Incident.

She truly couldn't think about The Incident, about what happened. She couldn't get past the guilt. How could she? He was their son. Her son. And she hadn't been strong enough to protect him.

Nate had also felt guilty. She knew that, but he had dealt with it long ago. He hadn't been there that night. He had been working. That was understandable. He had no need to blame himself. He had been making sure they had food on the table, making sure the lights turned on.

But she had been there. It had been her responsibility.

"Think Mike is going to be ok?" Nate asked, jogging her out of her head.

"Of course. He's a vamp. Plus, he's got friends like me and a trainer like Thomas. Who did Thomas have to help him? Anyone?"

"Well, he had his brother," Nate suggested.

Niki stopped walking and turned to him. "And you see how well that worked out."

"Valid point," he conceded.

She nodded her head down the street and started walking again.

"How do you know we're going the right direction?" he asked.

"Nathan Edwards. I swear. Just trust me. We continue down St. Peter's. We're going to pass *Harrah's Casino*. From there, we'll turn up Canal. It's another half mile on Canal before we turn on Bourbon."

Again, she shook her head with exasperation, and then hand-in-hand, they strolled down St. Peter's.

The street was dimly lit. Some lights flickered, and the rest were out entirely.

She'd walked down many a street like this, usually on the hunt for a rogue vampire den. No better vampire hunting ground than a poorly lit street with flickering lights in the dark of night. And no better way to fish them out of hiding than an unsuspecting female, drunkenly walking alone. The new ones made it too easy.

Fortunately, New Orleans was off-limits to vampires for hunting. One of the few laws vamps seemed to honor. They could visit, but they had to register just like Michael. Under no circumstance could they hunt. The rules were strict and well enforced. Sometimes even by a vampire's peers.

The buildings helped to block the breeze coming off the Mississippi River, but she could still feel the bite in the night air. Niki was thankful she was in jeans. They kept her legs warm. Her arms, however, were a different story. She'd kill for a jacket! More and more goosebumps rose on her arms with each gust.

Her thoughts wanted to drift back to Detroit, back to The Incident, but she refused. The last thing she needed to do was take a trip down

Memory Lane. Especially down *that* Memory Lane. That lane was filled with pain. A day would come that she'd have to confront it, but that did not mean today. Not at all.

The street lit up as they approached *Harrah's Casino*. The bright lights filled the air and set the late hour on fire.

Nate slowed down as they neared the doors to the casino.

"Want to gamble?" he asked.

"Don't we do that every day?" she asked in return.

"Yeah, but this would be gambling with our money, not our lives. Be a nice change."

Because his grin was as big as it was, she took a moment to actually consider it. "No. Come on. Bourbon Street, remember? Maybe we can find some food."

Nate's smile had waned when she had said no, but at the mention of food, his eyes perked up again.

"You know just how to speak to my heart," he said.

"Of course, I do, My Ebony Prince. Of course, I do."

They trudged past *Harrah's* and turned up Canal Street. Immediately, a brisk, winter wind tore through them. Canal was wider than other roads and faced the Mississippi. Nothing stood in the way to block the chill from the river. Niki felt it down to her bones and shuddered

"Oh, fuck me!" she exclaimed.

A few people walking along Canal turned their heads. Each person was dressed as though they had prepared better for this.

"Cold?" he asked.

"Yes, it's fucking cold, love. I prepped for an attack, not the damn weather. I have my silver whip around my waist as a belt, but I forgot to bring a fucking jacket. It's the middle of fucking winter, and I'm in a goddamn T-shirt."

She instinctively let go of his hand and crossed her arms over her chest, shoving each hand under an armpit.

A snort escaped Nate. He raised a fist to his face, obviously hoping he could catch it before it happened.

"Laugh it up," she snapped. "You keep going, and I'll steal your shirt. You can walk around in this wind topless."

Nate slid the bottom of his shirt up, rubbing his hand across his well-defined abs. "You sure you want me to do that? Might get a few dollars shoved down my pants and make you jealous."

"Then you can take those dollars and buy me a fucking coat that's functional and looks great on missions." She turned her walk into a quick trot. "Bourbon is another couple of blocks up."

A few moments later, she saw the streetlights illuminating their destination.

"About fucking time," Niki said, as they turned off Canal and onto the famous party street. The wind was blocked by the buildings on the narrow strip, raising the temperature by a dozen degrees.

Neon signs lined their path as they walked. Large crowds swarmed both sides of the street and down the center of it. The French Quarter had a different feel. Something Niki couldn't quite put her finger on. Whether it was the rich history visible everywhere, the wrought-iron balconies above them, or the bright purple, green, and yellow streamers and banners hanging from the buildings all around, she didn't know.

"Check out the window," Nate said, pointing next to them.

Niki knew better but still couldn't resist. Mannequins dressed in leather and lace lingerie stared back at her. She looked up at the neon sign. *Hustler Hollywood.*

"Why spend money on something that'll end up on the floor? Keep walking. I'm sure there's food that isn't also underwear farther on."

They continued down, and Nate hesitated in front of *Hard Rock* but didn't stop. Niki was glad. She was hungry but wanted something more authentic to the area.

The farther down Bourbon they walked, the more music poured into the street. A saxophone and stand-up bass played smooth jazz. The unmistakable sound of an accordion filled the air with zydeco. An electric guitar cried away the blues.

Her stomach grumbled. She was hungry and thirsty after seeing so many people drinking daiquiris from large slushy-filled tubes.

Souvenir shops rife with T-shirts popped up at least once on every block. Niki was tempted to pop her head in and find a nice comfy sweater to pull on over her T-shirt but decided against it. They'd stop to eat soon, and their temporary housing wasn't too far from the Quarter. She'd made it this far already.

As they passed a twenty-four-hour grill, Niki slowed. Her stomach finally got the better of her. She felt a hole in her middle and needed to fill it. The thought of midnight burgers immediately made her mouth water. Before she could come to a complete stop, Nate pushed her along.

"Wait," she said. "Let's eat here." She tried to stand her ground, but he overpowered her.

"Let's not," he said, his voice was absent its usual comical banter. This voice was no-nonsense serious. She knew how to read him. Something was off, and he didn't want it to appear as if something was.

She stopped resisting, grabbed his hand, and pushed it around her back, drawing in close to him.

Tilting her head up, he leaned down and kissed her. As he pulled away, he whispered, "We're being followed."

Josh sat comfortably in his chair chatting with Mike. With his headset on, he rested his back against the back of the wheelchair. Too often, he found himself slumped over the keyboard, his shoulders rounded, or his head propped up by one arm. Most times he had the audio playing through his computer speakers, but when Mike had wanted to have a conversation, he had switched the feeds on the earbuds, grabbed his Bluetooth headset, and eased back. As he told Mike about the Council, he raised his arms behind his head and peered up to the gray ceiling.

New Orleans wasn't a bad city. He loved the food even though the spice didn't love him back. Outside of the whole hurricane thing, he could handle the weather. Josh didn't care much for snow and freezing temperatures.

Staring up, he saw water stains on the ceiling. If this was a more permanent assignment, like tracking Silas had been, he'd want to liven the place up, put on a fresh coat of paint, make it feel like home. But since this was temporary, there wasn't any need. Intel secured the location, and beggars couldn't be choosers. There were plenty of worse areas where they could've been housed. At least he had a nice view of the park across the street, whenever he managed to look up from the computer screen anyhow.

"Josh, you're still tracking my location, right?" Mike asked.

"Of course. Why? Something wrong?"

"I have no idea where I am. How do I get back?"

He couldn't help but burst out in a rolling laugh. The man had the ability to remember everything that'd happened in his entire life, and second life, but he couldn't remember how to get back. Mike must've really been out of it while walking down the street. Or the conversation about the Council was that riveting. Josh naturally assumed the latter.

"I'll send you directions. You know your phone has a maps app, right?" He shook his head.

There were moments when he felt they asked him for help like this just so they wouldn't have to look up the information themselves. Sure, he was usually sitting in front of a big computer screen with his fingers casually perched over the home keys but come on now. They could easily find out some of the same information. Often just by asking the built-in AI.

"Yes, I know," Mike said. "But that also means I need to know the address of the new..."

Mike's voice trailed off. He didn't know the new address. Maybe that was a decent enough excuse.

I'm still giving him shit later, Josh thought.

"Sending you the address now."

Josh dropped his hands from his head and placed them on the arm of his wheelchair. He pressed hard with one hand, stretching his shoulder and back, then did the same on the other side. He was numb from his waist down, but he'd often joke that the soreness in his upper back made up for it.

Pressing up with both arms, he scooted closer to the desk and reached for the keyboard. His fingers expertly danced over the keys. Without touching his mouse, he shifted the window to his messenger screen, copied the address into the text bar next to Mike's name, and sent the message.

"What are you... How are you..."

"What was that?"

The message indicator didn't show "Read" yet. He knew Mike wasn't referring to anything he'd just sent him. Something had sounded strange in his voice.

"Mike? Did you get the address? Just plug that into the app, and it'll take you right back here."

Silence. He could hear Mike's breathing. It had escalated, almost to the point of hyperventilating.

"Everything ok?" Josh pushed. There was no reason why Mike wouldn't respond. They'd been having good conversation up until that point. Something was wrong.

Mike's voice confirmed his suspicion.

"Brit?"

At the next block, Nate nudged Niki, and the two of them veered off. With less people around, he picked up his pace, and Niki followed suit. Up ahead, the sign read Dauphine Street. Nate rarely paid attention to signs. He knew Niki was much better with directions than he was, but when it came to springing into action, his mind clicked into a different gear.

As they crossed over Dauphine, taking long strides to speed up, Niki asked, "How do you know we're being followed?"

He hadn't wanted to glance back yet. He feared that once their tail realized they'd been spotted, Nate and Niki might lose the advantage. "Noticed it on that windy street first. Whatever pace we went, so did they."

"They? Like you can't tell if it's a he or she, or like there's more than one?"

"More than one," he said.

They reached the other side of Dauphine, and he nodded to the right. Niki took the hint and went that way, taking them in the same direction they had walked on Bourbon, just now one street over.

"How many? Vamps or something else? Vamps aren't supposed to be operating here with ill intent." Her speech sped up as she spoke. As she did, her Australian accent became heavier.

"I hoped you would notice at *Hustler*. That's why I pointed at the window. You didn't pick up on it, though. I counted seven at that point. When I pushed you off the road, three more had joined the ranks."

Nate shot a glance in the store window across the street. He saw Niki's eyes go that direction also.

"How many do you see?" he asked.

"Eight, nine, ten...twelve."

"Twelve?"

"Yes," she said. "Are you sure they're following us? They're just a bunch of guys. I'm not getting any vamp vibes."

Nate wanted to discount his gut and tell her maybe they weren't. Maybe he was just being paranoid. But he couldn't bring himself to say that. He knew that wasn't the case. Seeing them here confirmed it for him. Sure, Bourbon was a busy street, and tons of people partied on it, but while Dauphine had some foot traffic, it wasn't nearly as busy. For a group that large to change streets at the exact same time as he and Niki, taking the same path, that wasn't coincidence.

They'd been tracked and followed before, usually when they were doing the hunting, usually on purpose. On the rare occasion when they weren't the hunters, he'd been better armed. Nate ran through a quick inventory in his head. Niki had her silver whip. He had a small knife he kept hidden under his belt. Unless Niki hid anything else, that was it. Inventory done.

"Turn left," he said.

One more street, he thought. *I'll give them one more street just to make sure.*

Niki turned left onto another cross street.

Nate stayed close behind her. He wanted to run but forced himself to keep their pace at a fast walk instead. If the group was following them, they were all together. He had no idea who they were or why they were tracking the pair. If the group scattered, there would be no way to know the answer to either of those questions. He knew they could take out a couple of guys each. They'd fought vampires and werewolves for fuck's sake. Yesterday, they'd cut the head off a damn she-devil. But a dozen guys? That was asking a lot.

"Turn here," he said as they approached Burgundy Street.

"Do you have any idea where you are taking us?" Niki asked.

"Not really. I just know we are walking the same direction only two streets over now. If we keep going this way, we'll be back at HQ, right?" Nate hesitated for a moment, second guessing himself.

"Great job, love. See. You can still surprise me at times."

The street was empty. The architecture still looked like Bourbon Street, but with less neon signs, daiquiri places, and souvenir shops. The jazz music also faded away, leaving them with only the sound of their breathing and racing hearts. Where two streets over, the lights and sounds filled the atmosphere and brought everything to life, Nate found they were now surrounded by the opposite. No streetlights. No store fronts. Just darkness and shadows.

Nate broke his own rule and spun around. The large group of men turned the corner. Twenty yards separated the mob from Nate and Niki. Obscured by shadows, each person appeared faceless. No expression. Nothing. They all marched toward the couple, their feet rapidly increasing in pace. Their shoulders slumped forward, and their fists clinched. Nate saw nothing but malice in their approach.

"Nathan," Niki said. Her voice quivered.

She never called him that unless something was seriously wrong. For a brief moment, her tone reminded him of when she had cried his name that fateful evening in Detroit. This didn't have the wail or the tears, but the fear was there. And for Niki Davis to be afraid, it had to be something bad. Something next-level bad.

Staring forward, a handful of figures appeared out of the shadows. Four total stepped into the street a block in front of them. Their fists were also clenched. Shadows also masked their expressions. More faceless paintings.

"Any thoughts?" she asked.

"Maybe they just want to talk," he said and slowed their pace. No use rushing headlong. They were surrounded.

"Really want to joke right now?"

"Why not?" Nate responded with a smile. "How about, you take the four in front, and I'll start on the group behind us? When you have some free time, you can help me out."

"Sounds like a plan," she said, turning just a moment too late, her eyes widening in horror.

As much as Mike had prayed he'd see her again, he had known he never would. He still had to close his eyes and imagine she was there. Even the times when he had heard her voice or felt her hand on his shoulder, he hadn't really seen her.

But now, Brittany was standing in front of him. He saw her with his own, open eyes. Her vibrant red hair flowed around her shoulders, a stark contrast to her soft, white skin. She wore the nightgown that she'd died in, but now it was unblemished. It was her, as if nothing had ever happened to her.

41

As the fist connected, the side of Nate's face erupted in pain. The taste of blood filled his mouth, and he staggered backward. A field of stars shot across his vision.

"Son of a bitch," Nate said and spat a wad of blood on the street.

The four in front ran at them. The sound of the mob at their rear grew louder, obviously rushing in for the melee about to begin.

Nate turned to stare at the man who just emerged from the shadows. The fucker had sucker punched him. He looked to be college aged. A tassel of brown hair flowed from under a backward baseball cap.

"You just fucked up, kid," Nate said and slowly shook his head. "I'd have waited for my friends."

Nate raised his hands into a fighting stance and clenched them into tight fists. With a speed the kid obviously wasn't expecting, Nate grasped the kid by his collar, and yanked him forward. The guy gave no resistance, unable to react fast enough. Nate cocked back his other arm and swung. His fist met the man's face with alarming force. Nate felt the ridge of the man's nose for an instant before it disappeared beneath his knuckles. A spray of blood flew from his face.

After the first strike, the man's eyes rolled back in his head, but the hunter was still furious. The fucker had sucker punched him! He pushed the guy back and pulled him forward again. With each strike, he felt another bone crack under his fist. After he landed the third blow, Nate let go, and the guy crumpled to the ground like a ragdoll.

"Niki?"

From behind him, she said while trying to contain her laughter, "I'll occupy the ones in front. You take the mob."

"Sounds fair."

By the time he swiveled around to the mob, the closest person was less than ten yards from him. The others were only a few feet farther back. A dozen men bearing down on them, and another four from the other side. Nate had no doubt Niki could handle her four, especially if they were all as lightweight as their bloody-faced friend.

For the first time, Nate got a good look at the men. Surprisingly, they looked like ordinary men with ordinary faces. He'd fought enough monsters to know normal when he saw it. Most of these guys were in their twenties like the lump of meat at his feet. Except for the pack rushing at him, he didn't see anything out of place about them.

Then he saw their eyes.

Each person's eyes were vacant. Their pupils so dilated only the faintest trace of white could be seen. He didn't know how they focused. Nate's first thought was drugs, but then he had a sudden realization that these men weren't in control of themselves; someone else was doing the driving.

Not that it much mattered. Their faces didn't contain that same lack of emotion. Instead, they had the look of rage, pure and simple. Puppets or not, their intention was to take the two down and out.

Nate knew that look well. Before getting his life in order, he'd grown up rough. He'd learned to fight by getting his ass kicked enough times. His size gave him a decent advantage, but it also made him a target.

Those days were long before Niki. He always thought of that version of himself as someone separate, someone he only needed to change into when things got really bad.

At the moment, things looked really bad.

He cocked his head from side to side, loosening up his neck, hearing the joints crack as he did. He gave his arms a quick shake at his side before raising his clenched fists in front of him again.

"Come on, assholes, let's go," he said as the closest person in the mob reached him.

Nate swung hard, connecting with the first guy's chin, his head whipping around insanely fast. As the next two arrived, Nate pushed one back for separation and delivered an uppercut to the other. When the guy he'd pushed back rebounded, Nate dropped him to the ground with a jab and right hook combination.

Before the guy hit the ground, another two had moved into his place, and three more pushed behind them.

He wanted to turn his head to check on Niki but knew better. With no idea how she was faring, Nate needed to make room between the two of them. He needed to keep his group from bleeding into hers. He reached both arms out to his side and ran forward, running over two and driving the pack back a few feet before his progress stalled. Planting his feet, Nate tried to push forward again, but the pile didn't budge.

He hoped that was enough.

The group surrounded him, and within moments, the mob swallowed him.

Nate held his arms up around his head, blocking anything from hitting him directly in the face. Blow after blow landed against Nate's arms, chest, and stomach. Fists pummeled his back and sides. Fortunately, he'd taken his fair share of body blows in his life. This was more of a nuisance than painful. If he could keep everything focused on his core, the group would tire, giving him a chance to take a few more down.

But, the weight of the mob on his back forced him to the ground. Nate dropped his hands to the gravelly pavement out of reflex to break his fall.

As soon as his head wasn't protected, a knee connected with his jaw and a boot with the side of his head.

For the second time that night, Nate saw stars.

He fell flat on the ground, his cheek pressed into the concrete. He had only a moment to register the coolness emanating from it before spinning onto his knees and curling into a tight ball. The last thing he needed was someone stomping on his head. Blows rained down on his back along with the sharp sting of kicks into his ribcage.

Nate told himself it was only pain. Pain he could take. He'd heal. Broken bones, broken ribs would heal. He just had to protect his head. Brain damage doesn't heal.

42

This is not good, Josh thought.

Brittany White obviously wasn't there, but Mike definitely thought she was. He wasn't talking to Josh, probably didn't even know he was still saying anything.

Any amount of comfort and relaxation Josh had been enjoying flew out the window. His mind went into overdrive, and he jumped into action. With his fingers still hovering over the keyboard, he flipped over to the communication window and unmuted his microphone for Nate and Niki.

"We have a problem!" he shouted. "Mike's in trouble."

Silence.

"Are you reading me? Nate! Niki!"

He knew he shouldn't have turned them down when he talked to Mike. He had gotten too comfortable, and now the team was split up and in trouble.

Fuck!

He flipped on all the switches so that Nate, Niki, and Mike were all active. The volume was cranked up as loud as he could make it go, hoping to hear something.

From Mike's side, he heard rushing water. According to his location, he wasn't far from the river, so Josh wasn't alarmed by that. He just needed Mike to respond.

Josh checked Nate and Niki's location on the screen. Their dots were two blocks over from the French Quarter and not moving.

"Fuck!" Josh said aloud and banged the top of his desk.

The keyboard jumped and the monitor wavered. Deep in frustration, he uncaringly slammed his fists down three more times.

Mike hadn't responded, and the sounds he'd heard from Nate and Niki weren't encouraging. The Night Crew needed more people. They weren't staffed like they should've been. Jax always liked a seven-person team. Even if only two or three were in the field at a time, it allowed for backup. Seven people. Not four. Well, really not even four. Three people and him.

He stared down at his legs, sitting uselessly in the wheelchair. He never felt sorry for himself. Just the opposite. He prided himself on what he could do despite being in it. The benefit he was to the team. Eyes in the sky. Keeping the cops distracted when they needed time. He'd even bragged about how he'd escaped from Silas when their last warehouse was attacked.

For one of the first times since ending up in the chair, he felt as useless as his dead legs. All he could do was sit, wait, and hope. No drone in the air. No backup team to call.

Josh switched channels on his communication console to the team channel, reaching out to all three at once, and opening the channels for full conversation.

"Mike! Are you there? Talk to me."

His eyes stared at Mike's audio meter. It remained dormant, nothing but static. Either Mike was being quiet, he'd taken out his earpiece, or it was no longer functioning. Josh hated all those options.

"Nate! Niki! Anybody?"

Their meters bounced ever so slightly. It sounded like a fight. Or like someone punching a slab of meat. Josh really hoped the slab of meat wasn't Nate or Niki.

With his arms still covering his head, Nate turned just enough to get a glimpse of where he thought Niki would be. He breathed a sigh of relief when he saw her still standing and about fifteen yards away. Men stood on each side of her. Nate saw three on the ground at her feet. As he watched, someone from his group ran at her when her back was turned, punching her in the back of the head. She stumbled forward and fell.

"Niki!" Nate shouted.

Furiously, he kicked, trying to separate from the group surrounding him so he could help Niki. As hard as he could, he thrust his foot backward. Based on the sound of someone gasping for air and the feeling when he connected, he had caught someone in the gut.

Despite his efforts, the mob still continued to kick his ribs and stomach. A lucky blow connected with his temple. This time, instead of seeing stars, he felt his consciousness waver. He needed to hang on. He couldn't let them beat him and Niki to death.

Flipping to their location map, Josh saw all three red dots on the screen. Nate's and Niki's dots were in the French Quarter about a dozen yards away from each other, and Mike's dot was a few miles away. None of them moved.

"Dammit, guys! I knew you shouldn't have split up. I fucking knew it."

Suddenly, the LED indicators on Nate and Niki's audio meters spiked red. Screams blasted through Josh's speakers, but they were quickly cut short. He heard bones crunch and bodies fall to the ground.

All Josh could think about was the massacre he just heard. Images flashed in his head, and he pushed them aside.

"Please respond," he said. Josh heard the quiver in his voice, even as he tried to be strong.

45

He fought to stay awake, and his vision split. Just when he feared he was about to lose the fight, the weight of the crowd let up, and the barrage of kicks stopped, replaced by fear-filled screams. Some ended abruptly. Others went on for a moment longer before they turned into gurgling sounds, as if their throats filled with blood.

Mike! Nate thought, his head buried under his arms, still spinning from the strike against his temple.

He knew the carnage an angry vampire could unleash. He'd seen the damage they could do. Usually once they did, though, the Night Crew was called in to exterminate said vampire. Not this time. Mike had just saved their asses. Nate found himself grateful this particular vampire was on their side.

Warm blood streamed over Nate's hands and against his forehead, bringing his focus back. There was no more screaming. Just the sound of his heartbeat in his head and the feel of his breath ricocheting off the pavement.

Nate rolled onto his back, not caring that he had dropped into a pool of blood. He raised his arm to his throbbing head and draped it over his eyes. The world still wobbled.

"Fuck, Mike, took you long enough," he said. "We were getting our asses kicked."

The long pause caused Nate's stomach to drop. Slowly, he lowered his arm and opened his eyes. He tried to raise his head and focus. Peering up, he saw two huge bat-like wings extending out above him.

46

She watched from the top of *Harrah's Casino*. Thanks to the light, Naomi didn't need to use any special ability to track the two hunters. But it wasn't the hunters she was tracking. It was Eileen.

Her sister walked through the crowd, two blocks behind the hunters. She stalked them, silently keeping her distance, but not letting them leave her sight.

Naomi wasn't exactly sure what her sister had planned, but once the hunters had passed under Naomi and headed for the Quarter, she got an idea. As Eileen walked past two men, she gently brushed her hands across the back of their necks. The two men dropped their phones, screens shattering as they impacted, and turned toward the Quarter. Eileen walked next to a man helping a woman out of a car and ran her hand along his arm. The man let go of the woman he was helping and joined the other two.

Eileen touched another three men before leaving *Harrah's* parking lot.

She was building her own little army.

By the time the hunters turned onto Bourbon Street, all of them were now fully under her control. Whatever she wanted them to do, they were going to do. They had no control and no inhibitions. They were puppets, and she was the puppet master.

Naomi extended her wings, relishing the form she was taking. She lowered her head as her wings reached their full extension. Her beautiful short hair disappeared, eyes changed into black nothingness, and skin turned into scales. When her transformation was complete, she flapped her wings a few times, loosening them up. High above the streets and people of New Orleans, she ran across the top of *Harrah's*. At the edge of the building, she leaped into the air and soared into the clouds.

The two hunters were no longer on Bourbon Street. They'd moved over and picked up their pace. They'd obviously sensed they were being followed.

These two were very good. She was already impressed that they had destroyed Angie. It had been a thousand years since a succubus had been killed, and yet, these two humans and the vampire had somehow managed it.

Eileen had also started moving faster. She touched a man holding hands with someone. He let go of her hand and left without saying a word. Randomly, she touched an arm, the back of a neck, or, once, even a cheek. The group had grown to over a dozen and began to close in on the pair from both sides. The hunters had become the hunted.

On the next street over, the duo stopped and confronted the puppet army. At Eileen's behest, they rushed at the hunters, attacking them. Naomi had seen as the male took the larger group, driving them away from the female. He had shown such chivalry, sacrificing himself for her.

That act of caring had touched Naomi's blackened heart. She knew she was going to help them. Her sister had sent an overwhelming force after the hunters. As good as she recognized them to be, she doubted they could handle so many.

The man fought valiantly. She thought back to the last time she saw someone take on that number at once, dropping as many as he did, before allowing the blows to land on his body. An Englishman she'd once known had fought with the same vigor. A Templar. She had watched him stand with a few hundred of his fellow knights at the Battle of Montgisard. Together, they had vanquished over twenty thousand of Saladin's army. This hunter fought with the same ferocity. If the hunter had a broad sword and shield, she was certain he'd have been as equally victorious over the men Eileen had sent their way.

Naomi circled above, her wings, such deadly instruments, holding her high in the air. As she admired the resourcefulness of the hunters, one of Eileen's puppets attacked the female hunter from behind. Not only did it seem to enrage the male, but Naomi found it reprehensible and dishonorable. A cowardly attack that couldn't be tolerated. Unfortunately, there were too many for the male hunter to fend off in order to avenge her.

With her wings arched, Naomi started her descent. She fell like a dagger from the heavens, her talons extended like knives, ready to plunge into flesh. Her first target was the coward, and she angled his direction. Her wings coiled across her back and down her legs, leaving nothing for the wind to catch and slow her fall. The cold air split around her scaled form. Anyone who saw her would only see a dark shooting star disappearing in the night. A dark missile headed toward the Earth.

The moment before she collided, the coward peered up and into her eyes. It was the last thing he saw before her eagle-sharp talons were buried in his chest. As fast as she fell, her claws tore into him and ripped his chest open, before she extended her wings and slowed. When the sharp claws of her feet gripped the hard pavement, she landed on the top half of the coward. Behind her, the legs still stood momentarily as if they hadn't yet realized the rest of the body was missing. One leg involuntarily kicked as blood spurted from the exposed pelvis before the lower half crumpled to the ground.

With a twist of her back, one of Naomi's wings shot out, plunging through the chest and right out of the back of the man standing next to her. Blood exploded from his mouth in a quick cough. When she withdrew the wing, he dropped to the ground, blood pooling on the street.

From behind her, Naomi heard the other men scream. That was a sound she had always hated. Men screaming. When she had grown up, men didn't scream. The only cries that men like her father or brothers had ever loosed were those in battle meant to evoke fear and terror into whomever was foolish enough to attack them.

Men screaming in fear? That made her angry. It didn't matter that deep down she knew those screams were truly from Eileen, yelling out of anger at her betrayal.

Eileen turned her army away from the hunted hunters and on to Naomi. Naomi saw Eileen's action for what it was, desperation and cowardice. Now, though, it was only a matter of time before she would have to face both Eileen and Lilith. Her betrayal would not be tolerated. When that time came, she would be ready to accept their punishment. For now, though, she intended to help the hunters.

The mob broke from their attacks on the two humans and turned on Naomi. They charged at her.

Eileen, why send them to their death like this? Such a waste.

She almost felt sorry for them. With man's weak-minded nature, they didn't have the ability to break out from under Eileen's control. That didn't stop Naomi from assuming a fighting stance, though. Her wings angled above her, their sharp bone ends ready to spill blood. Her clawed feet dug into the pavement, gripping the ground. Her taloned hands dropped to her sides, blood from her first victim still dripping from them.

Their assault lasted only seconds. As they approached, she used her hands and wings to impale, slice, and decapitate. The street turned a sticky, dark red hue, and entrails covered every surface.

With the last dying sounds fading, the male warrior rolled over.

"Fuck, Mike, took you long enough," he said. "We were getting our asses kicked."

He opened his eyes and saw Naomi standing over him.

"Oh, fuck!" he shouted and rolled away from her. He tried to rise, but immediately fell back down, clutching at his side.

Knowing her form was fearsome, she quickly changed back to the Naomi she preferred. The scales disappeared, and her short, purple hair and dark complexion returned. Talons became hands once again.

"You don't have to be afraid of me, Hunter. I'm not your enemy but be warned. My sisters are. You need to get to safety before she directs others after you."

Naomi reached into the back pocket of her jeans and pulled out a pair of gloves. She slipped them over her hands as the female ran to help the male. Naomi held up her gloved hands to show them.

"They are for your protection. Let me help."

"How do we know this isn't an elaborate ploy?" the woman asked.

Naomi gestured at all the bodies around them. "If I wanted to add you to the pile, I could have. You are both injured. Please let me help."

"Fair enough," she said.

Naomi gripped the male by the arm and helped him to his feet with ease. Seeing that he had trouble finding his balance, she put his arm over her shoulder.

"I'm Naamah, but you can call me Naomi."

"I'm Niki Davis, and that's Nate Edwards," Niki said.

"We really should be going before my sister sends more. Do you have a place we can go?"

"Yes," Niki answered. "Josh, are you there?"

"Oh, thank Christ!" Josh exhaled, giving an excited shout that rang Niki's ears. "You guys gave me a fucking heart attack."

"We're headed your way. Clear the table and get the med kit. And we're bringing a friend."

47

"What the hell happened?" Josh asked the moment Niki burst through the door. Nate followed closely behind, his arm draped over Naomi. Josh noted she didn't appear to struggle under Nate's large frame.

"You've got a lot to learn. But first, med kit."

Josh pointed to the shelf.

Naomi led Nate to the table. He sat his butt on it and laid back, sprawling across the entirety of it. The table legs groaned under his weight.

Niki grabbed the supplies from the shelf and rushed back to him.

"How you feeling, love? Want me to kiss it and make it better?" She tried to force a smile.

From the first aid kit, she pulled out gauze, alcohol, and bandages. After cracking open the alcohol, she doused the gauze with it.

"Take a deep breath."

The blood on his face had dried to a deep, sticky red. A dark shadow of bruises covered his sides and arms. As Nate tried to take a deep breath, he winced and favored one side.

Niki dabbed the gauze on his face and started cleaning off the blood. The gauze's color changed with each swipe, becoming darker and darker as she gently but efficiently cleared away the dried blood.

Each time she brushed over a new area, Nate gasped and then grimaced.

"Holy shit, that stings," he shouted.

"The alcohol or your side?" she asked, still cleaning the wounds on his face.

"Both. Fuck!" He tilted his head back, arching his back off the metal table.

Niki set the gauze down and looked at him incredulously. "Stop being a baby. You've had worse. Speaking of, sorry, love. This is going to be part of that worse." She moved her hands to his chest and started down his rib cage, feeling for broken ribs.

Nate bucked on the table. "Goddamn it, Niki! That hurts."

"Naomi, hold him down. I need to make sure nothing's broken."

Naomi moved around the end of the table and came up the other side. The whole time, Josh's eyes never left the newcomer. It was obvious he had a lot of questions, but he was determined to hold them until Nate was taken care of. She placed her hands on Nate's shoulders and carefully but unrelentingly held him on the table.

Niki kept inching her way down. Her fingers traced over each rib, meticulously checking for fractures. Each time, she felt Nate tense up, fighting against Naomi, trying to raise up, but unable to overpower her.

When Niki finally reached the last one, she said, "You can let him go."

As soon as her hands left his stomach, he exhaled whatever air he still held in his lungs and brought his arms up to his face. His entire torso deflated as he relaxed his muscles.

"Get up, whiner," Niki chided. "Nothing's broken. You're just bloodied and bruised."

"It sure fucking hurts like everything is broken," he said through clenched teeth, still laying on the table,

"Well, it's not." She moved her hand under his shoulders. "Raise up and pretend to be tough."

Naomi grabbed him under the other arm, and the two of them lifted his muscular frame to a sitting position. Niki wasn't sure how much she had actually helped, but at least he was up. She handed him another piece of gauze soaked in alcohol.

"Finish cleaning that pretty face. You're a mess."

She looked across the table at Josh who was still staring at Naomi. "Josh, this is Naomi. Naomi, Josh."

Niki looked at Naomi, and in that moment, something dawned on her. They had come to New Orleans to hunt a possible succubus. They had found one and killed her. Now, another one stood across from her, supposedly helping them. Niki felt her whole demeanor change. Nate had been hurt. Resentment took the place of appreciation.

"You," Niki said harshly. "Start talking. Now."

"And quickly," Josh said. "I can't get a hold of Michael."

48

She's not really here.

Despite telling himself that over and over again, he still wanted to believe it so badly. This wasn't just her voice. It wasn't an unseen touch or the memory of her scent. It was her, in front of him. His angel with the fiery red hair.

The distant echo of Josh's voice tried to find him. Mike heard it, but it rose from some unknown tunnel. Really, he didn't care. The voice buzzed in his ear, an annoying gnat. It was there, but he had no desire to listen. His entire focus was hijacked by the vision of his late wife.

But was it a vision? Mike thought he would know if she was merely an apparition.

She's not really here. It's just a figment of my imagination.

The voice in his head, some rational part of him, kept trying to make him realize it wasn't Brit, but the part of him that missed her wasn't listening. He smelled the sweet smell of (*Decay!*) vanilla and pepper wafting to him. Of course it was really her.

Unintentionally, his arm rose until his hand hovered just beside his ear. His fingers reached and pulled the earpiece out, setting it gently on the ground.

"Follow me," Brittany said.

Her words washed over him. A soft warm blanket wrapping around him on a cold winter day. They brought him peace. Peace from the vibrations. Peace from any guilt for almost attacking Niki. Peace from any obligation to the Night Crew. Peace from his need to drink blood.

His hand found his pocket. He removed his cell phone and placed it gingerly on the ground next to the earpiece.

"I'm here, Michael. Be with me."

The wind blew against her, sculpting the nightgown to her beautiful body. His eyes saw every sensual curve. The nightgown was sheer enough that he could almost see through it.

The nightgown Silas killed her in.

The voice tried to get through to him. Tried to speak truth to him. But it wasn't her voice. Its volume grew less and less with each attempt.

The landscape of New Orleans dissolved. Michael realized he no longer stood on a street in the Warehouse District. The midnight sky lit up, and the stars vanished. Instead, bright blue replaced it. A handful of white clouds dotted the sky. Small balls of cotton floating in the sea. The sun shined, bathing everything in its glow, including Michael. Despite being covered in sunlight, he didn't feel as he had before. No feeling of being trapped, held down by its harsh rays. No diminishing power or strength.

The warmth of the sun washed over him, and he smiled.

Around him, kids ran past. He looked up and saw Brittany only a few feet away, holding her hand out. She was in blue shorts and a tan shirt that she'd cut the sleeves off of. He remembered the day she had cut them off. A hot summer day like most in Texas. She had liked how soft the shirt was but had hated the tan line it gave her.

"It's a farmer's tan," she had told him. "I'm not a farmer."

"Just get a sleeveless shirt, then," he'd replied, but his advice had fallen on deaf ears.

She had promptly cut the sleeves off and slipped the shirt on. Most summer days, that shirt had either been on her body or in the laundry. It rarely made it all the way back to the closet.

Her hand extended out in front of her, beckoning him.

"Come on," she said.

He grasped it gently within his own. The feel of her smooth skin, soft and delicate, reminded him of so many days and nights. Comfort personified.

His eyes drifted to the green grass under his bare feet. Trees lush with leaves surrounded the park. Spaced out throughout the park were blankets. Families with children or couples sat on them with picnic baskets. Birds flew above and sang songs from the trees. In the distance, music played from a speaker on one of the blankets.

"This park..." he started.

"Was where we went when you first told me you loved me," she finished.

"But, how are we here?"

"We can be wherever you want us to be."

She led him through the center of the park. They passed random people and faces, transitioning from the park to their picnic blanket or vice versa.

A Frisbee flew through the air and fell at his feet.

"Little help?" a voice said.

Mike looked and saw a man with his arm held up. Across from him, a boy about ten stood waiting. He looked to be a carbon copy of the man who hollered at Mike.

This couldn't be real. Moments ago, he was in New Orleans. He was a vampire on a hunt. But as he felt the cool grass under his feet and the warm breeze blowing across his face, what was reality and what wasn't became harder and harder to distinguish.

Could he really be a vampire? Or was that just a dream? Monsters were nothing more than imagination. Creatures made up to scare both children and adults.

But walking in the grass under the sun? That felt real.

Mike bent down, grasped the Frisbee in his hand, felt the hard plastic as his fingers slipped around it. He stood back up and spun it, delivering a dart that the man caught out of the air.

"Thanks," he said and turned back to his son, his arm cocked to send the Frisbee in that direction.

Brittany moved her arms around him, gripping him around his waist.

"Never leave me," she said.

He shook his head. "Never."

The only thing he saw was her. The only thing he smelled was her. The only thing in the world he cared about was her.

49

Standing in the middle of the dance floor, Lily held Michael close, controlling what he heard, what he saw.

She smiled at what she was doing to him. Oh, the pleasure she was going to get from torturing him. She wondered how deep into the illusion she could take him and how many different ways she could destroy him by ripping Brittany away.

The two of them swayed to the rhythm of the music the band played in their heads. Two lovers wrapped in a sensual embrace, invisible amongst the crowd surrounding them.

Her blood boiled knowing he was responsible for Angie's death. As much as she wanted to rip his head away from his body, she resisted. He deserved worse than a quick death. He deserved to die a thousand deaths, and she was prepared to deliver each and every one.

50

"Who's Michael?" Naomi asked. Her eyes shifted from Josh in his wheelchair, to Nate sitting on the table, over to Niki standing next to him.

"Don't you fucking worry about it," Niki snapped back. "We appreciate the help, but we need some fucking answers."

Naomi glanced down. Her features softened. Niki couldn't tell if she was being sincere or if this was a ruse, another way succubi manipulated people over the centuries.

"What would you like to know?"

"How many of you are there?" Josh asked. He spun around to his computer. The screen showed Michael's location, and it hadn't moved.

"For centuries, it has been my three sisters and me."

"Four!" Nate exclaimed.

"Yes, there were four of us. There are three now that you have killed Angie."

"Angie," Josh said. "She said her name was Agrat Bat Mahlat."

"Our names have shifted over time to match popular culture. My real name is Naamah, but I've adopted the name Naomi. Agrat went by Angie."

"And the other two?" Niki asked. She wiped sweat from her face and noticed a sharp sting on her cheek. She grabbed another piece of gauze, poured alcohol on it, and pressed it to her face. After the initial sting, she wiped away whatever blood was there.

"Eisheth Zenunim goes by Eileen. She controlled the men who attacked you."

"We're going to come back to that," Niki said, unwrapping a band-aid and applying it to her cheek. "Who's the fourth?"

"Lilith. She goes by Lily."

"Lilith?" Josh asked. "Is she the Lilith of legend? First wife of Adam?"

Based on how his eyes lit up, Josh was almost starstruck. Niki didn't blame him. Before Angie, the oldest creature she'd come into contact with was a banshee from the sixteenth century. A creature as old as any of these was a rarity.

"Lilith is the oldest of us and the leader. The first created by Samael. She helped construct most of the legends that mention her name. I wouldn't put much stock in certain tales of her exploits. She's not too shy about embellishing a few details."

"So there's you, Eileen, and Lilith?" Nate asked.

"That's correct."

Niki thought about how hard it was taking down Angie. It had nearly cost all three of them their lives. The thought of one was a reason to pause. Assuming Naomi was really on their side, meant not one but two more threats they needed to hunt. If Naomi was really on their side.

"How did Eileen control those men?" she asked.

The muscles in her arms and sides tightened up with the memory of the fight. With the adrenaline rush finally waning, she knew the time for soreness was approaching fast. It was soon going to be time to recover. She pulled her arm across her chest, working out the growing stiffness in her shoulder. Then she crossed the other one, hoping to stay somewhat limber.

"We can control a person by touching them. As she walked past the men, she gently brushed an arm or hand. For some, especially men, that's all it takes. As soon as you fall under our spell, it's very hard to break free.

By touching those men , she was able to unleash them on you. They had no control and probably had no idea what was happening."

"That's why you're wearing the gloves." Nate pointed to her hands.

"I didn't want you to be persuaded. I saw how valiantly you fought, with chivalry and courage. I've not seen fighting like that for some time."

Niki noticed a slight blush across Naomi's cheeks. Was she flirting with Nate? She told herself the she-devil wasn't doing that. Plus, Niki never needed to worry about Nate. They'd been through a lot together. He wasn't going anywhere, just like she wasn't going anywhere.

"Does it work on women?" Niki asked.

"Sometimes, but the effect is usually different, unless you have certain proclivities. If you're strong-willed, you won't fall under our control, but we would have access to your deepest fears or desires and could project those into your mind."

"That's fucking terrifying," Niki responded.

Josh brought himself closer. "We need to wrap this up. Michael is still out there. But I have one last question. You said Lilith is the leader. What's her motivation? Is it to bring back Samael?"

"And why are you helping us?" Nate added.

Naomi's head spun from Josh to Nate.

Niki nodded and increased the intensity of the nod with each question asked. There was so much she wanted to know and understand about Naomi's kind. The more she knew, the better prepared she'd be heading into battle.

"Lilith speaks as if resurrecting Samael is the goal. I think that's because Eisheth and Agrat wanted that. I'm not certain if she truly wants him to return, or if she was just using the promise to control us.

"He's been dead for centuries, and she's been the leader. Her desires, her agendas, have been our motivating force. The men we've influenced...most throughout the ages were chosen by her. Each had a purpose. Whether it was to inflate her legend, or to keep us hidden from the Council, or to make sure we never wanted for anything. Everything was what she wanted, what she desired.

"Samael was ruthless and uncaring. We were his slaves, his concubines. We were created to serve his desires. After his death, we went into hiding. The Council feared our abilities."

"If you can control someone with a single touch," Josh said, "I can see why."

Niki thought about what Naomi was saying, about Lilith's motivations. "So, is resurrecting Samael even possible?"

"Samael prophesied his death and his resurrection. He said when and how it would happen and despite us trying to stop it, we couldn't. As powerful as the four of us are, it was out of our control. Power of prophecy. But he also talked about when the era ended, it would be time for his return. To usher in his resurrection will require one of us—since we are his bloodline—to mate with someone with an extreme power like no one before. Samael would inhabit the spirit of that offspring and return."

"Someone with an extreme power?" Nate asked.

"When the era ended," Josh added.

Niki looked up at Josh. "Where's Michael right now?"

Josh spun around to the computer. He pointed at the red dot. "Same place. Hasn't moved."

"Is Michael the vampire who was with you?" Naomi asked.

"Yes, that's him."

"His aura was very powerful. He could be the one prophesied. Agrat wanted to use him as a pet. Did she touch him? Take control of him?"

Nate nodded. "Yeah, he talked about how it felt under her control. How he didn't want blood anymore. Almost as if he liked being under her control."

Naomi moved to the door. "We need to find your friend. Hopefully, we're not too late."

Josh said, "Niki, I'll send you the address."

Naomi continued. "He's still hearing the siren call. Lilith is leading him straight to her. If he is the powerful one Samael spoke of, Lilith will either take him as her own to resurrect Samael or kill him so Samael will never return."

51

Despite the excessive amount of pain in his side, Nate picked up the abandoned cell phone and earpiece from the pavement, one in each hand. The cell phone laid flat in his palm. He turned his face up to Niki and Naomi.

"According to the map, you're right on top of him," Josh said into Nate's and Niki's comm's. Naomi was the only one without, but she'd told them she could hear the conversation just fine.

"I'm holding his cell and comm's, Josh," Nate said. "Shit."

"He ditched them, didn't he?" Josh asked, rhetorically. "Lilith is smarter than Angie. Angie just had him take out his earpiece, so I tracked him on his cell."

"Any surveillance cameras in the area?" Niki asked.

Nate assumed she was asking Josh so he could tap into them if they existed. He looked from one side of the street to the next, anyway. Either the cameras were well hidden, it was too dark, or none existed.

"I'm not finding any," Josh said.

"Damnit," Niki exclaimed. "How the fuck did we lose a vampire?"

"Well, it is New Orleans," Nate said and feigned a smile.

Naomi started to wander off. The look on her face caught Nate's attention. He watched her walk back and forth across the street.

"What the fuck is she doing?" Nate asked.

"Why don't you fucking ask her?" Niki responded, her tone bathed in sarcasm.

"They went this direction," Naomi shouted from a dozen yards away. She stood under a stop sign at an intersection.

"How do you know?" Nate asked, suspicion in his eyes, but he and Niki started that direction, anyway.

"I can smell Lilith." She saw the look on their faces and continued. "It's too subtle for humans to pick up on."

"What does she smell like?"

"Decay. Despite how much we try to mask it, the smell of decay, of death, is always underneath. Like I said, humans can't pick up on it, but other creatures can. If the vampire wasn't under her influence, he would've been able to tell. He's either under her control or—"

"Don't say the or," Niki interrupted. "We don't need to know the or. Let's go with he's under her control. He's strong, though. He'll break out of it. He did against Angie, and he can do it against Lilith," she said with hope in her voice.

Led by Naomi, the trio headed down the street. "I could hear you," she said to Nate. "I know you aren't sure if you can trust me yet. I assure you, you can."

"We're putting a lot of faith in you," he said. "We don't trust easily, and the last succubus we came across threw our vampire friend through a wall and almost killed the love of my life. With two trained hunters and a vampire, we barely made it out alive. Going against two succubi plus whatever else they can throw at us is a little unnerving. We're relying on you pretty heavily here. Do not fuck us over." He stressed the last sentence, clearly enunciating each word.

"They're my sisters because we are of the same blood. But do not worry. I've been of a different mindset than them for quite a long time. I'm not a ruthless killer. I try not to use my powers unless it's an absolute necessity. I've only fed on the willing and never to the point of death. I've fallen in love more times than I can count. At times, my sisters hunted for sport. Since the Council's disappearance, Lilith thought it safe to act more brazenly. She no longer felt the need to remain careful. It was acceptable to her to leave corpses lying in the street. She told Angie and Eileen it was time to resurrect Samael."

Naomi stopped walking and turned to them. "You question if you can trust me. Because of the assistance I've already provided, in the eyes of Eisheth and Lilith, they are the last two sisters. I'm dead to them."

Nate saw a look of both peace and sadness spread across her face. He felt for her. If they were successful in freeing Michael, he knew it would come at the cost of killing both Lilith and Eileen. Once that task was completed, Naomi would truly be alone. There wouldn't be any other succubi left.

"We're getting close. The scent is stronger, fresher. I've picked up both her scent and the aroma of blood. I assume your vampire has fed recently?" Naomi started walking again.

"He only drinks from a bag but yes. He didn't want to be hungry while hunting," Niki said from a few feet behind her.

"Wise for a fledgling. I think they're both near. Their smell has intensified, as well as other smells." She breathed in deeply, flaring her nostrils as she did. "Smoke, alcohol. There's a dance hall nearby. The smell is unmistakable. I would guess she took him there. Why? I don't know, but Lilith is cunning. Do not underestimate her."

Damned if the she-demon wasn't right. A block over, Niki heard music. Compared to the music blaring out of Republic, New Orleans, this was a lot more subdued. She didn't feel any of the deep bass forcing her heart into an unnatural rhythm. Instead of the steady, rhythmic beating, she heard the strum of an acoustic guitar and the high-pitched tones of a fiddle. Lilith had taken Michael to a country music bar this time.

The front of the building had darkened windows with neon accents advertising *Coors*, *Miller Lite*, and *Budweiser*. The entrance was a large brown door, propped open. A man in a cowboy hat and boots sat on a stool outside of the door. He checked IDs as people entered the club.

"Josh, can you pull up the schematics?" Niki asked.

"Why do you doubt me?" he responded. After a brief pause, he said, "I've got 'em. Relatively straight forward. Single story. Couple of wide-open spaces. Couple of bars. I've got your location."

"Thanks."

Standing across the street, Niki shot a glance at the three of them. She thought she was the only one who looked the part for a night out at a country and western bar. And only barely for her. She still had on her pair of jeans and a relaxed T-shirt. Instead of boots, though, she wore sneakers.

On the other hand, Naomi looked straight out of a punk rock band with her short, spiked black hair with purple tips, each hand covered with gloves that ran all the way up to her elbows.

And Nate was worse. He wore black jeans and a muscle shirt that wasn't covered in blood.

"We don't look the part," Niki said. "Think they'll let us in?"

"Leave that to me," Naomi responded.

Before Niki could object, Naomi started across the street. Niki looked to Nate and shrugged. They jogged a few steps, catching up with Naomi.

The man in the cowboy hat lifted his head, and his eyes danced between the three of them. His hat dipped down and rose up again as he looked from their shoes all the way up to their heads.

"Can I help you?" he drawled.

Niki heard the condescension in his voice and didn't appreciate it at all. If it wasn't that Naomi had already said she'd handle it, Niki would've kicked the stool out from under him, thrown a knee or two into his ribcage, and then put his hat on her head for good measure as she walked in, leaving him bleeding on the sidewalk. But Naomi had called it. Although Naomi wasn't part of the Night Crew, there was an unspoken rule amongst hunters. Sort of like calling shotgun when getting in the car.

Naomi took the glove off one of her hands and stepped close to the cowboy, maybe a little closer than he was expecting. He raised his chest up, sitting straighter on the stool. She then raised her gloveless hand up to his shoulder, placed it on his upper arm, and sensuously slid it down to lie on his hand.

As her hand went from the sleeve of his shirt to the skin of his arm, his eyes glazed over. Niki saw a distinct shift in his demeanor. His shoulders, which he'd held tall, relaxed. His back loosened and slightly bent forward. A smile spread across his face. When he looked at Naomi again, he had the air of a teenage boy in the midst of puppy love.

"Hey, Roy," she said, as if they'd known each other for years.

The cowboy never said his name and didn't have a name tag. So, Naomi must have picked up his name through her touch. Based on her powers, it was no wonder the Council had tried to exterminate them. Simply controlling people with a touch, reading their minds, the ability to force visions of pleasure or fear, not to mention the deadly strength. A lethal combination when in the right hands, much less the wrong ones.

"Do you think you can let me and my friends in?" she drawled, as if she was born and raised in the South. "We forgot our IDs, but I'm sure that's not a problem. Right, Roy?"

His smile widened and his cheeks flushed red. Niki didn't know it was possible for his eyes to look cloudier than they already were, but the more Naomi talked to the cowboy, the more vacant and clouded over his eyes became. His head drifted from one side to the other as if her words were a drug, and he was as high as a kite.

"Of course not," he said. All the earlier condescension in his voice had vanished, replaced with an airiness. "Never a problem for you, my dear," he said longingly.

"Thanks, Roy." She lifted her hand from his and brushed his cheek.

His eyes closed as she did, cherishing the physical contact.

"One more question," Niki said.

"Roy, my friend has a question. I know you'll answer her honestly."

Roy slowly nodded. "Of course. Wouldn't dream of lying to your friends."

"Did a gentleman come in here earlier? Pale skin? Wearing jeans and a jacket?"

"He probably would've been with a woman. Stunningly beautiful..." Naomi started.

"Not as beautiful as you," Roy objected.

The succubus smiled at him but continued. "She would've had long, straight black hair."

"I think I recall who you might be referring to. Yes, they came in a little while ago."

"Thank you," Naomi said. Roy leaned forward, hanging on her every word. "My friends and I are going in now. Have a great night."

"You, too," he responded as the three of them walked through the door.

"Holy shit!" Nate said.

"I second that," Niki added.

"My sisters love controlling someone like that. I don't. I don't want people to fawn over me because I make them. I want what's real and pure. What's the point of life if the relationships you form, the bonds you make are imaginary?

"They would control someone, drain them of their life energy, and leave them sick and rotting away, moving on to the next victim. I never did that. I prefer to love. It makes the bond so much stronger. It makes the energy so much more intense. And love replenishes the life force like no physical sustenance ever could. My sisters never learned that."

Niki looked at Nate and both smiled. "I know what you mean," Niki said.

As they stepped inside the club, Naomi slipped her glove back over her hand, pulling it up to her elbow.

Under their feet, the concrete sidewalk turned into a dark brown hardwood floor. The interior walls were lined with old barn wood. Bar seating ran around the outside. Neon signs of various beer brands cast odd shadows on the faces of those sitting under them. Posters for bands that'd played there in the past dotted the walls wherever they could. The open area they first entered into had a half dozen pool tables surrounded by patrons.

"Lilith will be on the dance floor with him, wanting to maintain very close contact." Naomi sniffed the air, bringing a long, deep breath into her nose. "They're both here. This way."

Naomi led them through the pool tables, through a small opening, and into another large, open space. This one had the same decor on the walls, but the middle of the floor was a sawdust-covered dance floor. A band played from a stage at the far end of the dance hall. A few high-top tables and bar stools stood just outside the dance floor.

In the middle of the dance floor was Michael and Lilith, swaying, but not to the music. Although Niki had never seen the demon before, she fit Naomi's description. She was strikingly beautiful with long, straight black hair. She wore a spaghetti strapped blouse that exposed all of her arms, which she lecherously had wrapped under Michael's shirt and around his back. Her head rested on Michael's chest, and where they stood, a light from above the dance floor shined directly onto them, illuminating the two of them in an angelic glow.

Niki almost threw up in her mouth. Thank goodness for her years of training.

Suddenly, Lilith raised her head from Michael's chest and looked their way. A devilish smile spread across her lips. On anyone else, it probably would've looked seductive, but from Lilith, Niki could feel malicious intent oozing from the grin.

"That's her," Naomi said.

No shit, Niki thought.

She reached for the buckle of her silver belt, ready to slide it off her waist and make it her whip instead.

Naomi's hand shot out in front of Niki, stopping her. "If you value your vampire's existence, don't do that. She has him in a trance. She'll break his mind and leave you to deal with the pieces. I doubt you want that."

Of course, Niki didn't want to have to kill Michael. If for some reason it came down to Michael or her and Nate... Well, she didn't want to think about that situation.

"A trance?" Nate asked.

"Think of it as a very, very deep drug trip. She found a memory and placed him there. He has no idea where he is or who he's with."

"How can you tell?" the hunter asked.

"I can sense it from his aura. It's dim but not like he's dying. More like it's somewhere else. Like *he's* somewhere else," she clarified.

"Then I'll just have a conversation and ask her nicely," Niki smiled. Despite Naomi's objections, she marched forward, leaving Nate and Naomi behind.

53

"Lilith!" Niki shouted. "Or do you prefer Lily? We need to talk."

Lilith turned her head away from Niki, ignoring her.

Niki stepped onto the dance floor, furious that Lilith was ignoring her. She took a deep breath, and her nostrils flared.

"Bitch, do not turn away from me!" she shouted.

Three couples standing in between Niki and Lilith stopped dancing and looked at the Aussie. Their faces showed both confusion and hesitation. They didn't know what was going on, but they wanted no part of whatever it was. Slowly, they backed up, moving off the dance floor and making room for the inevitable confrontation.

Lilith looked back at Niki with disdain.

"Are you the one who killed my sister?" she calmly inquired. Although her voice remained steady, Niki saw the fury in her eyes. Naomi had said not to underestimate Lilith. Sitting just behind those eyes, Niki saw a thousand plans, all of which involved getting her revenge for Angie's death. She needed to be careful, but despite her better judgment, she kept approaching and taunting Lilith.

"Do you see this belt I'm wearing?" Niki started. She grabbed the buckle. "I wrapped it around your sister's neck and held her in place while removing her head with a machete. Now, let my friend go before we're forced to do the same thing to you."

Lilith's eyes left Niki and continued past her. She then lowered them back. "I had hoped what Eileen had told me wasn't true, but it looks like it was. You killed one of my sisters and turned the other one against us."

"We didn't turn her against you. I'm pretty sure you did that yourselves. Now don't make me repeat myself. Let my friend go." She spat out each of the last four words, as if each one was a swear word.

"Why don't you ask him if he wants to go? He seems perfectly at peace in my arms."

Niki's eyes drifted over to Michael. His eyes reminded her of the cowboy at the door. Glazed over. He stared as if watching a movie only he could see. Of course he was relaxed and at peace. He was high on whatever drug she had fed him. Niki was going to kill her. And enjoy it.

"Mike," Niki said. "Hey, Mike! Are you in there, love?"

He showed no response. Wherever she had him, he was well buried.

"Mike!" she shouted while stepping closer. "Michael!"

His face turned toward her, giving her a fleeting moment of hope. An instant later, though, it was gone.

His lips curled back, revealing his fangs, and his eyes turned red. It wasn't his normal deep red. There was still a haze covering his eyes. Niki knew he was still being controlled, but she couldn't take the risk. He looked to be in full vamp mode, and she didn't want to hurt him.

Niki took a few steps back, not wanting to confront Michael and the succubus at the same time. Even though they had one on their side, with Mike's strength, she knew the chances of coming out on top were slim.

"Niki!" Nate shouted at her. "We need to go."

"Nate, I'm not leaving him," she responded.

"We need to go!" he repeated more forcefully, capturing her attention.

She backed up until she was closer to the other two. When she was a few feet away she turned around to face them. From over their shoulders, she saw a brunette stroll through the dance hall. She stood out from the other women in the club. Instead of wearing tight blue jeans and boots, she wore sandals and a long, flowing white dress. The brunette stopped at a table where a man and woman were talking. The woman's face had a puzzled look on it, like she didn't recognize the newcomer.

The brunette brushed her hand over the man's arm, and he stood. The woman started hollering, but Niki couldn't hear what she was saying.

Naomi turned around, following Niki's gaze as Niki rejoined them. Naomi spun quickly around, wide eyes pleading with Niki.

"It's Eisheth," she said.

Niki watched Eileen gently brush the back of another man's neck. She worked her way around the room, headed toward the dance floor, and brushing the arms of those dancing. With each pass, the men let go of their dance partners and followed after Eileen.

"Josh," Nate demanded. "We need a way out." He spun around to the front door.

Niki followed his lead, looking for an exit. A few of the men Eileen controlled were already huddled there.

"Three emergency exits and the front door," Josh answered. "One in the room you're in over by the stage."

Somehow Eileen already had two men guarding it.

"I can dispatch her men like I did earlier," Naomi said.

"It's not their fault. I'd prefer to lower the body count," Niki said. "If we can find a way out with minimal damage, that'd be ideal."

"There's an exit in the kitchen. That might be your best route."

"Kitchen sounds great, Josh. Where is it?" Nate asked.

"Go into the first open space. The entrance is in the back corner."

Niki saw two large men, one with a cowboy hat and the other with an LSU hat, standing in the doorway between the two rooms.

"We're going to have to throw a punch or two," she told Nate. "Naomi, don't kill them if we don't have to."

Nate bounced up and down on his feet. She'd seen him do that before, loosening up and getting his blood pumping. He snarled, his face angled toward the two men standing in the doorway, then he ran as hard as he could. Before the large man in the cowboy hat could react, Nate's shoulder hit him directly in the stomach. His cowboy hat flew off as the man's feet came off the ground. He landed five feet back from where Nate hit him.

The man in the LSU hat glanced at his friend on the ground and turned back around right as Niki punched him in the face. She felt his nose shatter under her fist and then kicked him back into the room with the pool tables.

From across the dance floor, Eileen's army started running toward the trio as they sprinted around the pool tables. Naomi hopped onto the first one and leaped from table to table. She landed at the door to the kitchen just before Niki and Nate arrived. Naomi twisted the door handle, but it didn't move. Locked. She squeezed down, and the metal handle crumpled in her grasp. She pulled the door off its hinges.

"Move," she instructed Nate and Niki.

Both moved out of her way as she threw the large metal door at the onslaught of men heading their way. The door collided with the first person and continued on, taking out two others in its path.

"Where's the exit, Josh?" Nate shouted.

"Straight ahead. It'll take you out the side of the building. I've already dispatched a rideshare three blocks over. It should be there when you get there."

"That's my man," Nate said with a huge smile across his face.

Up ahead, was the large red exit sign. The three ran through the kitchen as fast as they could. As she passed a small silver table, Niki kicked it over. She then grabbed any pots and pans sitting on the counter and threw them behind her.

Naomi ran ahead of the pair. The door in front of her had a crash handle in the middle and a chain wrapped around the bar, connected to the wall. She doubted the fire department would approve. When Naomi reached the door, she slammed hard. As she did, the thick chain broke free from the wall, ripping completely from its hook. The door swung open, and the chain fell onto the concrete sidewalk.

"Which way?" Nate said.

"Take a right," Josh said. "Go down two blocks."

Without slowing down, they turned and continued sprinting. Niki didn't look back to see if they were being followed. She didn't care. It was better to just assume they were and keep running.

"Take another right. Car should be there. Black sedan."

Just as Josh said, the black sedan was less than a block ahead. All passenger doors stood open, waiting on them. The driver sat with the engine running.

Nate hopped in the front seat, and Niki and Naomi slid into the back, closing the doors behind them.

"Good evening," the driver said. "Buckle up."

The second three seat belts clicked into place, he punched the gas, squealing the tires on the pavement, and the car lunged forward.

Niki glanced over at Naomi who had a strange look on her face.

"What's wrong?" she asked while gasping for air.

Naomi pointed at the driver. "Vampire," she said.

"Don't worry," the driver said. "I'm registered and in good standing."

54

Josh watched on the screen as the little red dots sped back to headquarters. Sweat soaked into his shirt, and he wiped more from his brow. This night had been a huge failure. He was at a loss for what to do next and needed help.

There was only one thing he could think to do. He initiated the conference call and queued it up on his second screen. Then, he waited for the team to get back.

Niki was the first through the door. Her face was flushed as she burst inside.

"He just fucking stood there," she shouted. "No, wait. First, he had the balls to flash his fucking fangs at me, and then he just kept dancing with her! We are so fucking fucked. And when he comes back from this. I'm going to remind him why he shouldn't fucking flash his fangs at me when I fucking flash castrate him! Fucking vampire!"

"It wasn't his fault," Jax said.

Josh had to swallow a laugh when she spun so quickly she nearly lost her balance.

Jax's face took up a third of the monitor.

"Holy shit!" she finally said. "You need a haircut and a shave."

Jax grinned. "Thanks, Niki. Where's Nate?"

"Right here, boss man," he said as he walked through the door.

"I'm not the boss man anymore. Mike gets that dubious honor, but first we need to work out a plan to get him back. He hasn't been a member of the Night Crew for long, but how many times has he already saved our collective asses?"

"We haven't given up on him," Nate said. "Niki's just pissed about the bitch he was dancing with and the other one who keeps sending innocent guys to kick our ass."

"Okay. So let's figure it out and make a plan."

Naomi stepped around the table and stood next to Josh, staring at the monitor.

With the team back and her standing there anyhow, he figured this would be as good a time as any to make introductions.

"First though, let me introduce you to Naomi, one of the three remaining succubi in the world. Naomi, the man with the stubbly beard and graying hair is John Sanchez, but we all call him Jax."

"I've been doing this a long time," Jax said. "I thought we knew everything. Should've realized that wasn't the case. From what I've heard, I'm really glad you're on our side."

Josh continued, "In the center window, with the long hair and pale skin is Thomas."

"You were Silas's brother," she interrupted.

"Something that I'm glad you can speak of in the past tense. He was misguided, but his ambition left us with quite a mess."

"So it seems," Naomi stated.

"And last, wearing the glasses on the far right, is Intel."

"I'm guessing you give the information that sends hunters after their victims?" Naomi asked, a hint of cynicism mixed into her voice.

"They aren't victims," Intel said. "We only go after threats. As long as you play by the rules, we're good. But since the four of you decided to fill the morgue, I had to send a team."

Nate grabbed two bottles of water and hopped onto the table. He handed one to Niki as she sat down next to him.

Meanwhile, Josh worried the exchange between Naomi and Intel was about to get ugly if he didn't jump in.

"Now that we have introductions out of the way, we need a plan, and I'm at a loss. Nate and Niki have been beat to hell."

"Hey," Niki said. "We still have a lot more beatings we can take, love. Don't go insulting us like that."

"Fine, Nate and Niki are exhausted." Josh rolled his eyes at the two on the table. This wasn't how he thought this meeting would go. "I have two exhausted hunters and a succubus to go up against two succubi and a vampire. I don't see the odds in our favor. If Mike wasn't under Lilith's control, that'd be different. Thomas, want to take a road trip?" Josh smirked, knowing the answer already.

Jax spoke up, ignoring the question. "So, you have two objectives. Kill the succubi and save Mike. I don't think we care which order at the end of the day, but I agree having him on our side from the beginning would make things a lot easier. Naomi, how do we break him out of whatever spell Lilith has him under?"

"The siren's call," she corrected gently.

"So how do we get him to stop hearing this siren's call?" he capitulated. "Does killing her work?"

"He was touched by Angie," Nate said. "We killed her, but Mike still heard Lilith's siren call."

"We haven't lost a sister since before Samael was assassinated," Naomi thought out loud. "Usually, whoever is touched is either released by the one who touched him..."

"Or is left doing a dried husk in the middle of the street impression," Intel finished.

"Something like that," Naomi said. Her tone screamed her displeasure at Intel's sarcasm.

Jax wisely interrupted the fight that was about to break out. "Back to my question, though. How do we free him from her?"

Josh glanced from the screen to Naomi. A silence hung in the air as everyone waited for her answer.

She slowly shook her head. "He's very strong-willed. He broke free of Agrat's spell on his own, but Lilith is more powerful. Her seduction, her call, is stronger. And she had him completely immersed in the dream. His aura was weak, split between the two worlds: the dream world and the real world. We'd need something more powerful, more intense to pull him out of wherever she put him."

"Yeah, I'll say. Michael's definitely strong-willed," Thomas agreed. "But that also plays in our favor. If we can start to break through to him, I know he'll do the rest."

"So, we will all do more thinking on how we can pry him back," Jax said. "But before we can do that, we have to find him."

"Where would Lilith take him?" Intel asked. "The four of you have been hiding for a thousand years. I assume you have multiple places that are both secure and secluded."

"We haven't stayed in any one place for a thousand years. We've moved so often that I've lost track. More than once, the Council nearly stumbled upon us.

"As to where she would've taken him, I think I know. Lilith has a lair. Her own and one that's personal to her."

"Great," Nate said. "So you're saying there's a secret sex demon dungeon lair."

"I think I've seen that porno," Niki said. She then added by pointing at Nate and saying, "in fact, I think we watched it together."

"Do you see what I had to deal with?" Jax asked Intel.

"I'm in the same room as the two of them so if anyone deserves sympathy," Josh said.

"It's where she would've taken him, especially if she thinks he's the one who can bring back Samael," Naomi said, ignoring the banter. "If Lilith and Eileen feel cornered, they will run. Although after Agrat's death, revenge is their only motivation. I don't know if she will want to wait for me to lead you to them so she can have it or if they will run. I also don't know if they'll take the vampire with them or kill him. He'd be a great tool if they can keep him under control and if they move locations."

Niki hopped off the table. "So, what I'm hearing you say is, and stop me if I'm wrong, you could be leading us into an empty sex demon lair or walking us right into a trap?"

"Unfortunately, those are the only two options."

"Niki," Jax said. "At least going in you'll know it's a trap. Plan accordingly."

"Thanks, love," Niki said, sarcastically. "You've been a huge help stating the obvious." She turned to the others in the room. "Why do you have him on this call?"

Josh rubbed his head. More Tylenol was in his very near future. A lot more.

"Thomas. Intel." Josh stated. "You guys have anything else before Nate and Niki get some rest?"

"We don't need rest," Nate objected.

"There's no reason to rush," Intel said. "Let me see what I can find out."

Naomi added, "If they are moving, they'll have already left. We don't pack. We just leave."

"And if they're staying," Thomas said, "you'll need your energy. Also, if," he paused, rethinking what he said, "when you break Michael free, he's going to be hungry."

The room went quiet.

"Thanks, team," Josh said, finally breaking the silence. "Intel, I'll send you the info on the lair. Night Crew out."

55

Niki awoke to the sun streaming through the windows. Next to her, Nate was still snoring on his side, his back facing her. She could make out the bruises down his side, across his arms, and around his shoulder. The other side looked just as bad. She knew it without needing to see it. She tried to think of the last time they took a beating even remotely close to this bad. The more she thought, the more she realized there hadn't been. This had been the worst.

But in the past, there were more of them. It wasn't just four. Jax never liked less than six. Seven was his preferred number. Six in the field and one with eyes in the sky.

They were already a man down when they had raided the school Silas had made his personal playground. If it wasn't for the urgency, Niki was certain Jax would've trained a new replacement for Scott before they attacked. They were lucky, then. Sort of.

It had cost Michael his humanity.

Nate rolled over onto his back. His arm went up to his forehead as his eyes slowly opened. More discoloration spread across his chest.

Propping herself up on her arm, Niki stared down at him. With her finger, she traced the bruises on his torso. She playfully took two fingers and walked them from his stomach up to his neck, forcing a smile from Nate.

"You up for this?" she asked. "Not one, but two succubi?" After a pause, she gently added, "And Mike?"

He brought his hand up to her upper arm and gently squeezed. "Doesn't really matter, does it?" he asked in response.

She closed her eyes and audibly exhaled from her nose. As she opened her eyes back up, she fought back the urge to cry. She wasn't a crier. She was Niki Fucking Davis. She'd killed more vampires than she could count. A few werewolves. A banshee, and once even a rougarou, which reminded her more of a deformed werewolf. And now she could add succubus to her bingo card.

But she didn't cry. Ever. Fuck that.

"For the first time in a long time, I'm a little scared, love." It pained her to admit it. As hard as it was to admit to Nate, her Nate, she knew she would never admit it to anyone else. She'd charge into any situation headfirst like she did. But this time, she was scared it'd be the last time she would be able to.

"I'm not a fan, either. I'd love to have a whole goddamn army with us. Instead, it's you and me fighting monsters alongside another monster. It's what we do. But, baby, I wouldn't want to do it with anyone else."

"You'd better not want to do it with anyone else." Her mouth curled up into a smile, but the threat was real.

Nate grabbed one of her triceps in each hand and flung her onto the bed, rolling himself above her. His biceps and shoulders flexed as he held himself there, staring down at her. After a few seconds, he bent his head down and kissed her. As they kissed, she wrapped her legs around his waist and spun around, throwing his back on the bed and sitting on top of him.

"Since when do you think you're the one in control?" she said, slipping her shirt off over her head and tossing it onto the floor.

56

"I'm tracking you," Josh said. "I have eyes in the sky this time, and I'm activating thermals as well."

Niki, Nate, and Naomi stood in front of a two-story house across from the sprawling grassy area known as New Orleans City Park. The park itself had luscious trees and a lake, as well as paths that crisscrossed throughout. As they'd driven close, she'd seen the signs for various things to do. The park housed the New Orleans Museum of Art, a botanical garden, a children's museum, and a number of other attractions.

"If we survive this night," she had told Nate, "we're coming back here. You're taking me to the Museum of Art."

"Since when do you love art?" he asked.

"Since I started saying things like, 'if we survive this night'."

"Fair enough."

Staring at the front of the house, she wondered if Naomi had the right place. The house had a baby blue door and a small balcony off a second-story bedroom. Seven red brick steps led up to the front porch, and columns supported the overhang. A white railing ran along the exterior of the porch. It was a beautiful, quaint little house with a tiny green yard in front of it.

"This can't be the house," she said.

"It's how we stayed so well hidden, and for so long. If we bought the most expensive, most luscious homes, others would notice. This," Naomi said, pointing to the house, "this is invisible."

Niki couldn't argue.

"Josh, are you getting anything from thermals?"

"No. It looks clear."

"Well," Niki said. "No time like the present."

Instinctively, she reached down to her side and felt the silver whip dangling next to her. On her other hip, a machete hung loosely. She had a .45 nestled into its holster behind her, clipped to her belt. Being fully armed gave her the only hint of comfort about this whole rescue mission. She hadn't been in her usual hunting uniform since they'd arrived in New Orleans. That attire would stand out in a nightclub.

There was no night club hunting today, though.

She glanced at Nate. He had a .45 on each hip, a shotgun strapped across his shoulder, and a machete at his side. Gazing at him all strapped up, she couldn't be more in love with him.

"Let's go kill some fucking succubi," she said. "No offense, Naomi."

"None taken."

Niki took a step forward. The moment her foot reached the sidewalk, she heard Josh in her ear. "Hold up a second."

Niki immediately felt her heart skip, and she froze in place. "What's wrong?"

"There's something you guys haven't done since you started this mission."

Niki turned her head to Nate, meeting his eyes. He also had a puzzled look on his face.

"Circle up and get your hands in," Josh told them.

Suddenly, it dawned on her what they hadn't done. She knew where he was going and took it from there. She turned, creating a triangle between herself, Naomi, and Nate. Niki's hand went in the middle, and

Nate's was there at almost the same time. Following their lead, Naomi did the same.

"There's a very real chance, we don't all make it out," she said. "Not only do we have two very powerful beings to deal with, but our friend as well. I'm scared. Josh, I hope you recorded that, because you won't hear me say it again. Now more than ever, we need whatever divine fortune we can muster. Now, close your goddamn eyes.

"Lord, protect us from evil as we deliver Your judgment to them. Amen."

"Amen," Nate and Josh echoed.

Naomi nodded.

"We haven't done that since Silas," Josh said. "Now, go save our vampire."

Niki took a deep breath and stepped a foot on the sidewalk. She half expected something else; she didn't know what, but something, to stop her again. When nothing came, she continued, leading the way down the gray concrete sidewalk, and up the red-bricked steps.

Her heart pounded the entire time. She suddenly realized that was the only sound she heard. No birds in the air. No traffic. Just the steady drone of her heart. She had to stop herself from marching in rhythm with it.

Once on the front porch, the wood creaked under her feet. Naomi stepped around her.

"I'll go first. I know the way." Naomi placed her hand on the doorknob and slowly twisted it. "Also, I know them. If anything's booby trapped, I want it to hit me first."

"By all means," Niki said, taking a step back.

Her mind drifted back to the booby traps Silas had set. Locking Nate in the gym. Trapping her and Jax in the cafeteria. He'd had the place ready for them. If it wasn't for Michael, they'd have been bled dry.

As the door swung open, a quiet squeal escaped the hinges, barely audible. Naomi eased her hand back as the door opened all the way. She took a hesitant step across the threshold, expecting something to happen. When nothing did, she noticeably exhaled.

Niki and Nate followed closely behind her. Nate held his shotgun, his hand around the grip, and his finger resting lightly on the trigger guard. Niki kept her hand resting on the whip, ready to strike.

Once inside the house, Niki examined their surroundings. From the furniture to the wall hangings, it looked as if it was waiting for a realtor to bring potential homeowners by. The pictures were stock photos. Couch, loveseat, and recliner were neutral colors and a matching set. Nothing in the house indicated anything about Lilith's personality. This was as bland and sterile as she'd ever seen a house. She wasn't sure what to expect from a creature that had lived for thousands of years who thrived on seduction and control; maybe a throne of skulls, pictures of her with various celebrities and world leaders, anything that pointed to the Queen of Demons.

"Which way?" Nate whispered.

Naomi gestured for them to follow her. She delicately placed each step onto the hardwood floor, not making a single sound.

She led them through the living room, down a short hallway, and into a second living space. This one had bookshelves that lined the walls from floor to ceiling. There wasn't an empty space in the room. A single chair sat in the middle of the floor.

"Avid readers when not seducing men?" Niki asked. She knew the sarcasm had to be apparent.

"The entrance to the catacombs is through here," Naomi said, ignoring the snide question.

She walked over to the bookshelf, placed each hand on a different shelf, and shoved forward. A ripple ran across her back. Niki thought Naomi was about to transform back into the gargoyle-like succubus, but then she heard a metallic click from somewhere behind the wall. The rippling stopped, and Naomi backed away.

Slowly, a seam appeared in between two bookshelves. With a hiss, the wall recessed. Niki doubted that, despite the apparent age of some of the books, the shelf was hermetically sealed, so she assumed some pneumatic system must control the movement. Once the wall moved back about a foot, Naomi gripped the edge of the bookshelf and slid the panel to the left, where it fit perfectly behind the next shelf, revealing a dark tunnel system that descended beneath the house.

"I haven't seen a secret passage in a library in a while," Nate joked.

He walked over to the newly exposed doorway in the wall and peered down. Immediately, his head shot backward, and his nose curled up.

"What the fuck is that?" he demanded, eyes watering. He appeared visibly sick, fighting back the urge to vomit.

As if she couldn't smell a thing, Naomi stepped into the stone stairwell leading below the house. "That's the smell of The Willing."

57

"The Willing?" Niki asked, as she started down just behind Naomi. The smell permeated the air, making it barely breathable. She focused on inhaling through her mouth and not her nose. Instead of smelling it, she was now tasting the foul stench. The pungent aroma was everywhere.

The light from the study penetrated only a few steps, so soon they were swallowed up by darkness. Niki placed her hand on the wall as she cautiously took each step. Moisture seeped in through the man-made—or succubus-made—stone cavern. The steps curved around, taking them below the house.

At first, Niki thought this was a hidden basement, but she soon realized this went deeper than a typical basement. A little further ahead, a soft orange glow brought the area into better focus. As they turned the corner, Niki saw wall sconces with lit torches hanging on the wall.

Naomi walked a few feet more and then stopped.

"They are here. Lilith would not have left the torches lit."

With the warm hue washing over the tunnel, Niki was able to see the gray stone blocks that were used to construct the underground structure. The curved stairwell flattened out and turned into a wider hallway. Every dozen feet or so, another lit torch hung from the wall. Also spaced apart along the walls were metal rings. A few of them had chains dangling from them.

Niki ran her hand across the cold, rusted steel. As she did, a thought crossed her mind.

"You never answered my question," she said to Naomi. "What did you mean by The Willing?"

"Something I'm not very proud of."

"We all have a past, love."

"The Willing are those so infatuated that they willingly submit themselves to us. They volunteer to be a sacrifice, to be kept close so we can continuously feed off of their energy."

Nate moved close to Niki, grasping the chain in his hand as well. "How long do they last to feed off of their energy?"

"It varies. Some last for weeks before all their bodily systems shut down. By that time, they're nothing more than skeletons; their flesh just draping their bones. Dried up husks. They have no control of their bodily functions anymore. They look more like the dead than the living. And all the while it's what they want. They smile all the way to the end. Happy and high on the drug we provide."

"Why the chains?" he asked.

"Lilith won't allow them to freely roam the halls, and they aren't allowed to leave. So, she came up with a solution. The best thing..."

"Chain them to the wall," Niki finished. "Prisoners in the dungeon, waiting to die."

"That was the unfortunate case, yes."

Niki imagined what that must've looked like. All that came to mind was a medieval crypt, something from the Middle Ages or the crusades. Lit torches lighting the way, men chained to walls or on the floor dying. Corpses with heartbeats happily waiting to die. The stench of shit, piss, vomit, bile, rotting, and decaying bodies filling the atmosphere. So much so that even now without any of them here, the smell of rot still lingered.

"This is New Orleans, and your dungeon is underground. What happened to your chained up group of Willing during Katrina? Or really when any hurricane hits here?" Niki asked as they walked deeper down the stone hallway.

Naomi didn't look back at her. Instead, she kept her eyes forward, navigating them along. Niki was glad. The more she heard about what the four of them had done to their victims, the more disgusted she became. She didn't even care that it was all at the behest of Lilith. There had to be some level of complicity from the other three. Lilith could be the ringleader, but it took all four of them to make it work.

"I'm sure you can assume the answer." The solemnity in her voice told Niki everything she needed to know.

"You let them just drown." The accusation lingered in the dimly lit tunnel. "At least vampires kill quickly. This is sadistic torture."

"You're the one who said we all have a past," Naomi said, finally stopping and turning around. "I'm not proud of what I've done. I've tried to distance myself over the centuries as best I could. I didn't participate in all of this. I fed off the energy of those I've loved. Like I said, it's a purer energy that way. Untainted by the effects of our powers."

"You were complacent in her atrocities. That makes you equally responsible."

Niki and Naomi stood toe-to-toe. Niki had become furious learning about how they treated people, keeping them locked up and left to drown, or drained to nothing but skeletons.

"Ladies," Nate said, stepping in between the two of them. "We can hash all of this out later. You two can throw hands and beat the shit out of each other after we accomplish our mission. For now, we have two she-devils to kill and a vampire to save. Can we work together, so we don't get killed down here?"

"Where are The Willing now?" Niki asked, seemingly ignoring her partner.

"Lilith discarded them after the Council went missing. She decided we would feed the old-fashioned way. They left bodies, and you guys showed up."

Naomi turned around and led them down another hall. The three remained silent.

"We're almost to her sanctuary," Naomi whispered.

Up ahead, Niki saw a stone entranceway. The top was arched. The same flickering torches lit the area on the other side of the wall as well.

"Naomi," a voice called out from within. "It's about time you came back home. Thank you for bringing us something to feed."

"She'll try to manipulate you," Naomi said, quickly turning to Niki and Nate. "It's what she does. Ignore her."

"Niki Davis and Nathan Edwards," Lilith stated. "Michael told me so much about you. He wants to say his goodbyes. He's going to be leaving with us. Unfortunately, you three will not be coming along. Well, maybe in spirit."

Lilith laughed. The sound echoed off the stone walls and ceiling. It bombarded them from all directions.

Niki took a deep breath. "Let's get this over with."

She stepped around Naomi and into the room with Lily, Eileen, and Michael.

58

The first thing she noticed was the cavernous size of the room. Niki couldn't tell how far they'd traveled underground. If she had to guess, they were somewhere back under New Orleans City Park. It was the only way city officials hadn't found this large of a structure. Any utilities would've been laid around the park instead of cutting through such a beautiful patch of greenery in the middle of the city. The park gave Lilith the perfect cover for her cavernous lair.

At the far end, the two succubi and the vampire stood together. Michael was in between the black-haired Lilith with her olive complexion and Eileen, the brunette who sent waves of innocent men to attack the hunters only for Naomi to strike them down. With Michael in the middle, it appeared as if he was the one in charge and the two of them were his vampire brides. Niki knew better, though. She knew they controlled him.

They were about twenty yards from Nate, Niki, and Naomi. It reminded Niki of Western movies where the good guys are on one end of the street and the bad guys on the other. A stand-off. High noon and everyone had their hand on their hip, ready for whoever drew their side arm first and opened fire. The unholy OK Corral.

No one said anything. Even Lilith had ceased her taunts.

Finally, Niki, unable to stand the tension, sang, "Red rover. Red Rover. Can Michael come over?"

Lily and Eileen exchanged a look. Their mouths opened into smiles that seemed both unusually wide and disorienting. They stared straight past him, as if the vampire wasn't even there. Their faces turned back toward Niki.

"You should be careful what you wish for, Niki Davis," Eileen said. "He'd much rather be with us. If you take him away, he'll be very displeased."

Thomas's words of caution floated through her head. That could be their way of saying Mike was in bloodlust already. He hadn't mastered control yet, which means they were essentially trapped in this room with him if he was in the midst.

Eileen turned to Mike, and Lily stepped closer to him, gently rubbing her hand down his face. She adjusted the collar on his jacket, straightening and pressing it against his shoulder, primping him as if they were a couple.

Mike's eyes narrowed, and a smile crossed his face as she touched him.

"Michael, my dear," she said, loudly enough for her voice to travel across the empty room. "The people over there want to take you away from us. Away from me! I know you don't want to go with them, but they are really persistent. Would you like them to take you away from me?"

Mike's head shook. It didn't look so much like he shook his head as much as it just moved. Niki knew they needed to break whatever spell the two had over him. Josh had told them something that he'd hoped would work, but it required them to get close, so they were going to have to fight.

"Fuck this," Niki said. She gripped the silver whip at her side, removed it from her hip, and let the end dangle by her feet. "It's time to kill these bitches."

Nate slung the shotgun from his shoulder to his hands, holding the forestock in one hand and clutching the pistol grip in the other. His finger again hovered right next to the guard.

On her other side, Naomi began to grow in size. Her features contorted and her wings spread wide. She became the true form of a succubus again; that gargoyle-like beast that was so deadly.

As soon as Naomi completed her transformation, her head a solid foot above Niki's, Mike's eyes changed. From across the room, she could see the bright red orbs pulsing in their sockets. He flashed his incisors, putting his fangs on full display.

The two succubi standing next to him shifted their form simultaneously. Any semblance of their former selves vanished. The three sisters were identical with one exception. A tuft of purple hair stood straight up on the top of Naomi's head.

Niki smiled. She had a way to tell who was who.

Naomi took a few steps backward. She dropped one knee to the ground as if doing a lunge, wrapped her wings around herself, the bony points just above her head, and then exploded forward like a missile, straight at Eileen.

59

The moment Naomi shot from her stance, Nate shifted every ounce of his focus to Mike. Naomi had told them she'd handle her sisters and keep their attention on her as best she could. Lilith and Eisheth would want revenge for her treachery. She promised them she could handle the two of them as long as Nate and Niki could handle the vampire.

And that was exactly what Nate intended to do. He knew he could take a beating. He just needed his window of opportunity to hopefully break Mike away from the siren call of Lilith. Mike had broken away from Angie. He could do it again with the right motivation.

To capture Mike's attention, Nate fired his shotgun at Lilith. He figured if he pissed her off, she'd send his friend. He made sure not to load the silver shot just in case. Normal slugs wouldn't kill him, just slow him down. Silver could actually hurt.

The slug hit Lilith square in the chest and drove her back a few feet. The look on her face was pure shock. She obviously wasn't expecting to be hit with anything like a heavy lead round. She had probably anticipated birdshot that would've cast a wider net but not been near as effective. Black blood oozed from the hole in her torso. She raised her clawed hand to the wound, then changed back to her beautiful female persona. When she did, the wound shriveled and closed.

She turned to Michael who stood watching. "I'm releasing your inhibitions. Kill without mercy. Kill for me."

At her command, Michael's facial features contorted. Nate knew older vampires could change their entire appearance, more than just their fangs and eye color. He'd heard stories of their faces changing, as if the underlying bone structure had shifted. It wasn't something he or anyone he knew had seen before, until it happened to Mike.

His eye sockets narrowed, intensifying his stare, and his nostrils flared. His cheek bones became more defined, creating deep shadows of dark, black lines. Vampire Michael was a beast designed for one thing, and at that moment, that one thing was to kill Nate.

Michael crouched, hands nearly touching the ground, and bounded toward Nate in large leaps. More animal than human. A cat leaping for its prey.

"Fuck me." Nate barely managed to get the words out before Michael was in his face.

With one swipe of his arm, Mike threw Nate into the wall, the shotgun still clinging to his shoulder. With an oof, the wind rushed out of him. Nate tried to refill his lungs with air but struggled to gasp enough. He had wanted Mike's attention, and he had gotten everything he had wished for. Before Nate had a chance to recover, Michael stood in front of him, pressing his forearm into Nate's throat.

Stars erupted. Nate used one hand to try and counter Michael. With the other, he fumbled with the shotgun until his hand found the pistol grip. Nate pushed the barrel into Mike's side as hard as he could.

"Sorry," he croaked out, and then he pulled the trigger.

The lead slug, which entered Mike's left side, tossed Michael a few feet away, where he landed on his back. It wasn't far, but it was far enough to give Nate a second to breathe. His throat burned, and he could feel it trying to regain its former shape. He also felt the thick blood draining down the back of his throat.

A moment later, Mike jumped back onto his feet.

"Josh, I hope you have something," he whispered.

Just before Michael could charge at Nate again, the silver whip wrapped around the vampire's neck. Mike's hands shot to his neck, trying to claw his way out of the whip's grasp. His mouth opened and he wailed in pain.

Niki braced herself, holding the whip as firm as she could.

"I know it hurts," she said. "We're trying to save you, dammit. Let us save you."

"I've got something," Josh responded.

Nate shot a glance at Niki, hoping she had their friend. He advanced closer to Mike. The shotgun, with the next round loaded and ready, firmly in his grip. Nate took the last step toward Mike when the whip slipped from Niki's hand. Mike immediately found enough slack to get his fingers through and pried the silver away from his skin. The silver must've burnt his hand as well, but he ignored it, gripping the chain and ripping it off him.

Free again, Michael lunged forward. He grabbed Nate by the neck and forced him against the wall once again. With Nate's back firmly secured against the stone, Mike raised his other arm.

Nate realized he could kick both of his feet. Mike may have held him in the air, pinned him against the wall, but his feet dangled a few inches above the ground. Nate was a large, muscular man. Being suspended in the air was new. He felt like a kid and immediately didn't like it.

He also didn't like the feeling of suffocating. Mike's effort intensified, crushing Nate's trachea with nothing but grip strength.

Nate felt his heart pulsing and the vertebrae in his neck separating. Shaking, he reached his hands up to his throat. Instead of fighting off Michael's hand from his neck, Nate moved one hand to his ear and removed his earpiece. Fighting through the black encroaching in on his vision, Nate placed both of his hands on Michael's arm, hoping for some leverage to ease the tension on his neck. With the earpiece clenched between his fingers, he reached his hand out and forced it into Mike's ear.

"Now, Josh!" Niki screamed.

Naamah gripped the ground with her feet. She encircled her body with her wings, the bony point of each meeting together just above her head. Every muscle in her body rippled, and she forced every ounce of energy into her legs. With a quick, sudden thrust, she fired herself from the ground, directing all her power at Eileen.

Lilith was stronger, older, more powerful. If Naamah tried to fight the Demon Queen first, especially with Eisheth's assistance, she wouldn't stand much of a chance.

But if she focused on Eisheth and trusted the hunters to distract Lilith, Naamah felt confident she could take out her sisters one at a time.

While hurtling toward Eileen, she heard the report from the shotgun. It echoed in the stone room, sounding more like a multitude of blasts than one.

Let one shot be enough, she thought.

An instant later, she collided with Eisheth. The point of her wings, the tips of her spears, caught Eisheth in the stomach, and the impact drove them both into the wall. Stone blocks cracked and crumbled behind them.

Naamah tried to unfurl her wings but couldn't. Eileen had her arms wrapped around her sister, enveloping Naomi inside the cocoon of her own making. With a quick twist, Eileen shoved Naomi into the wall and then slammed her into the ground.

As quickly as she could, Naomi dropped her wings and rolled out of the way. Eileen's taloned foot hung above her head. If Naomi would've waited a second longer, that foot would've pummeled her head into the floor.

"Traitor!" Eileen screamed at her. "Betrayer! We are on the verge of bringing back Samael." Instead of stomping on Naomi's face, she kicked her in the side.

"Why would you want to?" Naomi yelled, curling her wing next to her, hoping it would absorb some of Eileen's blows. Despite her efforts, enough of the impact filtered through that pain traveled up her side.

Naomi rolled and spun onto her feet.

"Why bring him back? He was a tyrant. Have you forgotten that?"

"He was our creator," Eisheth said. "He made us the magnificent creatures we are." She stood up tall and spread her arms and wings, showing herself to the entire room. "We are gods. You owe him everything. We owe him our loyalty."

Naamah thrust herself forward again. This time, she punched Eisheth in the stomach, then swiped her face with a wing. A long slice appeared down the side of Eileen's face, and in response she released a reverberating roar into their arena. Naomi threw another punch and swiped with the other wing.

This time, Eileen caught Naomi's wing mid-swipe in both of her hands. Naomi tried to tug it away but failed. Eileen gripped it tighter and tighter, resisting Naomi's futile attempt to escape. With the wing directly in front of her face, Eileen bent it in half.

Pain erupted through Naamah's entire body. Pain she'd never felt before. The top half of her wing dangled uselessly toward the ground. It was nothing but broken bones and torn membranes. And Eileen still held firmly onto the wing.

"You don't deserve what he gave you," she said, and with that, she tore the broken half of Naomi's wing from the rest and tossed it aside.

"You aren't worthy to be called one of our sisters," Eisheth continued as she ripped pieces of torn membrane from Naomi's wing.

Naomi fought to get Eileen off her back, but the excruciating pain immobilized her.

Eileen shifted her body and moved her hands closer to Naomi's back. One hand rested at the end of the wing, and the other drifted to the base of it.

"You don't need him," Naomi screamed through the pain. "Isn't one tyrant enough? Lilith doesn't want him here, either. She would have to submit and couldn't enjoy the power she has now."

She hoped to misdirect some of Eileen's hatred of her onto Lilith. Eileen didn't know that Lilith was lying to her. Naomi saw it, but Eileen was too blinded by her loyalty.

"You lie," Eileen cried.

A pulling and tearing sensation ripped down Naomi's back. She felt the joint connecting her wing to her body separating. Eileen meant to rip the wings straight off her back.

"Eisheth, I'm your sister. I'm trying to protect you from the one who is lying to you."

Each word was a struggle to say. Red hot pain coursed through her, plunging straight across her chest. A burning tear formed at the top of the knuckle that held her wing in place. Black blood sprung from the rip as Eileen continued to pull the decimated wing from Naomi's body.

"Eisheth Zenunim, you are killing the wrong sister."

That was the last Naomi could say before resorting to agonizing screams.

For a brief moment though, Naomi felt hesitation in Eileen. There was a slight faltering in her attempt to rip off the wing. A slight window of opportunity. It was all Naomi had hoped for, and all she hoped to need.

In that instant of release, that moment of doubt, Naomi dropped to the ground and twisted her body.

Eileen's grip had loosened, but it wasn't gone. She tried to reset her hold, but Naomi had already started her descent.

Naomi's wing pulled away, but by that point, she'd already committed. With her body falling and twisting, she curled the good wing and bent it, keeping the sharp point securely in front of her.

Ignoring the pain as Eileen's grasp ripped one wing away from her body, she used her velocity to drive the point of her other wing into Eileen's neck. The point met the soft fleshy tissue just under the jawline, pierced through the throat, and exited Eileen's mouth.

Eileen landed on the floor as Naomi completed her rotation.

The succubus planted her feet on the ground and heaved her remaining wing backward, withdrawing it from her sister's mouth and neck. Her dismembered wing laid next to the dying succubus. Black blood flowed down Naomi's back and spurted from Eileen's neck.

With her hands clutched to her throat, Eileen shriveled back into the beautiful brunette.

"Eisheth, have the decency to die as you once lived," Naomi gently chastised.

Writhing on the floor, gasping for air, but spitting out black ooze, Eileen's body shimmered once again. Her skin changed to a deep bronze, and her brunette hair blackened and formed into braids encircling her head. Her clothes became white linen.

"Eisheth of the Old Kingdom of Egypt, take your journey through the Underworld. May you reach Osiris and the Hall of Final Judgment. And may you plead your case well."

Naomi, wounded and hurt, fell to her knees next to Eileen.

"And good luck at the weighing of your heart, you Egyptian bitch," she said. "I hope Ammit devours the fuck out of it."

She spat in Eileen's face, then rose back to her feet, staring as the last of Eisheth's life flowed from her body, turning the gray stone floor dark and sticky. Naomi's form shifted away from the gargoyle, regaining her dark complexion and purple spiked hair once again.

Before Naomi could raise her head, Lilith pounced on top of her.

61

Josh spun in his chair. His finger hovered over the mouse, waiting for the signal. Sweat beaded down his face and chest.

"Now, Josh!" Niki screamed.

He clicked the button with the play symbol.

On the screen a video started playing. It was one he'd found after a handful of social media searches.

The image showed Mike, dressed in a rented tux, standing in front of a latticed archway that was covered in green floral. Directly in front of him Brittany stood dressed in a short white dress. Her red hair hid the small tiara that held her veil. A bouquet of flowers was in one hand. Michael held her other hand in his.

"Do you, Michael Anthony White, take this woman to be your wife, to live together in holy matrimony, to love her, to honor her, to comfort her, and to keep her in sickness and in health, forsaking all others, for as long as you both shall live?"

"I do," Mike said. The smile from his face lit the room, and a tear fell from his eye.

"Please, God, let this work," Josh prayed.

The video continued.

62

Naomi knew she should've been prepared for Lilith's attack, but after the brutal fight with Eisheth and her back still bleeding, she had let her guard down. For a single moment, she had turned her back on Lilith to take a breath. All she could do now was hope it didn't mean death for them all.

Lilith's violent impact threw Naomi to the ground. Her head bounced off the hard stone and stars cascading in front of her. Just beyond the golden orbs floating in her vision, the beast, the Queen of Demons, stood above her. She towered over Naomi, her gray, scaly skin rippling with fury.

Naomi couldn't move. She tried to rise but was pinned to the ground. Her arms were stretched out wide. Lilith straddled her, a foot on each arm holding her firmly against the ground.

There was nothing Naomi could do. She'd betrayed her sisters, turned against them. She had given aid to the hunters and killed one of her own. She deserved whatever punishment, whatever death, Lilith needed.

With her head turned up to the ceiling, Lilith let out an ear-piercing roar that shook the stone room.

The connection between Naamah and Lilith still existed. Naamah felt every one of Lilith's emotions, her rage, her betrayal.

"You want to be their savior?" Lilith screamed.

"I liked how things were," Naomi said through clenched teeth. "Why did you lie to Eisheth and Agrat? Why tell them you planned to resurrect Samael?"

At the mention of his name, Lilith back handed Naomi across the face. "Keep his name out of your mouth. You are no longer worthy to speak it."

"But you lied to them? What makes you worthy?"

"I was his first. I knew him the longest. When my god rejected me, Samael took me in. When my god left me to suffer at the hands of barbarians, Samael saved me. He made me a god in my own right."

"That doesn't answer my questions." The pain in her back was excruciating. The hole where her wing had been sent resonating pain up her neck and down her legs. "You don't want his return."

"Of course not. We don't need him anymore. We had each other. But your sisters didn't believe that. Their memory of him had become rose-colored. They didn't remember the tyrant. They wanted him back in order to grow the family, to have more sisters."

Lilith's claws ground into her arms.

"Why not keep us hidden in the shadows?" Naomi asked. "Why be so arrogant?"

"Arrogance is in my nature. Our nature. We thrive on lustful men. Men who think they have the power and the control, when in fact, it is ours."

She grabbed Naomi's throat. Naomi felt the force of her sister's grip crush her airways. Lilith stepped off Naomi's arms and picked her up from the ground, still crushing her neck. She pressed her sister against the wall.

Naomi struggled to breathe; her vision doubled.

"With you gone, I'll be the only one left."

Lilith grabbed one of Naomi's arms, forcing it out to the side. When it was fully extended, the Demon Queen shot her wing around her body, throwing it through Naomi's hand and burying it into the wall. She switched her hands on Naomi's throat and forced the other arm straight out. Once fully extended, she impaled that hand as well. The grip on Naomi's neck eased once she was suspended along the wall, pinned there by Lilith's wings, held up as if crucified.

"I'm going to rip your heart out of your chest as you ripped mine out by killing Eisheth. You slaughtered your own sister and aligned yourself with hunters. You are going to die, and then I'm going to feast on their life forces."

Naomi was powerless. Lilith was older and stronger.

With the talon of one hand, Lilith made an X like motion across Naomi's chest. Naomi's shirt spread open, and a thin black line of blood, one that matched the X, dotted across Naomi's skin. Searing pain shot through her. She didn't want to give Lilith the satisfaction of hearing her scream, so she swallowed it back down and dropped her head.

Lilith placed the point of her claw, still dripping with Naomi's blood, into the middle of the X. With just the tiniest amount of pressure, she began pushing her claw slowly into Naomi's chest. It broke through the skin with ease.

Naomi clenched her jaw. She wasn't going to make a sound.

A little more pressure and the claw started to grind into her chest bone. Lilith wiggled the sharp talon from side to side, drilling it into the bone. She drew out Naomi's suffering, making it as slow and as painful as she possibly could. Naomi was going to feel every moment of this.

Waves of blinding pain tore through Naomi's chest as her breastbone started to crack under the pressure. She heard tiny fractures as her sternum began to splinter. With each resounding crack, she fought the urge to black out. She would not give Lilith the satisfaction.

A shot rang out and echoed in the cavern, followed quickly by two more. The sound drew Naomi's attention away from her pain and onto the room around her.

The pressure drilling into Naomi's chest lifted, and her arms dropped to her sides. With all the pain in her chest, she had forgotten about the holes in her hands until blood started to flow in them again.

"Let her go, Demon Bitch!" Niki yelled.

Naomi gazed up and saw Niki with her gun raised and a trail of smoke drifting up from the barrel. Lilith had two holes in her wing and one in her side. Blood, thick and black, oozed from the wounds. Naomi leaned back against the wall, resting herself there.

Niki fired again and then raised her whip in the air. She quickly brought it down, cracking it directly in front of Lilith. She squeezed the trigger a few more times, continuing to fire rounds at the creature until the hammer clicked on an empty chamber. With the gun empty, she tossed it to the side and grabbed her machete, replacing the firearm with cold steel.

Their connection still intact, Naomi sensed Lilith's growing frustration with Niki, with Nate, and even with Michael at that point. The vampire would have been a nice asset, but he was quickly becoming too much of a hassle, thanks to the company he kept.

As Niki shot the whip forward, Naomi tried to warn her, but she was too weak to intervene. Niki cracked the whip again, and with stellar precision, Lilith snatched it out of the air. She yanked hard on it, bringing Niki closer. Too close.

Lilith reached out and grabbed Niki by the throat, lifting her up into the air.

"I'm not killing you yet," she said and tossed Niki to the ground.

Niki landed hard on her back a few feet away.

Lilith changed her form back into the beautiful, black-haired temptress. She gingerly stepped over to Niki and brushed the side of her arm. "Welcome to your nightmare, Niki Davis."

Niki's head and shoulders shot off the ground, as if she'd been electrocuted. Her eyes dilated, becoming almost entirely black before rolling into the back of her head. Her head fell back onto the stone floor, and her back arched, thrusting her stomach into the air.

She took a deep, gasping breath, and screamed.

64

He stood in the middle of the park with Brittany, their park. What had once been a beautiful, serene memory of the day he had first told her he loved her became something bizarre. The other people in the park, the dads throwing Frisbees with their kids, the kids catching it and throwing it back, the moms making picnic lunches, the lovers kissing on blankets, all menacingly turned toward the two of them. Then, they began to run.

Not sure what to do, he rushed Brit to the farthest reaches of the park, shielding her from the onslaught of attackers. He stood his ground as his combat training kicked in. He fought as if their lives depended on it. He wasn't quite sure why, but he knew they did. He was fighting for their lives.

This was all wrong. He promised Brittany he would never leave her, and he planned to keep that promise. He wasn't abandoning her again. He would be there for her and never let a monster like Silas kill her. If he never left, she'd never die in his arms. He'd never have to hear the sound of her chest gurgling as the life bled out of her.

Pain shot through his side and his back. It reminded him of the way people in his unit described getting shot.

A searing pain wrapped around his neck. Mike clawed at it, trying to remove whatever invisible force had latched on to him.

Nothing made sense. Why were these people attacking him? Why did they want to kill him and Brittany?

"I do."

The voice soared through the air. Michael looked up expecting to see the face of God staring down at him, even though that hadn't been the voice of God. It sounded like his voice.

"Do you, Brittany Mae Sharp, take this man to be your husband, to live together in holy matrimony, to love him, to honor him, to comfort him, and to keep him in sickness and in health, forsaking all others, for as long as you both shall live?"

Mike turned away from the angry mob of attackers and looked at Brittany. As the voice from the heavens said it, she mouthed, "I do."

The crowd surged past him rushing to slaughter his bride. But as they reached Brittany, they dissolved into nothing, vaporizing into a mist and ascending into the atmosphere.

The voice boomed again from the heavens, continuing their wedding ceremony. As it did, he turned around, and the entire illusion began to dissolve. The green trees melted away, a newly painted canvas splashed with water. Blue streaks of sky merged with the green of the grass. The entire landscape melded into a kaleidoscope of color until nothing but a blank slate of white remained.

With one last turn, he looked at Brittany again. At least she was still herself; she hadn't melted. Michael wasn't sure he could take the image of her melting away like one of the Nazis at the end of Raiders.

"You have work to do," she told him, as if it was just another day.

"Why do you push me away?"

She shook her head. "I swear. One day, you know you'll find someone and want to settle down."

"Not likely."

"We'll see. For now, though, your team needs you. They need their leader. There's still a fight taking place, and you're missing out."

Michael's head dropped, staring at the white canvas under his feet. "Where are we?"

"Lilith's mind trap. But you are strong, Michael White. You can break free and this time for good."

He looked up at Brittany. "How do I do that?"

She strolled over to him, placed her hands on his head, and tilted it down to her level. She placed a small kiss on his forehead. "You'll figure it out."

He closed his eyes, knowing he now stood alone in Lilith's mind trap. Although the landscape was now gone, the voice still droned on. He focused on the voice of the minister, their minister.

"You may..." with each word, the voice grew closer and closer to him. "...kiss the..." He began to hear screaming. Niki screaming. Nate screaming for Niki. Something's wrong with Niki. "...bride."

The voice vanished, replaced by a scream of sheer terror.

65

"When's daddy gonna be home?" Jamal asked his mom.

Niki stood at the edge of the playground; her mind gripped for a moment in terror.

I can't watch this, she repeated. *I won't watch this happen again.*

She knew where she was. Knew *when* she was. Lilith thrust her into her only nightmare. One she'd played out in her head over and over again. But this nightmare wasn't a memory or a dream this time. She wasn't seeing through her own eyes and wasn't only remembering what she had seen. She stood a few feet away from a younger version of herself. The one who still had to experience this scene play out and then figure out how to live again.

Lilith had captured her mind and sent Niki directly into The Incident. The night that had started everything. The night she and Nate had lost Jamal. The night she hadn't been fast enough, strong enough, smart enough. The last time she'd not been enough.

Niki's past self sat on a swing next to the five-year-old boy. His black, curly hair hung close to his scalp as he propelled himself forward, then backward. His facial features resembled hers more than Nate's. Although, at times, when he was being a little five-year-old shit as five-year-old's did tend to do, she thought he looked exactly like his father. His skin tone had more Nate than her. He wasn't nearly as dark as Nate, but Jamal definitely had more than the normal permanent tan.

Around them, it was a typical playground. A large playscape fully equipped with monkey bars, tunnels, platforms at multiple levels with mounted steering wheels, and slides sat in front of them. Behind them, a few more slides, a merry-go-round, another set of monkey bars, and another swing set. This one had five swings.

Despite Niki's narrow frame, the swing still fit tightly around her. It was not made for adults. Jamal was comfortable, though. He held onto the chains, his feet extended out in front of him as he swung forward and flipped around behind him as he went backward. He didn't need his arc to be too exaggerated. Just a little back and forth, as long as he did it himself, kept a smile on his face.

"Daddy will be home soon. He's working late tonight," young Niki answered. "We're having fun, though, love."

Niki watched her younger self and Jamal swing. She desperately tried to intervene, to run to that version of her, and to yell to scoop him out of the swing and run back home. Try as hard as she could, moving was futile. Her legs were locked into the ground. Even screaming was futile. She couldn't force any noise to come out of her throat. Lilith had locked her in place and silenced her. All she could do was watch, relive, and feel. Feel sadness for her younger self, frustration that she couldn't change anything, anger that the she-demon would dare try to use her son's death to hurt Niki.

"Mommy, I am having fun with you." Jamal's smile beamed from ear to ear. "Daddy is just more fun."

There was that five-year-old little shit that reminded her of Nate.

"Oh, he is, huh?"

Niki jumped off the swing and turned, standing directly in front of Jamal. As he swung closer to her, she grabbed his feet, holding him in place so he couldn't make the return trip.

"Stop, Mommy," he said through bouts of laughter.

"Who's more fun?" Niki inquired, shaking his feet from side-to-side, his back facing the ground. "Who's more fun?"

She briefly paused, giving him a chance to answer.

Through choked laughter, he looked up at her and yelled, "Daddy!" He stuck his tongue out and blew a raspberry.

Niki let go of his feet, crossed her arms in front of her, and turned around as if she was throwing a fit like a toddler. Taking large, exaggerated steps, she stomped off toward a set of picnic tables, leaving Jamal swinging.

Watching it all transpire, Niki wanted to scream at her younger self. Still, nothing came out. *Run. Grab him and run. Turn around. Don't move away from him.*

Despite all her mental pleas to the Niki who didn't know real monsters existed, the young woman marched all the way to the picnic table. Hearing Jamal's laughter grow quieter and quieter, she turned back to him and sat on the table top of the picnic table, placing her feet on the bench.

When they first arrived at the park, it was dusk. She wasn't sure how long they'd been there, but dusk had slipped into night. Two streetlamps, one on each end of the park, cast light across the playground equipment, creating patches of darkness. Each lamp emitted a low-pitched, humming sound as the electrical current coursed through it. The one closest to young Niki flickered.

Jamal jumped off the swing, landing on his feet, and ran to the Playscape. He grabbed onto a handhold on the hard rubber climbing wall. The wall only went up three feet with a platform at the top as a landing.

"Jamal," Niki warned. "It's getting dark. We're going to be leaving soon."

He quickly scaled the wall and stood triumphantly on the platform. "I'm gonna do the bars, then the slide, then we can leave." He turned and ran across the bridge to the next platform. The monkey bars were just on the other side of it.

As soon as Jamal went across the bridge, Niki knew her younger self could no longer see him. She watched as the young mother rolled her eyes, unable to warn her. "You do know I'm the mom, right, love? That means I'm the boss."

Niki tried to close her eyes, but even then, she could still see what was about to happen. It was like Lilith had removed her eyelids. She couldn't move, couldn't speak, and couldn't close her eyes. Niki involuntarily shook her head. Her whole body trembled; whether with grief or anger or frustration, she didn't know.

"Hurry up, Jamal," Young Niki shouted. "Daddy will be home soon. We still need to walk back to the apartment."

Niki heard footsteps, but only because she knew what she was listening for. Frustration welled up inside of her. If only the footsteps would've been quicker.

"Mommy," Jamal hollered. "Come here. Big doggy."

Young Niki hopped off the tabletop. "What was that, love?" she asked while striding toward him.

"Big doggy!" he yelled again.

Niki's perspective switched. Although she hadn't moved, couldn't move, the image did as if the camera angle adjusted. Whatever nightmarish mind powers Lilith possessed ensured Niki didn't miss a single, terrifying detail.

Helplessly, she watched the young Niki walk over to the Playscape, grab a bar, and fling herself onto the elevated platform. The moment her feet landed, she heard the growl. The sound sent a shiver down her spine and froze the blood in her veins. She'd never heard a dog growl like that before. It sounded feral, hungry, determined, and confident all wrapped together.

"Jamal!" she screamed. "Get over here! Now!"

The growling grew louder.

"Mommy, I'm scared. It's looking at me."

Young Niki saw Jamal standing next to the side of the platform. There was an opening where the monkey bars started. She couldn't see the animal, just her young child.

As Niki watched the events unfold, she cursed Lilith. Who the fuck did she think she was? Niki was so angry she could cry. But no tears came. Why would they? Nothing else was going her way. She was an incorporeal being. No real body. Only her mind, hijacked and trapped. She screamed inside of her head, but even the scream didn't drown out the growl. She needed those fucking footsteps to go quicker, but she already knew the outcome.

"Jamal," Young Niki tried to say, as relaxed and calm as she could. Her vocal cords, though, betrayed her as they still carried a tremor. "Jamal, don't turn around. Just take a few steps back toward me."

He sniffed. She didn't need him to turn around in order to know he was crying in fear. "Mommy," he said. It was all he would ever say.

Suddenly, the beast, so much larger than a dog, rose on its hind legs. It was the first time Young Niki was able to see it. The growl, as terrible as it was, didn't prepare her for this abomination. Raised up on hind legs, it stood well over six feet tall, towering over Jamal, even on the raised platform. The snout was long and slender. Sharp, fanglike teeth, caked in gore, lined the snout. A mixture of blood and saliva dripped from the numerous incisors. Black fur covered the monster's body except for speckled bald patches on both sides. It reminded Niki of a dog with mange except it looked to be well fed.

Before Young Niki could react, she heard gunshots. She'd been raised around guns and knew the sounds they made. She recognized the reports of two handguns and a shotgun. The rounds landed in the side of the beast who was staring at her son.

It yelped and staggered before falling to the ground. Yet, the growl grew more intense.

The three shooters approached quickly, but not quickly enough.

Niki started across the bridge as Jamal turned. Their eyes met for a brief moment before the beast sprung forward and latched its teeth onto Jamal's shoulder. The fangs sunk into the soft muscle between neck and shoulder. Blood poured down both sides of his shirt.

She saw her son's eyes open so wide that she saw only white before the monster dropped back below the Playscape, Jamal still firmly held within its jaws. The beast turned around and shot forward, using its powerful legs to cover ground faster than anything the young mother had ever seen.

Both women stood there and stared. They couldn't scream. Couldn't move. They just stared as the beast vanished into a clump of trees.

"You two, track it and kill it," the man with the shotgun said. He walked over to Niki. "Miss, I'm sending my team to find him. Was that your son?"

Still in shock and standing on the bridge between the two platforms, she turned her eyes to look at the newcomer. Slowly, she nodded.

"We're going to handle it. I'm sorry we weren't faster."

Young Niki continued to just stare at the man. He had a strong, square jaw and military-style buzz cut.

"Ma'am, I need you to listen. My team is going to take care of this. I need you to go home for now. Do you live close by? Do you need an escort?"

She nodded again. "Yes," she finally croaked out. "Close. His father will be home soon." Each word she spoke felt painful to say. She said each one at a time as if they were their own sentence.

"Ma'am, I'll help you home," he said. "I'm John. John Sanchez. But you can call me Jax."

Jax placed a hand on Niki's arm and eased her off the bridge and back onto the platform. Then the man jumped to the ground before turning to help her once again.

Young Niki's body felt numb. So many emotions coursed through her. She wanted to cry, needed to cry, but every emotion fought to explode all at once, clogging whatever emotional highway existed. Instead, she turned and began operating on autopilot.

Fuck you, Lilith, Niki thought as she watched Jax lead her away from the park and the other two former Night Crew members hunt for the werewolf. *Fuck you. Fuck you. Fuck you.*

Everything in Niki's view froze as if Lilith hit the pause button. The image shifted and stuttered, making Niki disoriented about her surroundings. Her stomach turned over and a wave of nausea hit her.

"When's daddy gonna be home?" Jamal asked his mom.

He was back on the swing. The memory reset.

Niki realized she was trapped in this memory. If Nate, Naomi, or Mike failed, she had no way of escaping this. She swallowed hard, knowing what she was about to see again.

66

Mike raised his head and almost put it right back down again as a disorienting wave hit him. The last thing he remembered was walking down the street after leaving the nightclub. This was not a nightclub. In fact, it looked like he was in a stone vault. Nate was a few feet away, crouched over Niki. Niki was lying on the floor screaming as tears slipped down her face.

Nothing made sense to him.

He heard applause in his head and reached up to his ear, touching the earbud. He placed his hands over both ears and bent his head down.

"Josh?" he asked. Flashes of his and Brit's wedding popped into this head.

The applause quickly snapped off. "Mike?" Josh nearly screamed. "Mike, is that you?"

"What the hell is going on?"

"Oh, holy fuck, that worked!" Josh exclaimed. "I was hoping that would fucking work, and it did. Sweet Jesus."

"Be excited later. I need a SITREP. And I'm fucking starving, which isn't good."

"Quick version. There were three more succubi. Naomi is a good one. The other two are bad. You were hearing Lilith's siren call which is apparently some kind of mind fuck. Naomi led Nate and Niki to Lilith's lair to rescue you and kill the baddies. I think you're caught up."

Mike raised his head. Across the vault he saw a beautiful woman with black hair. Two bodies lay on the floor at her feet. One of them, who looked like she had purple hair, rolled over. Black blood oozed from her body. The other body appeared lifeless.

Nate raised his head away from Niki and locked eyes with Mike. He reached for his shotgun, chambered a round as he spun, and aimed it at Mike.

"Easy, Nate," Mike said, cautiously. Obviously, something had happened while he was under. The black spot in his memory reminded him of the one Silas had given him many years ago. Hopefully, after this was all over, the team could fill him in on what happened. "It's me. I'm me."

Hesitantly, Nate eased his finger away from the trigger. "So Josh's idea..."

"I'm guessing it worked," Mike finished.

"Holy fuck, thank God." He let out a sigh of relief. As he did, Niki screamed again, and Nate twisted back around to her. "It's ok. Fight, baby. Fight."

Mike rushed over. He saw and smelled the blood on her. His stomach growled, and he was overcome with the instinct to open his mouth wide and bury his fangs into her. Instead, he slipped the end of his tongue under an incisor and eased down on the appendage, hoping the taste of blood, even his own, would tamp his desire temporarily.

"What's wrong?" he finally asked Nate.

"Lilith touched Niki, and now she's locked into some kind of nightmare." He wiped a tear from the side of Niki's face. "I can't get through to her, and whatever she's going through must be rough."

"Niki's tough. I'm certain she's doing some nice ass-kicking in her nightmare."

Mike looked up at the black-haired beauty across the room. She stood over the other one as if waiting for her sister to die.

"Which one's on our side?" Mike asked Nate.

"Purple. Black hair is Lilith." As Mike turned to address Lilith, Nate grabbed his arm. "She's a tough bitch."

He looked down at Nate, still wiping tears away from Niki's eyes, and nodded. When Nate dropped his arm, Mike dug deep into his chest, using Niki's screams as fuel for his anger and rage, and felt the monster inside of him rise to the surface. The heat in his eyes ignited. The colors in the room became vibrant. Everything appeared sharper, crisper. He was an alpha predator, and he was ready to prove it.

With supernatural speed, Michael ran at Lilith. He closed the gap between them instantly. He then used all that force to punch her chest as hard as he could. He felt her sternum give way as the impact flung her backward into the wall. Cracks shot through the stone.

She slid down the pulverized wall and landed on her feet. When she looked up at him, he saw her own rage. "For a fledgling, you are strong."

"Release Niki," he demanded.

She brushed away pieces of gray dust. "It's been centuries since someone has broken out of my call. Maybe I'm losing my touch."

"I'll say this once more. Release. Niki. Now." Michael cracked his neck and raised his hands in front of him, tightening his fingers into his palms.

"Release her? She's reliving fond memories. Over and over again." Lilith straightened up. Despite their distance, Michael heard the crushed sternum repairing itself. "What do you think you will do if I don't release her? What power do you think you have over me, Fledgling? I'm Queen of the Demons, First Wife of Adam, Oldest Among Us, First Lover of Samael. All of you," she pointed at Naomi trying to sit up on the ground, "to include her, are nothing more than a single hair on the back of a fly to me."

When she finished, her form twisted and changed. Her skin split and molted as she shed it off, revealing the gray-skinned beast underneath. In moments, she towered over Michael.

"Fuck me," he whispered.

Next to him, Naomi sat up on her hands and spat out a wad of black blood. "You are so full of yourself," she yelled at Lilith. "You believe your own lies. I've said it before, and I'll say it again. Your arrogance will be the death of you."

The beast roared at her, rattling the entire room with its echo.

Michael cracked his neck again, preparing himself for the fight. Behind him, he heard another scream from Niki. In retaliation and just to piss off Lilith, he held his fist further out in front of him and motioned for her to come at him.

"At me, bitch."

67

Lilith charged. She punched with one hand and then swiped at him with her wing. He dodged, dropped to the ground, and swept her feet out from under her. With her forward momentum, Lilith fell face first onto the stone floor. Her scaly cheek scraped against the ground as she skid, leaving slashes on her face.

As soon as she hit the ground, Naomi sprang up and onto Lilith's back. She gripped one of Lilith's wings in each hand and pulled back, bending the Demon Queen backward, causing her head and chest to rise.

Michael ran forward and began kicking her in the head while Lilith tried to toss Naomi off her. After the third blow from Michael, she moved her arms to block him. She caught his leg and tossed him backward like he weighed nothing. Despite his strength, she was still much, much stronger. He knew he had to be careful, or she'd easily overpower them.

As Mike worked to regain his feet, Lilith fought to free herself from Naomi. She rolled back and forth, each time making a little more progress. While he stood back up, Lilith managed to flip back around and kick Naomi off her. Naomi flew into the opposite wall, and more cracks appeared.

Michael, with his fists raised, ran at the Demon Queen again. He managed to land a few blows to her body before she grabbed him by the neck and picked him up like a misbehaving animal. He tried kicking her in the stomach, but he would've had more success kicking the wall.

"Mike!" he heard Nate yell. He glanced over and saw Nate holding the shotgun. Mike tried to angle away as the shotgun let out a deafening report.

When the bullet struck, Lilith roared in pain and anger. Fury burned in her eyes, but Nate pumped the gun and fired, again and again. The monster staggered backward at the sheer force of the impact, discarding Mike with ease and setting her sights on Nate.

Nate pumped the shotgun again, but this time nothing happened.

"Fuck!" he yelled out.

From his side, he grabbed the machete and held it out in front of him.

"Come on, bitch." He waved the machete around in front of him. "This is the same blade that took the head off that other spineless bitch. Care to be next?"

Lilith's black eyes turned to look at the vampire and succubus, both struggling to get up, and then returned her attention to Nathan Edwards. She shifted form back to the beautiful temptress.

"You're just a man." She stepped closer to him.

Nate, poised and ready, waited for the attack. With each step closer, the tension in his muscles increased. Finally, she was close enough for him to strike, but still he waited.

With snake-like speed, she darted one direction and then another, closing the gap, and moving in front of him and between his arms before he could react. He was in the perfect position to have given her a hug. Nate stood still, the machete in his right hand. Lilith was directly in front of him. He swallowed hard, expecting his head to be ripped off any second. Instead, she gently raised her hand and brushed his cheek with a smile on her face.

"Like I said, you're just a man."

As he stared into her eyes, a dribble of blood escaped the side of Lilith's mouth. She looked down and saw Nate's machete buried up to the hilt in her side, his hand still gripping it.

When she looked back, her eyes were wide and filled with confusion.

He pulled the blade out of her side and thrust it in again. One last time he brought the machete in front of him and stabbed her through the chest.

Lilith dropped to her knees. "How?" she asked. Blood poured from the sides of her mouth. "I touched you."

"What can I say?" He pulled the blade out again and held it even with her neck.

"You were able to resist. It wasn't the vampire. You were the one. You could've raised him." She coughed, sending black blood droplets across the floor.

He raised the blade above his head.

"I'm a one-woman man, and you're not the one woman." He swung the blade as hard as he could, cutting cleanly through her neck.

Her eyes rolled to the back of her head as the head tumbled to the side of the floor. Her body fell forward in the opposite direction.

There was a moment of peace before Niki screamed again. Nate realized she was still trapped in her nightmare.

68

"Michael!" Nate yelled.

Nate ran to Niki, gently lifted her head, and slid his legs underneath. Then he carefully rested her head back down on his lap and brushed the top of her forehead. "It's ok, baby. You got this."

Mike and Naomi scrambled to their feet and hurried over. Both limped, sore and broken. Additionally, Mike was once again fighting off hunger pains. His temporary solution had worn off.

"She's strong," Mike said. "She'll fight through whatever nightmare she's in."

"No, she won't," Naomi interjected. "Even if she's able to fight the fear, it'll still drain her life force. She'll wither away and die."

Mike turned to Naomi. "How do we break this? What do we need to undo it?"

Mike could feel the limits of his control being tested. Adding that to his fear for Niki, and subsequently Nate, had him frustrated and irritable.

"We need to break the nightmare loop. Let me try," she said hesitantly.

Michael listened to Niki's heartbeat. "I thought her heart would be racing, but it isn't. It's slowing. I don't know how much longer she can keep going."

Mike knew Niki had the mental strength to keep going, but physically, he wasn't sure. A heart, a body, could only take so much.

"Not helpful, Mike," Nate snapped back.

Naomi kneeled next to Niki. She took the gloves off and rested one hand on Niki's arm and the other on her cheek. Then, Naomi closed her eyes.

The men watched as Naomi's face changed and contorted, but unlike when she was transformed into her other form. This was more as if a grimace was struggling to break through. Her breath caught in her throat, and her face tensed.

Finally she sighed and shook her head. "I can't get through. Lilith locked her in tight."

Nate stared at Naomi. "Can we do the same thing we did for Mike? Have Josh use a memory to pull her out?"

Naomi shook her head. "I don't believe it'll work for her. Her aura isn't as strong as Michael's. Plus, she doesn't have enough time left." She glanced up at Michael. "But you may be able to reach her."

Mike took a step backward. "What? How am I supposed to if you couldn't?"

"Because my connection is only through touch, and as powerful as that is, your connection is even more so."

"What connection? I can't control minds."

Sweat covered Niki's forehead. Nate hated to see it. He knew she would've hated it, hated to be weak in any way but especially mentally. His heart crying out for what she must be going through, he carefully wiped it away. He hoped it would bring her physical comfort now and psychological comfort later. With his eyes beseeching, he looked up and held the vampire's gaze, hoping he would be right, hoping his idea would work. "You can do the same thing that Thomas did for you when he removed Silas's block."

Realization hit Mike, and his eyes went wide. He rapidly shook his head. "No, I can't. Thomas had to drink from me. I'm not doing that. Even if I did, I wouldn't know what to do afterward. Also..." he stopped himself. He wanted to say, "I don't know if I could stop," but he didn't want to vocalize that.

"Blood is the strongest bond," Naomi said. "It's the only way."

"We're in New Orleans. Can't we holler down the street and get another vampire? Go ask the registrar guy where the fuck another vampire is."

Niki's body tensed up again and pain shot across her face. Fresh tears flowed down her cheeks. "She doesn't have that much time. You know that. I know you do. You've got to do it."

"Nate. I...I'm..."

"You're scared you won't be able to stop," Nate said, finishing the thought that Mike couldn't. "You will. I'm not going to let you kill her, but right now, I do need you to save her."

Mike dropped to his knees. He looked up at Nate's red eyes and at the tears flowing from them. "Do not let me kill her."

Nate just nodded his head.

Looking down at Niki's face, Mike grasped her arm in his hands and lifted it up. "Sorry, Aussie." He took a deep breath. "Oh, for fuck's sake."

He opened his mouth wide, placed the soft underside of her arm against his lips, and sunk his teeth into her flesh. Immediately, his mouth filled with a taste like none other. Sweet and warm, it coated his mouth, his tongue, and flowed down the back of his throat. This was nothing like drinking from a bag or his thermos.

There was something different about the blood coming straight from the tap, so to speak. A purity. A carnal purity. The more he sucked in, the more he wanted. The more he craved to have. He couldn't get enough of it.

Mike tightened his grip as his teeth sank deeper into her arm. He didn't need to stop. This was natural. This was the way it should be. Vampires were meant to hunt. Meant to kill. Not drink through a straw. A vampire was supposed to feel the pressure dwindle as the prey's heart struggled to find blood to pump. As the life slowly drained from his victim.

As it slowly drained from Niki.

Niki.

This wasn't a victim. This was Niki.

He needed to stop. He needed to pull back.

Fight, dammit.

Mike felt his arms shake as they fought against his brain's order to let go, as they tried to ignore him.

Listen to me, dammit. Stop. Let go. Let go. Let go! Let...

"Go!" he said out loud as he pulled himself away from her arm, breathing heavily. He struggled to catch his breath, pulling in huge gasps of air, trying to fill his lungs.

"You're okay. I knew you were strong enough," Nate said.

"That makes one of us," Mike replied. "Drinking was the easy part. Now, let's see if I can figure out this mind piece."

He shifted his head from side to side, stretching out his neck. "Naomi, hold her legs. Nate, you got her head?"

He nodded.

"Good, from what I remember, I kicked like a son of a bitch when Thomas did this to me. Here goes nothing."

Mike relaxed the muscles in his arms and shook them out. It was the same motion he used when preparing for a fight. The similarity wasn't lost on him. This was a fight. He raised one hand and placed the tips of his fingers against her temple. He closed his eyes.

Come on. Work, goddammit. Thomas made this look so easy. He just touched the side of my head. Focus. Focus on Niki. I'm falling into Niki's head. Use the blood to find the path into...

69

...her nightmare.

Mike opened his eyes. He stood in a park surrounded by playground equipment.

He peered around before he heard a familiar voice.

"Jamal, it's getting dark. We're going to be leaving soon."

He followed the sound and saw Niki sitting on the top of a picnic table. Typical Niki. He didn't know Jamal, though. Mike leaned into his vampire senses and peered through the shadows to see a little boy. Beyond the boy, he also saw another figure standing at the edge of the park. Mike looked closer at the familiar shape.

Another Niki?

Mike's forehead wrinkled in confusion. He eased his eyesight back to normal and stepped out of the shadows. A slight breeze blew across his body, and immediately he knew something was off. The rank smell of raw, spoiled meat, blood, sickness, and wet dog attacked his senses. The urge to vomit rose up in his throat, but he swallowed it back down.

"I'm gonna do the bars, then the slide, then we can leave," the boy yelled back.

"You do know I'm the mom, right, love? That means I'm the boss."

A range of thoughts bombarded Mike.

The mom? Niki has a kid? If Niki has a kid, where is he now? Why hasn't she ever mentioned him?

At that last thought, everything clicked into place.

"Hurry up, Jamal," Niki shouted. "Daddy will be home soon. We still need to walk back to the apartment."

He glanced at the Niki sitting on the picnic table and at the one standing at the edge of the park. The one on the picnic table was doing the talking. The one at the far end must be his Niki, forced to watch whatever was about to happen while her life force was being drained away.

Mike sprinted around the equipment and ran up to his Niki. Her eyes widened as he drew close. She mouthed the word "Mike", but no sound came out. She pointed to her throat and shook her head.

He understood. She couldn't talk.

"We have to break the loop to get you out of here. On the outside, your body is dying," he said. Then, unable to think of something better to say, he added, "I'm here to save you."

Her eyes drifted up, and Mike knew she was thinking of a plan. After a few seconds, she pointed a couple of times to the playground.

"Your son?"

She nodded.

"Save your son to break the loop?"

More nodding.

She mouthed the word "Go".

"Save him from what?"

Very slowly, she moved her mouth. Mike picked up on what she silently said.

"Werewolf?" he asked, and she nodded. "That explains the smell, I guess. I don't have a weapon."

Niki shook her head. She pointed at him, then pointed at her head.

"Use my head. Thanks. Big help. Why couldn't you solve your way out of this?"

She pointed to her legs and tried to move them.

Mike gave an understanding nod. "You know, I'm still learning all of this stuff. One of these days, I need a monster hunting class."

A slight smile cracked her face as she shook her head. Michael wasn't sure if smiling in a nightmare was common, but maybe that was a good sign. As if in response to his optimism, her hand shot to her chest and a pained expression flashed across her face. Whatever physical toll her body was taking outside was starting to impact her here. Her eyes screamed fear, something Mike had never seen from Niki.

He turned back to the playground and ran. Time wasn't on their side.

The smell grew more intense the closer he moved to the Playscape. Rotted meat. Sickness. That was the only thing he could compare it to. Beyond being a werewolf, this one was sick. It was dying. The horrid aroma gave it away.

Jamal headed toward the smell. Then Mike heard the growl.

"Holy shit," he said and sprinted toward the playground equipment. He had to break the loop this time. Niki didn't have another rerun in her. He reached the Playscape, scaled up one of the slides, and stood on the platform next to Jamal.

"Who are you?" Young Niki asked from the picnic table.

"A friend," he answered.

The werewolf stood on its hind legs. "Damn," Mike said as it looked at him. It stood eye-to-eye with him, and he had an extra few feet off the ground. "You are one big son of a bitch."

The werewolf tilted its head and howled.

"Jamal, run to your mother. Now!" Mike commanded. When the boy didn't immediately respond, he grabbed Jamal's arm and started to drag him backward.

At the same time, he heard the other footsteps, followed by the gunshots. He knew the beast was going to be pissed. He grabbed Jamal and rushed him over to Young Niki who had moved to the bridge behind them.

"Run!" he hollered to them both.

The beast jumped on the top of the Playscape just in front of Michael, but instead of tearing into him, he looked around as if searching for the boy. This memory must be preprogrammed to attack the child. His heart broke for Niki.

Reliving Brittany's death through his UltraNet, his curse, devastated him. To relive the death of a child? Repeatedly? And only be able to watch? Mike knew he had to stop this. He couldn't let her keep going through this. Not on his watch. And not just for her physical wellbeing, but her mental state.

"Look at me, you mangy mutt," Mike yelled.

The hunters flanked both sides of the playground and fired again. Each shot only added to the werewolf's rage.

Standing on two legs, its head turned around and zeroed in on the movement. When Michael traced the beast's sights, he found Jamal and Niki running through the park. He prayed they were heading home.

The beast lowered itself back down onto four legs and bent its hind legs, preparing to leap.

"No, you don't." Mike caught one of the back legs as it left the ground, dragging the werewolf back down, well short of its target. Without looking at him, it kicked, trying to throw him off and break loose.

Claws tore through his arms and shoulders. No matter what, he wasn't letting go. This was just a memory. Once he got out of Niki's mind, he knew he would be just fine. But first, he had to get Niki out of her own mind.

More gunshots rang out.

He smelled rancid blood seeping out of the holes.

"Use silver, for fuck's sake," he shouted as more shots pummeled the monster. He held on for dear life, not letting it move any further. When he glanced up, he saw Niki and Jamal far away and breathed a sigh of relief.

The beast's resolve started to diminish. The kicks stopped, and it collapsed on the ground. Even when it stopped moving all together, Michael didn't let go of its hind leg. He held it pressed against his body, pinned between him and the ground.

He heard the footsteps circle around him. "You can let go. We killed it."

Mike, face buried in the ground, managed, "Are you sure? Why weren't you using silver? Doesn't that stop a werewolf?"

"We were," another familiar voice said. "Takes more than one shot."

Suddenly, Michael felt the hot end of a shotgun against his neck.

"So, Vampire, why am I not blowing your head off right now?"

Mike let go of the werewolf's leg and rolled over, staring up at Jax. "Because I just saved them. And you wouldn't reward that by killing me. Would you, Jax?"

A slight click happened as Jax slowly eased the hammer on his gun. "I'm not sure how you know my name, but you're right. If you get out of line, The Night Crew will hunt you."

"Oh, I'm aware."

Mike hopped onto his feet and started trotting toward his Niki. As he did, the ground felt odd, as if walking on a sand dune. Every step became harder and harder. The memory stuttered around him, like an old tape skipping. The image itself distorted and warbled, then dissolved, leaving only him and Niki.

She ran to him and hugged him.

70

Mike tossed his head back and took a deep breath. He fell back onto the stone floor.

Niki opened her eyes and blinked a few times before sitting up, trying to get her vision steady. As she started to rise, a wave of dizziness hit her, nearly sent her back down, but she fought through it and managed to stay upright. After a moment of staring around blankly, trying to figure out what happened, Niki finally realized she was no longer trapped in that nightmare but back in reality. She had no idea how long she'd been under. After the tenth time of watching her son die, she had stopped counting.

Nate's large and familiar arms wrapped around her, and she clung to them, using his touch to firmly ground herself. Between Nate's comforting embrace and the soreness coursing through her body, she didn't want to move.

Next to her, Mike pulled himself up. Naomi sat in front of her.

Niki remembered.

Just before she went under, they were fighting Lilith. Panic flooded her body, and she started to scurry across the floor, darting her head from side to side, and flailing. Her breathing became erratic.

"She's gone," Naomi said calmly. "We won." Naomi, solidly but gently, placed a gloved hand on her arm.

"I got you, babe," Nate reassured her. "I got you."

She gripped his arm desperately and the tears began to flow. Her body heaved up and down as she sobbed into Nate's chest. Grief for what she had lost then, for what she had gone through; relief that it was over; knowledge that she had survived, would survive; gratitude and love for the people surrounding her. All those things she set free through the soothing release of tears. Everything she couldn't do in the nightmare rushed out of her, because now she had Nate holding her.

She didn't have to go through it alone.

"What was in there?" Nate whispered above her head.

Niki hoped he wasn't talking to her. It wasn't anything she'd be able to talk about for a long time.

"A park..." Mike started.

"Got it," Nate interrupted. He sniffed, and Niki felt a tear fall onto her shoulder. Through choked back tears, he said again, "I got you."

Niki wasn't sure how long she sat. Eventually she raised her head, and stared into Nate's eyes for a heavy but understanding moment. Then she turned and looked at Mike. She raised her arm to look at the bite mark.

"Did you bite me?" Her voice was hoarse, gravelly, and incredulous.

He nodded. "They made me," he said defensively, hand raised and backing up.

"Was that the first time you actually bit someone?"

"Don't make me talk about it."

A smile spread across her face. "Ah, love, I popped your cherry. Was it as good for you?"

71

Once the team arrived at their headquarters on Jackson Square, Josh began the conference call queued up. Intel and Jax were on the monitors. Josh sat in his chair in front of them while Niki, Nate, Mike, and Naomi each rested around the table in the make-shift conference room.

"We have a problem," Intel said.

"Guess that means no rest for the weary," Mike said. "What's wrong, Austin?"

"Her," he said, nodding in the direction of Naomi.

"Her?" they all began at once. Mike raised his hand.

"We have no idea what powers she has. She's been hiding away for a thousand years. She's dangerous!"

"Wait a minute," Mike said. "She saved every last one of us. We owe her. I'm not going to take her out after all she's done for us. Nor am I asking my team to do that. That'd be like turning our back on those who helped us in Afghanistan."

"Mike," Naomi said, looking at Mike. "Thank you for your kind words." She turned her head back to the monitors.

"I understand your concern. I have no intention of using any of the powers that I have. I only have one desire, and that is to sink my toes back into the sands of my homeland as I did when I was a girl."

"What happens when you change your mind? How do we trust that you're no longer a threat?" Intel demanded.

"Anyone could be a threat. Even you. I give my word I will stay in contact. I also promise to work with you. Identify my powers, my weaknesses. I have a wealth of knowledge I've accumulated over the centuries. You will know my location at all times. If you feel I'm not living up to whatever arrangement we make, you may send one of your hunters to eliminate me."

"Do you want to resurrect Samael?"

"If I did, I wouldn't have helped your team to begin with."

"Okay," came the reply. After a long moment of silence, "Let's work out the arrangements."

"Intel," Jax interrupted, "we do have other things to discuss as well."

"What's going on, former boss man?" Niki asked.

"First, you're packing up shop and heading back to Dallas. You all need some R and R. Mike, Thomas is waiting for you to continue training."

Nate peered over at Mike and saw the expression on his face. "He's actually doing a lot better with his control," Nate tried to add hopefully.

Niki chimed in. "It's true. He only bit me once."

She held up her arm, sending the five of them in the conference room into laughter.

Looking back up at the monitors, though, there was no laughing happening.

"The absence of the Council is starting to be felt," he continued. "We're getting reports from all over about Accord violations. Teams are being deployed but we are having more issues than we can stamp down. The ripple Silas started hasn't stopped. It's growing."

"What do you need?" Nate asked.

"Be ready. We're still searching for the Council. I would like to restore some order."

"As the new guy," Mike started, "I have to ask. What if the Council members can't be found? Worse, what if they're dead?"

Both Jax and Intel simultaneously dropped their eyes. A large gap of silence hung in the air.

"Let's hope that's not the case," Jax said. "For now, get back to Dallas and take advantage of some well-deserved rest."

The Night Crew will return

Acknowledgements

First, as always, I'd like to thank my wife, Terri. Without your constant encouragement and support, none of the stories I write would be possible. As my first reader, your feedback is vital to making each story as entertaining or terrifying as it is.

Thank you, Joe Mynhardt and the entire team at Crystal Lake Publishing. Your support and belief in The Night Crew Series is humbling. I'm honored to be part of the Crystal Lake family and excited to see how far we can take my team of monster hunters.

Thank you, Maarten Van Vuuren, for the absolutely amazing cover art.

And as always, thank you, constant reader for spending some time inside my head. I hope you enjoyed the team's journey through New Orleans. Just wait for their next mission.

Be sure to follow me on Facebook or TikTok @BradRicksAuthor. Also, like and follow The Night Crew Podcast where I do a deep dive into all things that go bump in the night as well as talk to your favorite authors. You can find The Night Crew Podcast wherever you listen to podcasts.

Until next time.

About the Author

Brad lives in Central Texas with his wife and a house full of teenagers. A life long horror fan, Brad pulls inspiration from both classic literature like Stoker and Poe and modern works like Stephen King and Clive Barker. Although new to the publishing world, Brad has always loved to write and tell stories. His debut novel, a supernatural thriller titled "Fear Not The Dead", came out in July 2024.

THE END?

Not if you want to dive into more of Crystal Lake Publishing's Tales from the Darkest Depths!

Check out our amazing website and online store or download our catalog here.

https://geni.us/CLPCatalog

We always have great new projects and content on the website to dive into, as well as a newsletter, behind the scenes options, social media platforms, our own dark fiction shared-world series and our very own webstore. Our webstore even has categories specifically for KU books, non-fiction, anthologies, and of course more novels and novellas.

Readers...

Thank you for reading *The Night Crew II Bloodlust*. We hope you enjoyed this novel. If you have a moment, please review *The Night Crew II Bloodlust* at the store where you bought it.

Help other readers by telling them why you enjoyed this book. No need to write an in-depth discussion. Even a single sentence will be greatly appreciated. Reviews go a long way to helping a book sell, and is great for an author's career. It'll also help us to continue publishing quality books.

Thank you again for taking the time to journey with Crystal Lake Publishing.

You will find links to all our social media platforms on our Linktree page. https://linktr.ee/CrystalLakePublishing

Follow us on Amazon:

MISSION STATEMENT

Since its founding in August 2012, Crystal Lake has quickly become one of the world's leading publishers of Dark Fiction and Horror books. In 2023, Crystal Lake officially transitioned into an entertainment company, joining several other divisions, genres, and imprints, including Torrid Waters, Crystal Lake Comics, Crystal Lake Games, Crystal Lake Kids, and many more.

While we strive to present only the highest quality fiction and entertainment, we also endeavour to support authors along their writing journey. We offer our time and experience in non-fiction projects, as well as author mentoring and services, at competitive prices.

With several Bram Stoker Award wins and many other wins and nominations (including the HWA's Specialty Press Award), Crystal Lake Publishing puts integrity, honor, and respect at the forefront of our publishing operations.

We strive for each book and outreach program we spearhead to not only entertain and touch or comment on issues that affect our readers, but also to strengthen and support the Dark Fiction field and its authors.

Not only do we find and publish authors we believe are destined for greatness, but we strive to work with men and women who endeavour to be decent human beings who care more for others than themselves, while still being hard working, driven, and passionate artists and storytellers.

Crystal Lake Publishing is and will always be a beacon of what passion and dedication, combined with overwhelming teamwork and respect, can accomplish. We endeavour to know each and every one of our readers, while building personal relationships with our authors, reviewers, bloggers, podcasters, bookstores, and libraries.

We will be as trustworthy, forthright, and transparent as any business can be, while also keeping most of the headaches away from our authors, since it's our job to solve the problems so they can stay in a creative mind. Which of course also means paying our authors.

We do not just publish books, we present to you worlds within your world, doors within your mind, from talented authors who sacrifice so much for a moment of your time.

There are some amazing small presses out there, and through collaboration and open forums we will continue to support other presses in the goal of helping authors and showing the world what quality small presses are capable of accomplishing. No one wins when a small press goes down, so we will always be there to support hardworking, legitimate presses and their authors. We don't see Crystal Lake as the best press out there, but we will always strive to be the best, strive to be the most interactive and grateful, and even blessed press around. No matter what happens over time, we will also take our mission very seriously while appreciating where we are and enjoying the journey.

What do we offer our authors that they can't do for themselves through self-publishing?

We are big supporters of self-publishing (especially hybrid publishing), if done with care, patience, and planning. However, not every author has the time or inclination to do market research, advertise, and set up book launch strategies. Although a lot of authors are successful in doing it all, strong small presses will always be there for the authors who just want to do what they do best: write.

What we offer is experience, industry knowledge, contacts and trust built up over years. And due to our strong brand and trusting fanbase, every Crystal Lake Publishing book comes with weight of respect. In time our fans begin to trust our judgment and will try a new author purely based on our support of said author.

With each launch we strive to fine-tune our approach, learn from our mistakes, and increase our reach. We continue to assure our authors that we're here for them and that we'll carry the weight of the launch and dealing with third parties while they focus on their strengths—be it writing, interviews, blogs, signings, etc.

We also offer several mentoring packages to authors that include knowledge and skills they can use in both traditional and self-publishing endeavours.

We look forward to launching many new careers.

This is what we believe in. What we stand for. This will be our legacy.

Welcome to Crystal Lake Publishing—Where Stories Come Alive!

Thank you for purchasing this book

9 781968 532093